NOTHING HAPPENED AND THEN IT DID

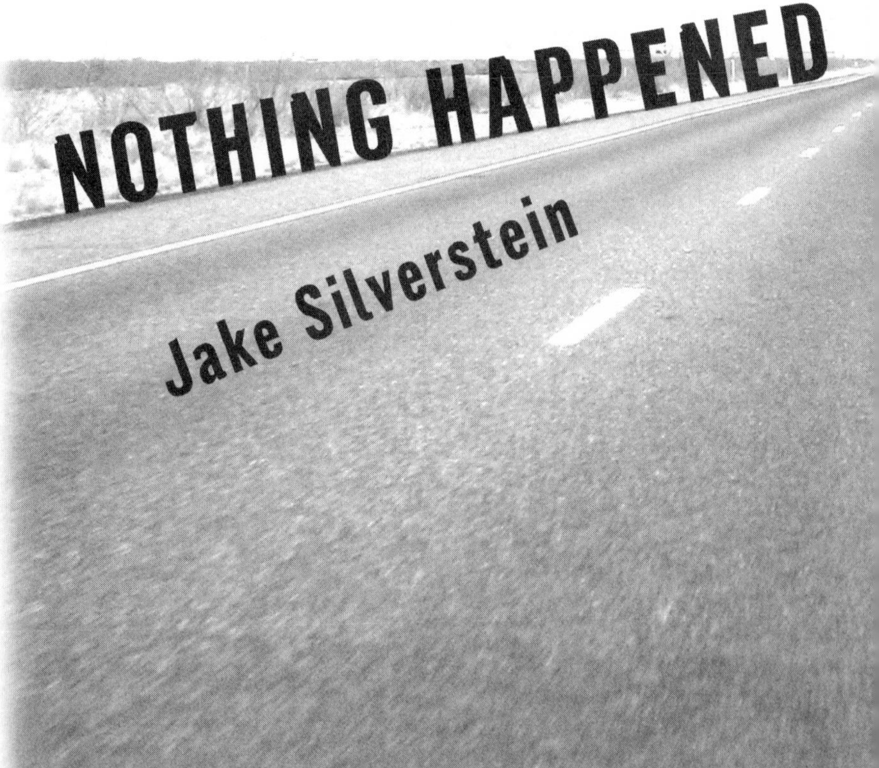

NOTHING HAPPENED

Jake Silverstein

AND THEN IT DID

a chronicle in fact and fiction

W. W. NORTON & COMPANY
NEW YORK LONDON

Printed in the United States of America
First Edition

Portions of this book appeared previously, in slightly different form, in *Harper's* magazine.

Manufacturing by Courier Westford
Book design by Lovedog Studio
Production manager: Anna Oler

Library of Congress Cataloging-in-Publication Data

Silverstein, Jake.
Nothing happened and then it did : a chronicle in fact and fiction /
Jake Silverstein. —1st ed.
p. cm.
Summary: Fact and fiction vie to tell the story of a young journalist bedeviled by the devil and seeking greater truth. The timing couldn't be better—as scandals erupt over journalists and memoirists who've cooked their books—for a work that explores our difficulty in separating fact and fiction, while explicitly demonstrating how they differ and what they share. In prose so fine and wry it makes the back of your neck prickle, Jake Silverstein narrates a journey he undertook through the American Southwest and Mexico, looking to become a journalist. His picaresque travels are filled wtih beguiling and hilarious characters: nineteenth-century author Ambrose Bierce; an unknown group of famous poets; a twenty-first-century treasure hunter in the Gulf of Mexico; an ex-Nazi mechanic shepherding an old Mexican road race; a stenographer who records every passing moment; and various incarnations of the trickster devil. As bold, ambitious, and funny as it is unconventional, *Nothing Happened and Then It Did* is a deep and lasting pleasure.
ISBN 978-0-393-07646-2 (hardcover)
1. Silverstein, Jake—Travel—Fiction. 2. Journalists—United States—Fiction. I. Title.
PS3619.I5527N68 2010
813'.6—dc22

2009053127

W. W. Norton & Company, Inc.
500 Fifth Avenue, New York, N.Y. 10110
www.wwnorton.com

W. W. Norton & Company Ltd.
Castle House, 75/76 Wells Street, London W1T 3QT

1 2 3 4 5 6 7 8 9 0

for Mary

I, Cuauhtencoztli, here I am suffering.
What is, perchance, true?
Will my song still be real tomorrow?

—*Cantares Mexicanos*

contents

fact **fiction**

Preface

THIS BOOK TAKES PLACE ALMOST ENTIRELY IN REMOTE areas of Northern Mexico and the American Southwest, with a brief excursion to New Orleans. It chronicles a period of five years during which I ranged back and forth across this territory on long lonesome highways and wide quiet main streets and bone-white caliche roads, seeking to gain a livelihood. The desert environment was incidental to my aims, which might have been as easily pursued in friendlier climes, but it quickly bent them to its mood. In the unshaded sun, thoughts twist like timbers, turning from memory to fantasy to silence. There are people who make their home in this region and speak of its unspoiled beauty. That may be. But the beauty is pitiless and unusual, and the hard dark mountains furnish no refuge, and the effect of prolonged exposure is often to leave you wondering what is real.

This is evident in the first written accounts of travel through the Southwest. During a period of roughly two decades in the sixteenth century, a series of Spanish conquistadores clanked across this land, looking for gold to pillage and Indians to baptize or slay. Full of marvel and fright, the reports they submitted to the king of Spain are often prefaced with reassurances that what follows has not been fictionalized. "Novel or, for some persons, difficult to believe though the things narrated may be, I assure you they can be accepted without hesitation as strictly factual." So begins Alvar Nuñez Cabeza de Vaca's story. He was one of the sole survivors of an expedition that started in Tampa Bay in 1527 with four hundred men and ended, nine years later, when four naked, bearded, leather-footed survivors staggered out of the wilderness in Northern Mexico (several hundred miles from the location of my chapters V and VI). Cabeza de Vaca offered Spain the first glimpse of this terra incognita and he was justifiably concerned that the king would be disposed to doubt his tale. "Better than to exaggerate, I have minimized all things," he wrote. "It is enough to say that the relation is offered to Your Majesty for truth."

The same could not be said for the report turned in three years later by a Franciscan friar named Marcos de Niza. Friar Marcos had been sent into the mysterious expanse to investigate a passing mention by Cabeza de Vaca of "towns of great population and great houses" in what is now northern New Mexico. Fearful and unadventurous, Friar Marcos likely never made it past the Sonora Valley, but he fabricated a gripping tale of reconnaissance that includes a magical unicorn, Indians who scrape sweat from their bodies with golden spatulas, and a city so gigantic that it "has no end." Most important, he claimed to have found the "seven cities of gold," a mythical settlement of untold riches that had been the lodestar of Spanish exploration since the twelfth century. His fraud was discovered a year later when he returned with more than three hundred Spaniards, who were outraged to discover "a little, crowded village, looking as if it had been crumpled all up together," in the words of the expedition's chronicler. Somehow,

Friar Marcos escaped with his life, ever after to be known as the "Lying Monk."

Why did the friar lie? Historians have chewed on this for centuries. Some insist that he was a pawn of the viceroy or that he was misled by exaggerating Indians, aggrandizing guides, or even the air itself. "Since the rarefied atmosphere of the southwestern deserts is very deceptive," explained a pair of New Mexico historians in 1928, "it may be that the pueblo appeared much larger than it really was."

A long sojourn in the Southwest provides another explanation. It is unquestionably true that the desert is deceptive, but this may have more to do with its giant solitudes than its refractive atmospheric phenomena. To travel for hours over hundreds of miles of treeless flatland without seeing a soul is to be forcefully reminded of your inherent aloneness in the world. The immense unpeopled grasslands flecked with ancient plants diminish notions of a human community. What human community? By the end of his trip the friar was traveling across this barren without his companions. I can confirm that it is not unusual, in such situations, for the curtain between the real and the imaginary to lift. Alone on the plain, a man tells himself stories about who he is that draw from both domains. Fact and fabrication are opposites only where there is a society to verify or deny; for a man in isolation—and who is not?—the two share a greater taxonomy.

Though I have succumbed to the same desert solitudes and the same fictive impulse as undid Friar Marcos, I have taken great pains to avoid his fundamental error. Within this chronicle, every attempt has been made to separate the fact from the fabrication. Chapters identified as the former can be trusted not to deviate from what happened in real life, regardless of how novel or incredible they may seem; events related in chapters of the latter category are wholly invented. I do not wish to deceive by passing off fiction as fact, as so many have done, only to permit the real to mingle with the imagined, as it does in the deserted labyrinth of the mind.

–J. S.

NOTHING HAPPENED AND THEN IT DID

Chapter I

IN FAR WEST TEXAS, ON THE SIDE OF THE HIGHWAY that runs south from Marfa to Presidio and across the Rio Grande into Ojinaga, Mexico, there is a small green sign that reads, PROFILE OF LINCOLN. Under these words an arrow points west at the jagged foothills of the Chinati Mountains, where you can make out the sixteenth president's profile in the ridges of rock. He lies on his back, forever staring at the sky, his gigantic head inclined gently, as if on a pillow. The short brim of his stovepipe hat has afforded him little shade over the years, and his brow is black from the scorch of the sun. His lips, such as they are, appear cracked and turned down, his forehead wrinkled with worry, his gaze fixed ahead as if in contemplation of some profound bafflement. He seems to wonder, How in God's name did I end up here?

The term Far West Texas refers to that portion of the state that lies west of the Pecos River. It is dry and sparsely populated. The urban centers are El Paso and Midland-Odessa, both of which are located about three hours from Marfa, the little town where our story begins. On the way you pass vast ranches, though you do not see many cows. This is the Far West Texas range. Since the first big boom, in the years after the Civil War, the local cattle industry has been a business in decline. Encouraged by cheap land, and then discouraged by the never-ending drought, Far West Texas cattlemen went about setting up some of the largest and emptiest ranches in the West. As you drive south the situation worsens. Some ranchers in Presidio County, the seat of which is Marfa, routinely run herds as thin as one cow per two hundred acres.

The human population throughout the region is as sparse as that of the bovine. In five Far West Texas counties that cover as much ground as Massachusetts, Connecticut, and Rhode Island combined, there are barely fifty thousand people, most of them clustered in small, dusty towns scattered over an emptiness that would be absolute were it not for the occasional thirsting Hereford. The scout W. B. Parker appraised the area thusly in his 1856 account, *Through Unexplored Texas*: "For all purposes of human habitation—except it might be for a penal colony—these wilds are totally unfit."

Parker's assessment was meant for the prospective human settler, but to another sort of immigrant this desolation held great appeal. His story is not one you will hear the civic boosters tell, but in the bars and fields you might ask a friend. When the devil was expelled from heaven, he was made to select a dwelling place on earth. Looking to prove a point, he bypassed anything remotely paradisiacal. Green valleys, cheerful streams, and lush orchards did not detain him. With a sneer, he flew over bountiful farmland and wooded hills. Then he came to West Texas. Numerous topographical features are named to recognize his selection: Devil's River, Devil's Lake, Devil's Backbone, Devil's Ridge, Sierra Diablo, Diablo Plateau, Cerro Diablo. Among the county's older residents, it is not uncommon to encounter the belief that he can still be found living in a cave on the side of a mountain overlooking Presidio and Ojinaga.

IN OCTOBER 1999, when I was twenty-four years old and intent on becoming something, I purchased a 1982 Toyota Corolla, painted it green, packed it with my meager belongings, and lit out for Far West Texas. My plan was to become a journalist. It was not my first plan. My previous plan had been to become a poet, but several years into this plan I had begun to feel that I was spending too much time sitting alone with a pad of paper, and not enough time in the world. Journalism, though I had no experience in it, seemed like a good way to be in the world. I had read a book in which a journalist was described as "a roving eyeball looking for truth," and this had appealed to me. I wanted to be roving and felt that I was capable of being an eyeball. My idea was to learn the trade at a newspaper, where I would amass some clips and eventually turn up a story significant enough to sell to a magazine, whereupon I would be launched into a career as a freelance journalist.

I had been mulling this new plan for a while without doing much to initiate it, when it came to my attention, through a chance seating arrangement at a wedding that placed a friend of a friend adjacent to the editor of the *Big Bend Sentinel*, Marfa's weekly newspaper, that one of the *Sentinel*'s reporters had recently resigned. The editor of the paper, Robert Halpern, was not deterred by my lack of experience, and in a relatively sudden turn of events, I managed to secure the vacant newsroom chair. I left my home in California on the day after Halloween, the Corolla's dashboard covered in candy that melted before I'd made Phoenix. I arrived in Marfa on a Saturday night. A crowd of girls asked me what I was doing.

"I'm moving here," I announced.

They had a good laugh over that. "You'll never make it," one of them said. "The boredom will drive you crazy."

The *Sentinel*'s staff was extremely small. I covered the school board, the city council, the county commissioners, the drought, the Border Patrol, crime, cows, the post office, the Southern Pacific line, the D.A.'s race, and anything noteworthy in Valentine, a flyspeck town thirty miles east. Sitting through council meetings, I developed a good ear for Mayor Fritz Kahl's rambling pontifications. I wrote a long story about a local man who spent six months each year working as a helicopter pilot in Antarctica. "Write that what I miss most is the chile verde at Mando's," he told me.

I found a position as a caretaker on a bygone cattle ranch at the edge of town. The new owners were frequently out of town and wanted someone around to keep their flowers and fruit trees alive and their paths weeded. In the evenings I'd drag water hoses around the property, stumbling over clumping bluestem grasses as I stared at the star-filled sky. South of the property lay sixty-odd miles of desolate hills and plains, then Mexico. I lived in a small adobe building with cold tile floors. Behind my little house was an even littler house, a miniature built by the previous owners for their daughter to play in. It had a miniature broom and a miniature stove. When I watered the pansies around its porch I liked to stick my head in the miniature windows, pretending I was a giant.

▪ ▪ ▪

ABOUT THREE MONTHS after I started working at the paper I got a phone call from an old Marfan who wanted me to find an article about him in the newspaper archives. He had been a war hero. He'd misplaced his old clipping and it was getting yellowed besides. He didn't remember the date of the article but there was a big old picture of him on the front page. Could I look for it? This sort of request was common at a newspaper that sometimes felt like a huge community scrapbook, and I had performed the same service many times before. On this day, though, I got sidetracked. In one of the giant archive books, I came across a letter to the editor from the December 20, 1990, edition of the paper that contained, after some opening remarks, the following sentences:

> Neither [Pancho] Villa nor his men had any involvement in the disappearance of Ambrose Bierce. Bierce died on the night of January 17, 1914, and was buried in a common grave in Marfa the following morning, in a cemetery then located southwest of the old Blackwell School and across from the Shafter road.

I knew a few things about Bierce—that he had written a book of clever, ill-humored definitions called *The Devil's Dictionary*, that he was considered a great misanthrope, that he had disappeared somewhere in Northern Mexico, and that his disappearance had never been solved. I read on. The author of the letter was a man named Abelardo Sanchez, from Lancaster, California. He had been born in Marfa in 1929 and had lived there until he was sixteen, when he joined the Air Force. In 1957, he was driving from California back to Marfa on a Mexican highway when he picked up an old man named Agapito Montoya in San Luis, Sonora. When Montoya learned his driver's destination he piped up, "I been there, during the Revolution." Sanchez, who had a keen interest in the history of that war, encouraged his passenger's tale.

As Sanchez's letter explained, Montoya had been a soldier in Antonia Rojas's army, which fell to Villa's at the Battle of Ojinaga in January 1914. Montoya survived the battle and with three friends began heading south, toward Cuchillo Parado. Along the way, they came across an old man who "appeared quite sick from a cold." He was trying to fix a broken wheel on a horse cart.

The old man asked the soldiers, of which Montoya, at seventeen, was the youngest, if they could help him find Pancho Villa, about whom he intended to write an article. They laughed at him and told him they were trying to get away from Villa. The old man's conditioned worsened through the night, which the soldiers spent nearby, and in the morning he shifted his aim and asked if they might help him get across the border and up to Marfa. He offered to pay them each twenty pesos. The soldiers agreed. Sanchez's letter continued:

> During the trip they heard of different books he had written including one that my narrator recalled with the word devil in its title he said his name in Spanish was Ambrocio. My narrator also recalled that years later while visiting in El Paso, he recalled the name of a dairy milk that sounded just like Ambrocio's last name. On the second day after crossing the Rio Grande they were captured by elements of the Third Cavalry which was rounding up stragglers who had crossed the border. Bierce by this

time had pneumonia and could hardly speak, my narrator recalls him repeating a doctor's name in Marfa that began with the letter D.

Neither the soldiers, whose English was poor, nor the old man himself, whom sickness had rendered mute, could convince the troops that he was an American, and he was loaded into a wagon full of wounded and dying Mexicans. Several days later, while interned in Marfa at Fort D. A. Russell, Montoya and his friends learned from a cavalryman that the old man had died and was buried in a common grave.

I photocopied the letter and took it home. Later that night, after I'd finished my watering, I sat under a pecan tree beside the empty cattle pens and read it two more times by moonlight. The next day I checked out some of its clues. I found that a Price's Dairy had existed in El Paso from 1904 until 1970 and that in 1908 a doctor had moved to Marfa from Tyler and opened a small practice. His name was Joseph Calhoun Darracott.

I spent the next few weeks in the Marfa Public Library, learning more about Bierce—his strange childhood in Indiana, his entry into the Civil War, his years as a journalist for Hearst's *Examiner*. There were various theories regarding his disappearance. A writer named Sibley Morrill contended that Bierce had gone into Mexico as a secret agent, dispatched by Washington to spy on the Germans and Japanese, who were plotting a sneak attack with the Mexicans. Joe Nickell, an occult detective, argued that the whole Mexico story was meant to give Bierce the privacy he needed to go to the Grand Canyon and plug himself in the head. The most popular theory had Bierce killed in the Battle of Ojinaga, his corpse burned with the other dead to curb an outbreak of typhus. What is certain is that he departed Washington, D.C., on October 2, 1913, with Northern Mexico as his stated destination. "Don't write," he wrote to a San Francisco acquaintance on September 30. "I am leaving in a day or two for Mexico. If I can get in (and out) I shall go later to South America from some Western port. Doubtless I'm more likely to get in than out, but all good Gringos go to Heaven when shot." All his final letters had this macabre tone. He was seventy-one years old and his health was failing. To his niece he wrote: "Good-bye—if you hear of my being stood up against a Mexican stone wall and shot to rags please know that I think that a pretty good way to depart this life. It beats old age, disease, or falling down the cellar stairs. To be a Gringo in Mexico—ah, that is euthanasia."

IN 1861, Bierce shipped off to fight in the Civil War with the Ninth Indiana Volunteer Infantry Regiment. He was eighteen years old. During the war, he was promoted to second lieutenant and shot in the head by a rebel marksman. The fighting had a profound effect on him, forever tilting his humor toward the dark. Forty-eight years later, as he made his way from Washington to Mexico, he stopped to visit all the battle sites of his youth. He toured Orchard Knob and Missionary Ridge, Chickamauga, Snodgrass Hill, Hell's Half-Acre, Franklin, Nashville, and Corinth. At Shiloh he spent a whole day sitting alone in the sun. In New Orleans he let himself be interviewed by a newspaper reporter, who observed, "Perhaps it was in mourning for the dead over whose battlefields he has been wending his way towards New Orleans that Mr. Bierce was dressed in black. From head to toe he was attired in this color." From New Orleans he made his way across Texas. The final letter to his niece, dated November 6 from Laredo but sent November 5 from San Antonio, said, "I shall not be here long enough to hear from you, and don't know where I shall be next. Guess it doesn't matter much. Adios." For most of November and December he was silent. His last letter was posted from Chihuahua City, Mexico, on December 26, 1913. It was addressed to his secretary and stated that he planned to leave for Ojinaga the following day.

The gloom of Bierce's last letters would not have surprised his friends and readers. Death haunted nearly all of his work, from the war-mangled bodies in his Civil War stories to the mysterious demises in his collection of ghost tales *Can Such Things Be?* He favored the *coup de foudre*. A man is buried alive, then dug up by two medical students, then bludgeoned to death when he sits up panting in his coffin. An inventor, and champion of the machine, is strangled by his automaton chess player. A killer is pardoned, but the man carrying his pardon can't transmit the message because everyone in the capitol has left to watch the hanging. In "An Occurrence at Owl Creek Bridge," the reader is tricked into believing the dream of a hanging man that he has actually escaped the noose. In "Chickamauga," a little child wanders out to play in the forest. He roams about until he comes to a clearing where a plantation is on fire: "Suddenly the entire plantation, with its enclosing forest, seemed to turn as if upon a pivot. His little world swung half around; the points of the compass were reversed. He recognized the blazing buildings as his own home!" One of Bierce's many nicknames was "The Laughing Devil."

The more I learned about Bierce, the more credible Sanchez's letter looked to me. His version of Bierce's end was so Biercian.

It did not swerve from the expected with so much velocity as a Bierce story, but it swerved all the same. A proud old man of letters, intent on finishing his life on a valorous note, sallies forth into a war-ravaged nation in search of a heroic death before a firing squad or in the heat of battle. But at the country's border he succumbs to illness and must beg for help in a language he barely speaks. Hours of unglamorous confusion and agony pass. His identity, which he has sought to abandon, he now discovers he can no longer convey. Surrounded by strangers, he expires and is buried in an unmarked grave. It was hard to ignore the similarity between this anticlimax and the one outlined by the definition of "dead" in *The Devil's Dictionary,* which consists entirely of a quatrain by Squatol Johnes, one of the fictional poets Bierce quotes throughout the book:

> Done with the work of breathing; done
> With all the world; the mad race run
> Through to the end; the golden goal
> Attained and found to be a hole!

It all seemed convincing, and one morning I called Abelardo Sanchez at his home in Lancaster. He did not demonstrate much familiarity with Bierce, referring to him repeatedly as "Bryce" and to his masterwork as "*The Devil's Advocate.*" He said that before his conversation with Montoya, he "didn't know Ambrose from shinola." Even after that, he had no idea that Bierce's death was an unsolved mystery. What prompted his letter to the editor was the 1989 movie *Old Gringo*—starring Gregory Peck as an oddly sentimental Bierce—based on Carlos Fuentes's novel of the same name. Indignantly, Sanchez told me how his letter was briefly picked up by some local historians and then dropped. "But there is no question in my mind," he said, his voice rising. "Ambrose Bryce, the author of *The Devil's Advocate*, is buried in Marfa."

ACCORDING TO ARCHAEOLOGISTS, the desert is one of the best places to dig for remains. In the arid soil, clothing can remain intact, free of rot and rain, for hundreds of years. The only more preferable places for grave digging are the Arctic Circle and Mount Everest, where even bits of flesh stand a chance against decay. Sanchez's letter stated that Bierce's grave was southwest of the old Blackwell School and across from the Shafter road, which runs down to Ojinaga. But how far southwest of the school? Past the trailer park? Before Jerry Agan's house? Under Jerry Agan's house? And what did "across from the road" mean? It didn't make any sense. A horse pasture that ran along the west side of the old Shafter road seemed promising, but a late-night trudge through the clods yielded nothing. None of the Marfans I talked to knew where the old cemetery southwest of Blackwell School was located. Some of them seemed to think it had been moved.

I was considering the matter one morning over some fresh donuts and a watery cup of coffee at Carmen's. On the helicopter pilot's recommendation, I'd tried the chile verde at Mando's. To me it didn't touch the hash they slung at Carmen's. The dining room featured a wraparound mural depicting key episodes in the region's history—Indians squatting around a fire, Spaniards in helmets and codpieces striding down from the hills, cattle grazing on ranches. It was easy to get lost in the pictograph, crude as it was.

A friend named Michael Roch came in. He said he had heard

I was looking for a graveyard near the Shafter road. "Oliver Cataño took me down there once on horseback," he said, "and I remember my horse stepping over a grave. It was just outside Mr. MacGuire's ranch. There wasn't much there. I don't know if I could find it again, but I could try."

We drove along Alamito Creek. This is a dry creek that runs more or less parallel to the Shafter road. Kids use it as a playground and adults use it as a depository of sand and gravel. Every now and again, if there has been rain in the Davis Mountains, it will gush a brown torrent for a day or two, never failing to surprise a few people who have forgotten its original function. A few months before, a man had inadvertently drowned his horse in the creek. He had gotten in the habit of staking the animal at various spots along the creek bed where there was some forage coming up. There the poor animal had been, grazing on a tether, when the flood came tumbling down on him. All manner of things were borne away by these two-day rivers. During that same rain that swallowed the horse, I saw a telephone pole go flying past on the current, pursued by a live goat.

Michael and I walked down the dry bed. I hadn't had time to go by the house for a shovel, but there was some orange surveyor's tape rolling around in the back of the Toyota. I grabbed that and some plastic tent stakes. If we found anything, I could return with picks and spades and a bar. Michael stopped and scanned the horizon. I could see his eyes slackening, waiting for the moment of recognition. "It was somewhere down this way," he said, climbing up the east bank of the creek.

We walked through a field of abandoned cars and other weathered artifacts. A washing machine. One of those old fat-jigglers with the straps still on it. A tub. He ducked through a barbed-wire fence and I followed him into a large dusty field, where we stood around for a few moments before ducking through another fence into another field. Two horses wandered around listlessly. It was quiet and hot. A discarded bottle had filled all the way up with dust. It was packed solid. I picked it up to see how much it weighed.

"I guess it could be another field," Michael said, "but this feels like the one."

We tromped up and down, running our eyes over each contour of the ground, each nub of desert grass and greasewood bush. I looked underneath a mesquite tree. Michael snapped a bean pod off one of the limbs. We looked at each other. "It's strange," he said. "I really thought it was over here."

TALK OF GRAVEYARDS led to talk of devilry. A friend named Frank Quintanar told me about the time, thirty years ago, that a stranger showed up at a Marfa dance. This stranger was handsome and well dressed, and he quickly found a girl to take his arm. Laughing and shrieking, they spun around the floor. As the dance wound down, a boy in the crowd noticed that the stranger had the feet of a chicken. The boy screamed and pointed. The stranger vanished in a puff of smoke. It was the devil.

"And that is why Marfa will never be prosperous," Frank said. We were at the bar.

In another of Frank's stories the devil appeared as a little red demon with horns. He stood outside the kitchen window of one of Frank's friends, steaming. Then he drifted off. Neither of these little episodes seemed very devilish to me, but I was missing the point. This devil, or at least the Far West Texas version of the devil, was not interested in death and mayhem. He liked to play games with people. He once appeared to a group of Presidio children as a burro with no tail. The children, amused, ran to tell their parents. When they returned, the burro had vanished. Another time, a woman saw a dancing rabbit with no front legs. She reached for the rabbit, the rabbit disappeared, and she grabbed a cactus. The cactus gave her a minor infection.

It all made a kind of hell-born sense—the Laughing Devil bungling his end, the actual devil laughing. Was not the devil's mountaintop cave said to overlook the very spot where, according to Sanchez, Montoya and his friends found the old gringo fumbling with his broken cart? Maybe the devil's trail could lead me closer to Bierce.

To find the devil I went to see Saul Muñoz, a man old enough to know him. Don Saul lived down on the border, in a blink-and-you-miss-it town called Redford. Even though it was more than eighty miles away, Redford fell under the purview of the *Big Bend Sentinel*'s Local News section, and I knew a few people down there. It was a dusty place. There are people who claim that Highway 90, running east-west through Marfa, is the real border, and that everything south of it might as well be Mexico. I never exactly agreed with those people, but if I were made to debate them on this point, I would not bring along Redford to aid my rebuttal. I drove the Toyota down the main paved road and parked at Don Saul's crumbling house perched on a crumbling hill.

Don Saul was from just across the border in El Mulato. Most of his life he'd been a shepherd. On the mammoth ranches to the north and east, he would spend up to eight months at a time wandering with a herd of sheep. He worked alone, slept in caves, and now and again he would slaughter one of his own flock to feed himself. In later years he was a ranch cook. Around the time I went to see him, he was spending his time at home, watching a black-and-white television with a broken contrast knob and smoking pack after pack of Fiesta cigarettes.

He was happy to have the visit, and we sat in his dark, cool kitchen, drinking water from chipped coffee mugs, talking softly in Spanish. I waited until the pleasantries had concluded, then presented my cards. I was looking for Ambrose Bierce, and I had reason to believe the devil had been involved in his disappearance; did he, Don Saul, know where the devil was or how to find him?

"What?" he said, waving away a cloud of smoke.

I repeated my question. Had he ever seen the devil?

"There is no death and no devil," he told me, speaking slowly so I could understand. "We make death and we are the devil."

He started talking about water—how important it is, how to find it, what to do when there isn't any. He rattled off a series of maxims about hydration. "Water brings work," "No water means no life," "When it rains on a man's land, he's got everything." He cursed the drought a while longer, and lamented the slipping away of the old ranch life. None of it had anything to do with my question.

"I was once a cook for thirty men!" He shook his head. "Those days are over." As he spoke, a young man politely stuck his head in the room. He was tall, with a friendly smile. Don Saul got up to pour him a mug of water, and the young man mutely nodded his thanks and sat on the bed in the corner. Don Saul fished another Fiesta from his crumpled pack and sat back down.

"What about animals?" I asked him. There were many folktales in which the devil took the form of an innocent creature. Perhaps I could help him to remember. "Have you ever seen an animal that seemed strange in one way or another?"

He thought about this for a while, burning down his cigarette with long, slow intakes of smoke.

"*Pues*, owls have their own language," he said, as if he had finally found something that would interest me. The young man nodded. I knew that it was common for witches to take the form of owls in local folktales, so I asked if he'd ever seen one.

"A witch?" he asked.

"*Exactamente*," I said, glancing sidelong at the young man, who continued to grin as if we weren't discussing the direst sort of characters.

Don Saul gave me a disappointed look, then launched into a long argument about how every supposedly extraordinary phenomenon has an ordinary explanation. I could only understand about half of what he said, since in his eagerness to make me see his point he had begun to speak more quickly. The last thing he said was, "An owl is a bird." A silence fell over the room, and we listened to his dry tobacco crackle. I sat back in my chair. The young man was still smiling at me. What did he know?

"A friend of mine did see a witch one time," Don Saul said after a while, exhaling a large cloud of smoke and peering through it intently. "She was flying around in front of his campfire."

"A real witch?" I asked, grasping my pencil.

"Of course not," he said, having a good laugh. "It was his hair hanging in front of his eye. We are the witches. We trick ourselves."

He walked me outside into the scorching midafternoon sun. I thanked him for his time and asked if we might take a photograph. The young man took my camera, lined us up against an adobe wall, and silently shot two pictures of us squinting into the sun.

THE *SENTINEL* PUBLISHED every Thursday. We'd finish pasting up the pages Wednesday night around ten, whereupon Mr. T, a retired herpetologist with bad knees, would drive them up to the printer in Pecos, wait around for the issue to be run out, and then race back home with the bundled stacks, arriving just as the old battered ranch trucks pulled up to the office and the old crusty ranchers came inside to lay fifty cents in the cigar box and amble off with the news. Thursday morning through Sunday evening were days off, and my watering schedule left me plenty of time each week to prowl around.

The Sanchez letter was a decade old. Surely I wasn't the first to turn it over. I needed the advice of a trained professional. After two annoying conversations ("Don't chase fireflies," one man told me), I found my way to Glenn Willeford, a professor in the Center for Big Bend Studies at Alpine's Sul Ross State University. He referred to himself as a "Bierce-chaser." I made an appointment to see him the next day.

Alpine is twenty-six miles from Marfa. Most towns in Far West Texas are about thirty miles from each other, since they were water stops on the railroad before they were towns. Alpine has a population of around fifty-eight hundred, a two-screen movie theater, a lumber store (WE PUT THE PINE BACK IN ALPINE), a McDonald's, an Amtrak station, and the state university. The university's mascot is the lobo, or wolf, but a cast-iron longhorn with a gigantic rack stood at the campus gate, calling to mind a passage I had just read from Colonel Richard Irving Dodge's account of life in nineteenth-century Texas: "Every bush had its thorn; every animal, reptile, or insect had its horn, tooth, or sting; every male human his revolver; and each was ready to use his weapon of defense on any unfortunate sojourner, on the smallest, or even without the smallest, provocation."

I parked in the visitor lot. A teenager was picking cigarette butts out of the flower beds with a spear. Willeford's office was in the basement of a brick building, in a corner of a large storeroom. The storeroom was full of archaeological artifacts and office supplies and boxes of brand-new novels from a western series with titles like *Pony Express*, *Carry My Message*, and *Across the Crevasse*. His desk was wedged between two crates. "No one bothers me down here," he told me. Willeford was first drawn to Bierce by the Civil War stories. "I think his experiences in that war embittered him," he said. "But they made him think about the hereafter, and what men are like, and God. Vietnam did the same thing to me." Willeford had just finished writing a short paper on the Bierce mystery, and one of his central projects had been to refute the Sanchez letter. He handed me a copy. Mortified, I accepted it. Three things became clear in rapid succession: (1) Sanchez's letter was full of holes, some of them serious, some minor; (2) it was unlikely that Ambrose Bierce's bones would ever be found; and (3) I would make a terrible historian. The historian must develop an immunity to the suggestions of coincidence and the chance meetings the world throws up in his path. Apparently none of that means anything.

But what about intuition? I put the question directly to Willeford. He dismissed it with a wave of his pen. He had begun to annotate all the glaring errors in my copy of the Sanchez letter:

"One week after the battle? Pneumonia killed a lot faster than that." "This was ten dollars U.S. at the time. Not much inducement." "Unlikely." "Contradictory." "Impossible!"

"I don't think he'll ever be found," he said when he was finished. "But I'm not going to quit looking. You don't know anything until you look."

By the time I left Alpine night had fallen. I poured myself a cup of coffee at the Town & Country and began the short, lonely drive. About halfway through, after the road bends down out of Paisano Pass, I pulled over at the spot where tourists come from all over the country to watch the sky over Mitchell Flat for the so-called Marfa Mystery Lights. The lights streak across the horizon; they hover in the air; they have, on occasion, approached certain viewers, like friendly ghosts ("The Lights of God," Captain Manuel Pedro Vasco called them in 1617). Science has never explained the lights, and many people who have lived in the vicinity their whole lives have never seen them. I sat on the hood of the Toyota. Some tourists had parked an RV nearby and set up for their all-night vigil. "Do you see anything?" I heard one ask the other. I knew that the odds were against them getting any more out of the experience than videotape of the headlights on the Shafter road. Yet every week more tourists came, fooled themselves, slept in their cars with binoculars, bought T-shirts. The plain before us was as black as the brew in my cup. Willeford could annotate till dawn. I still believed Sanchez.

IT WAS NOON when I arrived in Mexico, and after a quick lunch and some sketchy directions from the woman at the taquería, I headed for the mountain on which, as legend had it, I would find the devil waiting for me in a cave. I turned right at the decrepit Hotel Ojinaga and rumbled along a terrible road, past the military *campamento* and the *tortilleria* and over the railroad tracks. The outskirts of town were a mess of old adobe houses, satellite dishes, chickens, and faded political slogans painted on cinderblock walls with shards of broken glass in place of barbed wire. At the end of the road I could turn either right or left. My lunch lady's directions did not include this fork. The mountain was straight ahead, a small white cross shining from its summit in the fierce sun. I stopped in at a small market called Abarrotes "Nellie."

The butcher in the back of the store was mindlessly working some sort of awful-looking meat product in a huge tub. His arms were bloody up to the elbows. I couldn't take my eyes off him as the woman behind the counter gave me directions. From the look on his face, you would have thought he was icing cakes. When a girl walked into the store he raised one gore-encased arm and waved.

Following Nellie's directions, I took the right turn and drove along a road far too wide to be a real road, kicking up a cloud of dust that had completely obscured the store by the time I was a hundred feet away. Past the last house, the road turned left and crossed half-buried train tracks. A small cemetery, overgrown with mesquite trees, marked the beginning of the trail to the mountain. I nudged the Toyota along this bumpy road, easing around rockslides, spinning the wheels as I came up from dry creek beds. She wasn't the right vehicle for the job, but I was discovering that she could be made to understand the exigencies of a given situation remarkably well. The road forked continuously.

What looked like flags marking the route to the mountain turned out to be white plastic bags blown into the thorny ocotillos along the road; their distribution was by no means uniform, but one seemed to appear before me each time I thought I'd picked the wrong fork, as if some unseen hand had called together wind, trash, and flora to lead me straight to hell.

I parked my car at the base of the mountain. The parched earth spread around me. A breeze blew, but it blew hot and dusty. I started up the trail, which split into two trails, which split into four trails, and although each trail led to the same place, the route I chose took the most difficult ascent. I clambered up a steep devil's slide, kicking loose rocks that crashed violently down the mountain to settle in the talus below. I grabbed a root and pulled myself over a small cliff on my stomach. When I reached the summit, I sat at the base of the twenty-foot white iron cross cemented into the rock and caught my breath. This was a serious cross, very high-power, designed to protect legions of souls from the foulest demon. Pieces of cinderblock kept the votive candles around it from falling down the mountain.

The wind picked up. Chinati Peak towered from the other side of the valley. According to legend, the devil would string a tightrope between these two summits and prance back and forth, tormenting the villagers below. I gazed down from his perspective. There was the gully where the gringo writer's cart broke; there, the clearing where he found the soldiers, the thicket where they slept; across the river, the hillside where they were captured by the cavalry and loaded into the wagons.

It was all very devilish, but where was the devil? Around and around, I searched the summit for his den. The spines on a cactus pointed me in opposite directions. From the dust, an old Fanta bottle cap stared up at me like a dead eye. I did not find the cave.

I GOT BACK to Ojinaga just as the stores reopened after siesta and went looking for Bryant Eduardo Holman. Holman was an old mudlogger—an oil-field hand—who had moved to Presidio from Roswell, New Mexico, years before, married a Mexican orthodontist, and opened up a native crafts store called Fausto's. He always kept a close eye on local politics, and when I was in town I would drop by his store to hear the newest plot he had uncovered and peruse the blankets and masks. On occasion, his intel held enough water to warrant an article. When I arrived, he was in the back, by the birdcages, posting something to his website.

"You wanna find the cave?" he said. "Sure, no problem."

We took his brown Isuzu Trooper. He drove as fast as he talked, spinning another hairy tale about municipal corruption and swaggering drug kingpins, and in what seemed like an impossibly short time we were back at the base of the mountain.

"It's just up here," Holman said, striding up the path.

I had been all wrong to head for the summit. Only a quarter of the way up the mountain, Holman veered off the left side of the path, climbed down a rock to a sandy ledge, and intoned, "Welcome to the *cueva del diablo*," in a spooky voice. He jumped down inside the cave and launched into a confusing account of the devil legend, which involved Cabeza de Vaca, Pancho Villa, and the Aztec god Tezcatlipoca, commonly known as "Smoking Mirror." "To really understand what's going on here," he said, rubbing his hands, "you need to know about the four unlucky days and the powerful syncretism that Cabeza de Vaca, who was by the way the first *curandero*, brought to this region. But even then, this is really ancient stuff. It goes back to the Uto-Aztecans and their tales about spiders in caves. Before that, even."

The cave was L-shaped, opening out to the valley and up to the sky. It was about ten feet deep and ten feet tall. Here was his mountain; here was his cave. I climbed down beside Holman and stood in the shadow.

Hello?

I had come for the devil and found a garrulous folk-art dealer. When I turned back to him, Holman was explaining why he counted John Reed as the father of American journalism. "It all begins with him crossing the border and getting in with Villa," he said.

Holman started down the mountain. He had pretty small feet, I noticed. Down at the Trooper a police truck pulled up. The road was a dead end, miles and miles from town, but the two fat cops in the cab were not interested in us. They explained that they were looking for a stolen Mustang with doors that were a different color from the body.

A FEW DAYS LATER I was sitting at home reading a story of Bierce's entitled "The Stranger." In the tale, the ghost of an old prospector visits the campfire of a group of "gentleman adventurers." This is in the Arizona desert. The men do not know he is a ghost straightaway. They take him for a "witless fellow," and a "harmless lunatic," an itinerant driven crazy by the desert. The narrator observes:

> We were not so new to the country as not to know that the solitary life of many a plainsman had a tendency to develop eccentricities of conduct and character not always easily distinguishable from mental aberration. A man is like a tree: in a forest of his fellows he will grow straight as his generic and individual nature permits; alone in the open, he yields to the deforming stresses and tortions that environ him.

Was this what had happened to me? Outside my window men from a local nursery were toiling, installing an automatic irrigation system for my landlords that would soon fulfill all my watering duties with the flip of a switch and the punch of a code. These men and I were natural enemies, and during the week that they were laboring on the system I tried to avoid contact with them. The month before, knowing they were coming, I'd laid out and planted several new beds of carefully selected native flora—*Chrysactinia mexicana*, flame acanthus, blue salvia, skullcap, and black dahlia—intending to establish my value as more than a mere dragger of water hoses. But no sooner had I installed the last of these tender shoots than a gray cloud of locusts appeared on the horizon. Within a week Marfa was swarming with the brittle insects, and all that remained of my garden was a few spindly stalks and some half-chewed foliage. When the crew from the nursery arrived to commence my obsolescence, I stood at the window and watched as they pointed at my tattered plants and laughed.

The study of Bierce I'd undertaken had filled me with dark suspicions. How strong a grip on things did I really have? Was I awake, living out my days, or had I perished in some hideous accident—the Toyota run down by a two-ton truck on the Shafter road—and was now beholding the mishaps of my former life through the eyes of a wraith? Had I found the devil after all, only to return with no memory of the meeting?

I peered through the blinds. A few of the men had gathered around a partially dug hole about a hundred feet from the miniature house. They stood in a semicircle, pointing at the ground and gesturing with their tools. The sun was low, and the sky was beginning to turn colors. A younger man with a shovel hopped down into the hole and began to dig; in no time he was up to his ribs. His shovel seemed to hit something hard and he dropped to his knees, out of sight; the men above peered down into the hole, then quickly waved him back up. Working together, they shoveled all the dirt back in a flurry of scoops. The whole thing had taken no more than ten minutes. When it was done one of the men stood over the spot and crossed himself.

I did not have to wait long to see what that hole contained. Within the hour the work trucks bounced off the property, gravel crunching beneath their heavy tires, and rolled smoothly onto the blacktop toward town. When the music from their radios had faded into the night, and when the screen door had slammed shut with its three diminishing bangs, I stood outside on the open plain.

The wind blew. Along the northern horizon, at intervals, great flashes of silent heat lightning surprised the dusky sky. Dried leaves rasped out a greeting on the cement walk. One miniature window of the miniature house had been left open. The white curtains behind it fluttered softly, hung still, and fluttered once more, like a lady getting seated at the theater.

I crossed the yard to the area where the discovery had been

made. There was no trouble finding the spot. In the center of the dirt yard, by a tree stump, a multitude of boot tracks pointed inward around a depressed patch of ground. I grabbed a trowel, fell to my knees, and began to dig. The dirt had been shoveled once already and it came away easily. By my side the pile grew, until I was down in the hole, smelling the earth, throwing the clods up over my head. Finally, my fingertips met with that which would not give—a wide, flat stone. I sat on it and scooped out the dirt to find its edges. It was a large rectangle, three feet wide and six feet long. I swept the surface clean with my hands and, bending low, blew across it, my cheeks filling and emptying with air, the dirt particles flying up off the stone and into my face and hair. I staggered to my feet and stood on the stone. The wind died. The plain was quiet. The stone was blank.

IN FAR WEST TEXAS, on the side of the highway that runs south from Marfa to Presidio and across the Rio Grande into Ojinaga, Mexico, there is a small green sign that reads, PROFILE OF LINCOLN. Under these words an arrow points west at the jagged foothills of the Chinati Mountains, where you can make out the sixteenth president's profile in the ridges of rock. It is not so easy to see—the vast sameness of the landscape confuses the eye—and many travelers who stop fail to find the accidental monument. Sometimes I pass them on my way up and down the Shafter road. Their cars are parked along the shoulder, fifty feet past the sign, in positions that testify to abrupt stops; their cameras swing idly from their shoulders; they stare and squint, furrowing their brows, their lips curling into profoundly baffled grins.

Chapter II

THE CATTLE KINGDOM AROSE FROM THE ASHES OF the Civil War. Four years of gruesome battles, hopeless cruelty, decimated farms, pulverized hamlets, and the deaths of more than six hundred thousand teenagers and young adults had concluded in a paper truce, following which Confederate soldiers returned to Texas to discover gigantic herds of wild longhorns multiplying unmolested on the plains, and the Union boys got home to hungry industrial cities. In view of this perfect harmony of supply and demand, remaining differences were put aside. Human blood was replaced with bovine. Over the next fifteen years, five million Texan cows were butchered in the northern slaughterhouses. The men who raised and delivered the cattle were known as cattlemen and cowboys, captains of a rough, romantic industry, the glory of which, alas, was short-lived. Overproduction soon caused beef prices to crash, barbed-wire fences and railroads made trail drives impossible and unnecessary, and new settlers chopped the open range into smaller and smaller parcels. The decisive blow came in 1884, when the Far West Texas rancher was walloped by the first of what would prove to be an unending series of droughts. During the next hundred years, his occupation would be gradually stripped of its panache by one blistering dry spell after another. Yet in the face of mounting evidence that his particular swath of the Great American Desert was unfriendly to the blooded English beef cow (a hapless but delicious beast that had replaced most of the tough native longhorn stock by the turn of the century), he borrowed more money from the bank, bought more feed for his dwindling herd, and waited for the weather to break his way. And this was where I found him, reflecting dimly in his daily routines the once-magnificent adventures of the cattle kingdom.

Our acquaintance began innocently enough, with an article for the February 3, 2000, issue of the *Big Bend Sentinel* entitled "Drought Taking Toll on Ranching." In the previous three years, local gauges had recorded an average of just four and a half inches of rain per year—the worst output in history. Cows were starving, crops perishing; every month another operation went bust. I was sent out with my notebook to take the measure of the pain. By this point, Halpern had quit dispatching me to school board and city council meetings. I had a tendency, exacerbated no doubt by the stresses and torsions of my maddening quest for Ambrose Bierce, to dwell on odd little details of a scene—the collection of snow globes on the superintendent's desk, the matching brown shoes worn by three out of eight county commissioners—and overlook the actual news. The week that the city council had voted to limit the number of horses residents could keep within city limits I had devoted most of my article to the belt buckles on the citizens who had signed up to speak against the motion. This led Halpern to decide that I would be better suited to feature writing. He assigned me profiles of a local paraplegic who painted with his toes, a cook who'd been churning out chicken-fried steaks and chile verde at Mando's for thirty years, and a beekeeper. For the drought story, I spent two weeks roaming the dustlands around Marfa, peering into ranches that looked like giant sandboxes, drinking burnt coffee with the man at the Ag office, reminiscing about old dry spells with cowhands at Carmen's, and kicking the dirt with young, anxious cattlemen leveraged up to their eyeballs.

I was happy with these assignments, but there is only so much you can do with a two-week deadline and five to eight hundred words. You can't explore the history of toe-painting, for instance, or dwell for more than one column inch on the curious life of Lorenzo Lorraine Langstroth, the "Father of American Beekeeping," a clergyman who took up hive-stacking as an antidote to severe depression. And while in both of these cases I was ultimately persuaded that Halpern's reluctance to publish my overlong submissions made newspaper sense, the drought story was a different matter. Water, as Saul Muñoz had explained, is everything. "No water means no life," he had told me, and it was increasingly clear to me that there was never any water in this corner of the country. When Cabeza de Vaca stumbled through the region in 1535, he noted that the local tribes, whom he dubbed "the Cow People," had ceased to plant corn because they knew it wouldn't grow. "They begged us to tell the sky to rain," he wrote in *La Relacion*, the first written chronicle of the region. "We promised we would pray." To Halpern, a native of this parched plain, the barrenness of the Far West Texas ranch may have been unremarkable, but as a newcomer I was obsessed by the question of why anyone would persist in such a punishing locale.

My article provided no answer. "Since the only kind of help

that will truly amend the situation comes from the skies," it concluded, "there is little to do in the meantime but cut losses and wait." Yet even as Mr. T raced off to Pecos with the broadsides, I knew there was more to say. A quote from Kelly Hargrove, whose family operates a large spread in south Presidio Country, lingered in my thoughts. "The clouds come, but they don't bring anything," she had told me. "They're just empty. That's one thing you get used to, living out here. Those empty clouds."

I hung on at the paper for another five weeks, writing about Valentine's Day at the post office and the new high school basketball coach, but all I thought of was the drought. What kept families like the Hargroves from pulling up stakes? It was as if some baleful force had lured them out here only to withhold the sole element required to make a go of it. Didn't anyone warn them? I pored over rainfall records at the Farm Service Agency. I read *The Time It Never Rained*, Elmer Kelton's famous novel about the infamous 1950s drought, and *The Great Plains*, Walter Prescott Webb's engrossing 1931 study of the arid West. "East of the Mississippi, civilization stood on three legs—land, water, and timber," Webb explained. "West of the Mississippi, not one but two of these legs were withdrawn—water and timber,—and civilization was left on one leg—land. It is small wonder that it toppled over in temporary failure."

On March 9, I resigned from the *Sentinel* to devote myself full-time to the drought. This was the magazine story I'd been waiting for, and so long as my debt did not exceed what I hoped to ultimately sell the article for, I figured it was reasonable to finance the reporting and writing with a credit card. This was not an entirely rash move. Halpern had been kind enough to help me get a brief story proposal into the hands of a fact-checker at

National Geographic whom he knew from his days at the *El Paso Times*. The fact-checker, Ted Langhorne, was nearing sixty years old, at which point he intended to retire from the magazine business, but he took an interest in me. He'd grown up poor on a farm in southern Virginia, and the experience had produced in him a wagonload of scorn for the rural life and an unquenchable thirst for stories that seemed to confirm it, such as broke ranchers raising bony cattle on the parched desert range.

Langhorne would make no commitments, but he indicated that the door was ajar, if not open. The debt limit I'd settled on was $4,000, or fifty cents per word (the novice rate, I'd read somewhere) for eight thousand words, which seemed the minimum number into which the decline and fall of the cattle kingdom could be crammed. With my minuscule expenses and the occasional spot work I could find working for local tradesmen, $4,000 represented a vast expanse of time, and I happily plunged into research, driving the Toyota for hours and days all over the area, to Crane and Upton and Iraan and Sanderson and even out west into little towns in New Mexico where the cashiers at the gas stations knew the yearly rainfall down to the tenth of an inch. I met worried ranchers biding their time in coffee shops and feed stores and slightly less worried ranchers stuck behind desks at their day jobs. Free of the newspaper's quick deadlines and need to stick entirely to the point, I found myself passing hours at the library in illuminating sidetracks about Paleolithic climatology, plate tectonics, Mongol horsemanship, and the Civil War. Periodically, a sense of the vastness of my subject would overcome me, and I'd recall with amusement the meager ambitions of "Drought Taking Toll on Ranching."

It is hard to say when exactly the project began to falter,

except that by late summer it was impossible to ignore the fact that six months had passed and I had written nothing but reams of notes. Part of the problem was that none of the ranchers I'd met were willing to say much. Far West Texas cowmen can be a laconic bunch, given to yes-or-no answers and affirmative nods. What appeared to me to be a great tragic subject was summed up by many of these weatherworn elders with no more than a shrug. The most elaborate explanation was from Cleat Lovell, whose family ranch south of Fort Stockton had been perennially torched for six generations: "You can buy an old horse that's skin and bones, and bring it on home, and feed it up, and as soon as it gets loose it'll run back to the pen where it's starved its whole life. Because that's home."

An offhand comment of Kelly Hargrove's haunted me like an unheeded warning. "There's not much to say about a drought," she had told me back when I interviewed her for the *Sentinel*. There was some truth to this. Sitting down to write each morning was like trying to swim in an empty pool. I knew how many inches it had rained in Ozona in 1918, what hay cost in the 1960s, and the correct order of the eight grades of USDA beef, from Prime down to Canner, but I had no story, no people talking. And I was running out of money. Among other things, I had miscalculated how much gas I'd need for all the fruitless driving around the plains in search of a good quote.

One afternoon in August I dialed Langhorne's number and left a long message about some new developments I was sorting out. As soon as I hung up, the message began to seem foolish. No doubt Langhorne, with his keen eye for facts, would see right through these vague excuses. I waited an hour or two, then left another message. This time I described the piece's calamitous panorama and read him a few lines from *The Time It Never Rained*. Within twenty minutes this too had come to seem like a bad move. A third call would only make things worse. I let it rest. Three weeks later he called back.

"They might have a little something for you over at *The New Yorker*," he said.

"*The New Yorker*?"

He said he'd been emailing with a friend at the magazine about me. I should call them. They wanted someone local for a piece they were doing on Midland. At that point, everyone was doing pieces on Midland, since it was where George W. Bush had lived when he was an oilman, and now it looked like he might get elected president.

"What sort of angle are they looking for?"

"Angle?" Langhorne mumbled. "How should I know?" I could always sense that he was reading something while we spoke, checking some facts.

"Should I send them clips?"

There was a sound on the other end of the line like a sneeze being caught in a library.

"They're not looking for a *writer*."

"Oh."

"Their piece is already written. They're sending a photographer and he needs a driver. I thought you could use the money."

MIDLAND IS THREE HOURS from Marfa, north on 17 and east on 20 across the ancient seafloor of the Permian Basin. Abandoned granaries and windblown old gas stations dot the vast dead ocean where once there were giant purple sponges and wavy grasses and strange life-forms mucking around the hills. It's a lonesome stretch. The boarded-up houses and weedy dooryards reminded me of an evocative passage I'd recently jotted down from *The Great Plains*: "A drought never produces panic. It comes too insidiously and slowly . . . the smallest cloud in the burnished sky offers hope until at last there is no room for hope. One can flee from a flood or a storm, but one does not flee from a drought. In too many cases by the time hope is lost, the means of fleeing have departed."

Soon pump jacks began to appear in the dusty fields, tilting lethargically at the earth, drawing up the liquefied fossils left by those cartoon creatures of the distant past. Who was to say the same fate wasn't in store for us, to have our crushed remains refined into fuel for some unknown future civilization? The idea preoccupied me through Odessa, into Midland, and down Wall Street into the city's small clump of skyscrapers. Midland's nickname is "the Tall City" even though its skyline is not particularly tall, because it rises dramatically out of a flat plain. A friend in Marfa, who'd grown up in Odessa, had described these downtown office towers as "oil-thermometers." When oil is good, he explained, they fill up floor by floor with executives shouting into phones and driving golf balls down the hallways; then oil goes bad and the fever breaks, starting at the top floor. With a few minor exceptions, oil had not been terribly good since 1982. Some of the thermometers had boards on the lobby windows.

Downtown was deserted. Pointless stoplights clicked up and down their partial spectrums for an audience of no one. The first living thing for blocks was a red-coated valet standing out in front of the hotel fiddling with his chin strap. We were staying at the Hilton, and it was for this as much as the daily driver's rate ($200) that I'd agreed to the job. Two nights pinned tightly between the fresh sheets of a fine hotel might do me some good.

"Sir?" The desk clerk peered at me from behind a polished stone ledge.

"I'm with *The New Yorker*," I told him.

"Yes, sir. Mr. Riemers is waiting for you in the lounge."

The lounge was full of bad abstract art and large couches upholstered as tight as drumheads. The photographer sat on one of them, barely making a dent in the cushion, studying a city map. His name was Jonas Riemers. He looked to be around fifty-five, maybe sixty, at the cusp of old age but disinclined to enter in. He wore a mesh vest with pockets all over it. Under it he had on a close-fitting black T-shirt. His face was rugged and red. A few strands of light blond, nearly white hair drooped over his forehead. The rest was swept back in a loose ponytail. There would be no mistaking him for a rancher, or an oilman, or a tourist from Oklahoma. A light meter swung on a cord around his neck. We made our introductions quickly. His grip was as strong as his German accent.

"You are living here?" he asked.

"South of here."

Frowning, he set off at once. "We will need some coffee," he said, crossing the lobby with a long, loping stride. The valet had only moved the Toyota into an alleyway next to the hotel and run it up on a slope of gravelly grass. He was saving the good spots. "This is the car?" Riemers said. I'd spent so much time driving the thing around it had become obvious it belonged to me. Riemers eyed it critically. "It will not break down, will it?"

"No, no, no. This is an '82, when they were still putting the famous 3TC engine in there."

"'Eighty-two? 3TC ?" He didn't look convinced.

We headed next door to a café called the Ground Floor. The countergirl was impressed with Riemers; he had that magnetism that can make an older man attractive to a teenager. She eyed his vest and the light meters hanging from his neck and giggled when he waved a paw at the pastry display and told her to give us "a selection." I carried the tray. Riemers came over and spread out his map, and we started to go over it while we drank the coffee and ate the pastries. One of them had a homemade blueberry filling, which you don't get much of anymore.

"They run only one shot for this George Bush story," Riemers said, putting on a pair of red-rimmed reading glasses and pouring a large amount of cream into his coffee. "What I like to do is make a sense of the place on several pages, you know, with the photos and the space in between them. But for this story there is only one shot." He rubbed his face and looked at the map. "Have you ever seen many pictures of Midland?" he asked me. I shook my head.

"I have seen none," he said, "except what there is for promotion at the airport. There are no pictures of Midland. Nothing has been done. This is different from New York. In New York, everything has been done. New York is too often recorded in photographs."

He stood up and slowly circled the table, squinting at the map. "What is the shot?" he mumbled. "In two days I must understand what there is about this Midland, this George Bush city, that can be captured in one shot." Riemers said all he knew about Midland was what he had seen on the old television show with J.R.

"That was Dallas," I told him. "This is West Texas."

"Yes. What is the difference?"

"The devil lives out here."

Before we could get into it, a man came up to the table grinning from ear to ear. "Let me guess," the man said. "Y'all're from *The New Yorker*!" He stared at us, waiting for a response. "I'm Bill Northcutt. The old poke that took around y'all's reporter gal." He handed us each a business card that said WILLIAM NORTHCUTT — MINERAL RECOVERY. "Deborah What's-her-name."

"Deborah *Gallatin*?" I said.

"That's the one," he said. "Sweet little honeydew."

"Deborah Gallatin's writing this article?"

"She told me they'd be sending us some photographers too," Northcutt said. "When I just saw you over here with the map I figured, *shoot*, those're them."

Riemers offered him a chair and they immediately got right into the map, discussing the looks of the different neighborhoods and the angle of the summer sun. Northcutt said he and Deborah Gallatin had hooked up in the same way, crossing paths in the Ground Floor on her first day in town. Before long, he'd agreed to be our guide as well. He had a pudgy round face with small button ears on either side. Riemers offered him some pastry, but he declined, pointing to his belly, which was straining the buttons of a white shirt. It was one of those Texan bellies that are similar to certain Mexican bellies—taut despite tremendous girth. Up top he wore a crumpled white boating hat with pairs of perforated grommets on either side of the crown. It was a peculiar hat to wear, so far from any navigable waters, but it had the look of an old favorite.

Northcutt seemed like the type to be driving a large air-conditioned vehicle, and I feared his addition to the project might negate my contributions entirely. Leather seats and cupholders! Clean carpets and unscathed upholstery! Why would *The New Yorker* pay someone to wait at the Hilton while these two roared around town drinking Big Gulps and powering up and down the windows? But Northcutt said he was having a new transmission put in. We claimed the Toyota and rolled onto the Midland streets.

Riemers wanted to start by looking at a few oil pumps up close, so Northcutt directed us down South Lamesa to a field near the interstate, where he had me park behind a dumpster. Out in the field a handful of pumps rocked slowly. While Northcutt and I waited at the car, I fished for information about Deborah Gallatin's working habits. I'd read dozens of her stories and profiles; more than once, while struggling with the drought material, I'd turned to her well-known piece about the demise of a family farm in Kansas, with its grand yet modest opening line: "Here in the land of the Wizard of Oz and Jesse James, there is nothing that can keep a small piece of the past from disappearing, not wishing, not fighting." It seemed a stroke of tremendous good luck to have paired up with someone who had spent time observing her in action.

"Did she use shorthand?" I asked him.

"She may have. She was always writing."

"Did she have any special routines?"

"What she does is she just mostly spends time with folks, you know, following them around. She followed Gene Dudek right into his house and sat in the corner watching him eat dinner in front of the TV. He said it was like when a dog knows he might be getting some scraps—that kinda look."

Riemers stood very still underneath a pump jack, aping the gentle nodding of the horselike head. He glanced at his light meter. Squatting down, he snapped a couple pictures. Then he turned and began to walk back toward us.

"What did she do if someone didn't have much to say?"

"It wouldn't matter. She would just stick with him, buy him a donut, wait in his car. She can spend more time looking at a thing or person than anyone you know. Hours could pass, or even days. She's a patient little thing. Most of the time they wouldn't even be talking about the governor or about oil."

"What would they talk about?"

"Oh, this and that. Just talk, is all. She knows how to talk to a person."

Riemers ducked through the fence. He stood beside Northcutt and stared back out across the field.

"This is not the shot," he said.

"I AM FROM GERMANY," Riemers told Northcutt, as we headed across town, "and I always say that Germany is the Texas of Europe."

"That's interesting," Northcutt said.

"Like you, we have the rustic cuisine. We have the physical strength. We have the past of living off the land."

Northcutt thought about it for a moment. "Well, we have those old Germans to thank for introducing the Mexican to the accordion," he said. "Have you ever heard a Mexican whaling away on one of those boogers?" He tapped my shoulder. "Find him one of them AM stations where they have them."

I spun the dial, looking for a *ranchero* to corroborate Northcutt's point. The Toyota's antenna had long since been snapped off, and most of the radio band was fuzz. Riemers stuck his head out the window and squinted up at the sky, then made a tiny note on a notepad he kept in his vest. Northcutt asked him about it and he explained that the light was much too strong for taking pictures right now, so we'd spend a few hours scouting around, trying to just locate the shot. It would be one shot and it would have to capture the whole archaeology of the place, he said. If we found it, we'd come back at dusk or early the next morning.

"What's this picture you're aiming at taking?" Northcutt asked him.

Riemers said he wouldn't know until he saw it, but it was out there somewhere and all he had to do was look. When he found it he would know. "I compare it to love at first sight," he said. "You are ready to recognize that person when you see her. You have seen her in your head already."

Riemers scouted all day, directing me around the city on impulsive jags and loops. Broken signage gave him a particular thrill, but anything derelict would do. He seemed to be looking for an image that would capture the feeling of a bust. Northcutt tried to play tour guide, but Riemers kept sidetracking his excursions, crying out "Left!" or "Right!" at the sight of some decayed motel board or rusting factory.

We were roasting in the Toyota without air-conditioning, but Riemers liked the old car. He said it reminded him of the cars in Ghana, and besides, having the windows down gave him a better connection to the city. "Connection" was a favorite word of his. He was always connecting with things. He liked to go up to a building and touch the side of it. Sometimes he picked up trash, looked at it very closely, and then tossed it back in the gutter. During several stops I saw him lie down on the ground and look at the sky. Anyone watching us might have thought he was some kind of crackbrain detective dispatched by headquarters as a last resort when conventional sleuthing had failed to locate a fugitive's trail.

When he wasn't searching for clues, he grilled Northcutt about local people and things, and Northcutt was happy to oblige. He knew all the stories, knew everyone's name, and even had dates. Deborah Gallatin had been lucky to run into him. "That fella there," he said, pointing out a freshly painted house with a black iron gate around it. "He owns all the pawnshops."

"Tell me about this oil business," Riemers said. "It is a good business, yes?"

"It can be," Northcutt said. "You have to keep your eyes open, though. You can't trust people like Jeremiah Hillard. Turn left here."

I turned onto a leafy road and headed north. "Who's Jeremiah Hillard?"

"A wolf in sheep's clothing. But that was in East Texas. Out here it's a more spacious industry, you see, because it's a reef. East Texas you've got a known structure. West Texas is an unknown structure. There's no telling where that oil is."

"So how do they find it?"

"I'm glad you asked that," Northcutt said, rubbing his hands together and squeezing up between the front seats. He told us that a while back he'd acquired the rights to a high-torsion pendular device for graphing petroleum deposits. A man from Palm Springs named Finley had invented it, and Northcutt had bought the patent off him and spent several years refining the technology and rethinking the marketing. He'd changed the name from the "Petroleograph" to the "Petro-Pointer," was one thing. When a prototype was ready, he tried to pitch it to the big oil producers and drilling outfits, but the going had thus far been tough.

"Have you ever heard of the experiment where they put monkeys in a cage with a banana hanging above a ladder, but whenever a monkey climbs up to get it, the scientists turn a hose on him?" Northcutt asked us.

"No."

"After a while, what they found was that no monkey would even *try* for the banana anymore. They were too sick of getting hosed. But then they started changing out the monkeys. And when a new one went up the ladder, all the old ones would screech at him to get down. Bit by bit, they replaced every old monkey with a new monkey, but what you still had was a bunch of monkeys that wouldn't go after the banana, even though they'd never actually been hosed themselves!"

He leaned forward and looked around for a minute, then told me to take a right at the next street.

"Point of that story is that's how company policy gets set. Why do they do it this way? Because that's how they did it before. And that is exactly how it was with the Pointer. Folks were scared of it because it hadn't been done before."

Riemers thought about it a minute. "Maybe monkeys only want to eat bananas because they see other monkeys eating one. Maybe if a monkey was really to think about it, he wants to eat something else, like a muffin."

"It has to be bananas. How is any monkey going to ever get to know about muffins?"

"Maybe he thinks for himself. Isn't this the point of your story?"

Northcutt was silent for a moment. "You have an interesting view of things," he said. "Go ahead and pull over here." I stopped in front of a pinkish building with pine trees around it. There were no curtains in the windows. "This was one of the governor's houses when he lived here," Northcutt said. "I brought Deborah by here a couple times."

Riemers got out and stalked around a bit, picking needles off the trees. Northcutt and I waited, leaning against the hood.

"What did she do when you brought her here?" I asked him.

"Well, she was peering in that window for a while, and when she came back I asked her what about it and she said you could learn a lot about a person from what kinds of carpets they had in their house. Isn't that funny? Of course, they might not have been his carpets when he lived here. That was some time ago. Listen, you understand why it has to be bananas and not muffins, right?"

"Did she write about the carpets?"

"Oh, I don't know. She was always writing. She would pull over now and again and just scribble some things down in her book every so often, but I never asked if it was the carpets."

Riemers came back shaking his head. "This is not the shot," he said.

FOLLOWING THE ARAB oil embargo, the population of Midland grew from around fifty-nine thousand to around ninety-two thousand. According to Northcutt, people came so fast there wasn't anywhere for them to live, and little tent-and-trailer cities bloomed wherever there was an empty field. Apartment buildings shot up. Then in 1982 the price of oil plunged, the drilling rig count sunk by fifty percent, and the banks began to fail. Brand-new houses couldn't be sold. Tents and everything else that wasn't firmly established vanished overnight. The oil-workers drifted off down the lonesome western highways with their families crammed in truck cabs, and no one filled the vacancies they left all over town. We drove past street after street of empty and overgrown houses and apartment complexes, with cracking sidewalks and walls and small desolate courtyards strewn with sun-bleached trash.

"Where is everyone?" Riemers said, when we'd stopped for Northcutt to make a phone call at a gas station.

Northcutt came back from his call looking nervous, but when Riemers asked him about it he said it was nothing. Sure, he said, he was in a bit of a hole, but he fully expected his luck would soon change. He said the oil and gas business was like that—one day you were rationing toothpaste and the next a man was asking what sort of handrails you'd like on your yacht. "My motto is, 'Opportunity knocks,'" he said. "That's why I left home. It wasn't knocking."

It turned out that Northcutt had grown up on a cattle ranch. His father had died some time ago, and now his mother was working the place herself, even though it was financial suicide in Northcutt's opinion. "Even when Dad was alive that place had bad margins," he said. "Mom's an old woman and oughta be someplace where they can look after her, instead of fooling around down there, and now with the drouth so bad."

"It is very bad?" Riemers asked.

"Now they're sayin' this one could end up worse than it was in the fifties. That's what I told Deborah. These ranchers out here like my mother, God bless her, they're just hanging on to nothing and don't know how to let go. Times have changed but they haven't changed themselves. I told Deborah it would be a good topic for one of her articles."

"Left!" Riemers shouted, but I just slammed on the brakes and swerved awkwardly off the road into an empty parking lot. Riemers shrugged and got out.

"The Blue Star Inn," Northcutt said, pointing to a restaurant. "In the eighties, you could go in there and one whole wall of the place would be loan officers eating chop suey and waiting—"

"Did you really tell Deborah Gallatin to write a story about the drought?"

He smiled. "Nobody tells that cute little bullwhip what to do. I said it could be an interesting topic for her."

"What did she say?"

"She thought I was right about that. Said she'd look into it."

"*What?* She did? When was this? Do you know if she did?"

Riemers swung open the passenger-side door. "This Midland is a strange place," he said. He told me to head straight down the road toward a blank billboard. I could barely make out the destination. My head was swimming. A haze had descended before my eyes. I drifted down the street without seeing it and double-parked a few feet from the curb. Riemers hopped out and stood beside the car, snapping away.

"Listen," I told Northcutt, "this is important. When was she here? When did this happen?"

"June, I believe it was. So, what is that? Three months ago?" He rapped his knuckles on the door panel. "Isn't it funny how long it takes them to write these magazine articles?"

Riemers climbed back into the car. "A very strange place,"

he said. "There is the sense of increase and then decrease, like a dry lake. Like the Permian Basin, yes? I read about this. It is a dry ocean?"

"That's right," Northcutt said, "only don't believe that junk about decayed marine material. Petroleum is a distillate of the atmosphere."

"The atmosphere?"

"There are formations that have no marine connection that have oil in them. Hard to explain, right? It is until you understand that there's methane gas all through the atmosphere, particularly around Pluto, and what it did was to precipitate out of the atmosphere during the formation of our own planet."

"It rained oil?" Riemers said.

"You're familiar with the Bermuda Triangle? All that is, is frozen methane gas from the bottom of the sea that breaks off and floats to the surface in that area and destroys the water's buoyancy."

"I had no idea."

"Nobody does. Now, see, what the Pointer does is register a presence of these qualities. It's got a pendulum of a specific mineral composition and it registers these atmospheric elements, stuff you'll never hear a geologist talk about."

I drove aimlessly down a sun-bleached four-lane boulevard flanked by cracked sidewalks and empty car lots, waiting for a direction. At an uncovered bus bench a woman blazed in the sun holding a newspaper over her head for not much shade.

"So what's in the pendulum?" Riemers asked.

Northcutt belly-laughed. "Nice try," he said.

▪ ▪ ▪

IN THE MORNING I took a shower, made a pot of coffee in the bathroom, and watched the news. The networks kept showing a clip of George Bush talking to some factory workers in Oregon. "I was raised in West Texas," he told them, "far away from the center of power." I polished off two pots of the weak bathroom brew, then dialed the number on Northcutt's business card.

"Listen," I told him. "I can't fool around about this. I need to know if Deborah Gallatin is working on a drought story. Is there anyone else out here she might have talked to?"

"I did tell her to call Mom," he said.

"Your mother? Did she call her?"

"I don't know. Mom and I haven't spoken in eleven and a half months."

Before I could stop him, he launched into the story. He had plans all ready to create a demonstration area for the Pointer out on the family spread, but his mother was blocking him. She was determined to keep the place a working cattle ranch in order to honor his father, who disliked the sight of an oil well. It seemed to Northcutt like a lot of foolishness that would pass with time, but then Northcutt's sister Diane married a man named Vasquez—a "Mexican vaquero," Northcutt called him—and the two of them had moved back home to help with the ranch. Northcutt claimed that with Vasquez always clanking around the house in his spurs, there was never any way to get his mother to think straight.

"Can you believe it?" Northcutt said. "Here I'm offering them a way to make some real money, and all they want to do is ride around after those cows all day. What a waste of time and money!"

I got the number and dialed Northcutt's mother immediately. An answering machine picked up. "You have reached the Palo

Verde Ranch," it said. "We have been here since 1937. You couldn't leave a message then, but you can now."

We spent the morning scouting and shooting sites even more depressing than what the previous day had turned up—a shotgun shack near the train tracks with a drooping clothesline; a derelict motor court's broken sign, spelling CRE TM OR - VACANCY against the sky; a grimy row of oil-field suppliers on the interstate between Midland and Odessa; a pool store with empty pools upside down on gravel; a billboard in the form of a postcard that read, DEAR PERMIAN BASIN, IF YOU TURN AWAY FROM WICKEDNESS AND SEEK MY FACE I WILL BLESS YOU. LOVE, GOD; a for-lease skyscraper reflecting a used car lot in its tinted glass windows; gaudy sixties-era restaurants that looked abandoned until I noticed a lone waitress sponging menus at the counter; empty streets and old buildings; back alleys with pallets askew; shadows of a parking garage.

Riemers snapped hundreds of photographs, but none of them satisfied him. He ran his hand through his hair over and over again, grumbling about the lenses he'd brought. We picked up Northcutt at lunchtime, and he took us to some well-thought-of barbecue joint, an old place with the ceiling smoked black, where the food came on butcher paper and the clientele was a mix of truck drivers, day laborers, and office workers with their ties tucked into their shirts. It was the largest group of people we'd yet encountered in the city.

"How was Mom?" Northcutt asked me.

"She wasn't there."

He laughed. "You need to wake up pretty early to get Mom on the phone. Vasquez has her out in the truck by sunup."

Riemers shoved his brisket around on his butcher paper and

frowned. He kept asking for sauerkraut, unable to believe they had none. Every few minutes he checked his watch and peered up through a greasy window at the position of the sun. Halfway through the meal I slipped away and tried Mrs. Northcutt on a pay phone in the parking lot. My heart raced with the ringer. Maybe Deborah Gallatin had never even considered writing a drought story. *Brrriiing*. Maybe when this was all over I would pay a visit to Palo Verde Ranch myself. *Brrriiing*. Maybe Northcutt would convince his mother to talk to me. The answering machine picked up.

As the afternoon wore on, an air of desperation began to overtake our small party. Riemers kept shouting for me to pull over. He'd hop out, shoot a roll of film, then mope back to the car and bang the dashboard in frustration. He'd grab a new roll out of his vest, rip the top off the plastic container with his mouth, and spit the lid ferociously down into the passenger boot. His ponytail had loosened with all the tumult and stray white hairs orbited his head. Every hour or so I'd dial Northcutt's mother, and each time the answering machine would pick up. As for Northcutt, he was far quieter than he'd been the day before. Twice, while we were waiting for Riemers, he asked me if I knew anything about the vending machine business, specifically whether the foods being unperishable made the margins any better than they were for a straight grocery store, with its rows of produce and high overhead. By six o'clock all three of us were exhausted, silently plunged in our own thoughts. I drove for more than half an hour without a single stop or a single word. We passed abandoned schools, rusting train cars, peeling billboards. Nothing.

■ ■ ■

"HOW ABOUT WE GET a bird's-eye view of things?" Northcutt asked.

He said he could get us up on top of one of the downtown skyscrapers if we liked. Riemers shrugged, and soon we were pulling up to the base of one of the towers. Every parking spot on the street was available. "You're gonna like this," Northcutt said. He made a few calls from a pay phone, and twenty minutes later we followed him to the service entrance, where twin brothers named Grady and Brady were waiting for us. Through the strange ways of the universe, these twins, both of whom were wearing Dallas Cowboys jerseys, had come to oversee the operation of this skyscraper, and somehow Northcutt knew them well enough to call in the favor. As we rode up in the elevator, he said to them, "They're taking the pictures for that reporter gal I brought by."

"Jesus," one of them said, shaking his head. He looked at Riemers and checked his watch. "You're not going to want to spend the night up there too, are you?"

On the roof the city spread out below us as it had on the map at the café. Only now we could see the edges of it, where the buildings petered out and the nothingness commenced. No trees or lakes or rivers. No real hills. No scattered homes. Gazing out at the "vast country," as Walter Prescott Webb had called it, I felt an odd sense of possession. What did Deborah Gallatin know about these plains? Had she read Webb's book? Did she know that, during Francisco Coronado's expedition across these flatlands in 1541, the Spaniards were constantly getting lost until they found some Indian guides who reckoned their course by taking note of the sunrise every morning, firing an arrow in the direction they wished to travel, and then marching until they found the shaft? Without the sun, they could not keep their bearings. There was nothing else. And yet the sun was also a nemesis, since there was nowhere to escape it either. Had Deborah Gallatin ever thought of that? Had she driven the desert highways long enough to start talking to herself? Had she stared at the vast emptiness and been reminded of Ozymandias, king of kings, whose crumbled monument in the Egyptian desert inspired Percy Shelley's famous poem, with its famous last line: "Round the decay of that colossal wreck, boundless and bare, the lone and level sands stretch far away"?

"There!" Riemers said. "Right there!" He was standing at the edge of the roof, staring at a neighborhood just west of downtown, a run-down area of shotgun shacks and dead trees. We had driven around there the day before. All the streets were named for states.

"What is it?" Northcutt said.

"The shot."

"Well, let's run down and get your equipment."

Riemers looked at him. "The shot is not up here," he said. "It is down there."

We raced through the empty streets. Riemers had a pretty good sense of where we were headed, but every few blocks he would shout, "Stop!" and hop out of the car to look around. Then he would jump back in and tell me where to go next. Soon we were in among the streets named for states. Ramshackle sheds with rusted tin roofs lined weedy blocks of gnarled trees. No one was outside except a small child we'd seen the day before, digging holes in his side yard with a knife.

"Stop!" Riemers jumped out of the car and ran around in a circle, looking up at the buildings poking up out of the downtown. The street dead-ended in a rental yard. A chain-link fence surrounded a few banged-up cement mixers, a Rototiller, and untidy stacks of scaffolding. The gate was padlocked, with a small hand-painted sign that said DOC'S RENTALS - NO TRESSPASSING. Riemers was moving fast now, and there was something strange about the way he was moving. He hurried back and forth on the sidewalk with the camera held to his eye, taking small, stiff steps to avoid tripping. He stalked across the street and tried another angle, glancing nervously at the sky. He backpedaled up the block and tried it from there. He slammed on a new lens and ran around an empty lot.

Northcutt and I sat in the car and waited. "What's your opinion of those little go-me-rounds for children they put out on the sidewalk in front of the Quik Sak?" Northcutt said.

"What?"

"Do you think a man could make some money on those?"

"What are you talking about?"

"I never put much stock in them. They're known to break down on average five times a year and require costly repairs. That's why you never see any kids on them. Most of them are broken if you took a closer look. And what's it cost to run one? A quarter? Two quarters?"

Two dogs started barking, and we turned to see Riemers swinging a leg over the fence around the rental yard. He'd taken off his camera and hung it from a pole, and now he was straddling the fence, one leg on each side, and the dogs were hopping and twisting just beneath his feet. One was a Doberman and the other looked like a blue heeler, which is a strange dog to use for guarding cement mixers, but maybe there was more to the business than that. Northcutt ran over and shook the fence.

"Good Lord! Get down from there!" he shouted. "Those dogs'll kill you!"

Riemers said he was trying to get to the little shed office in the middle of the lot. That was where the shot was and the light was running out.

"You're not gettin' there now," Northcutt told him. "That's for sure."

Riemers's voice was level and calm. "These dogs are pussies," he said. "You should see the dogs in Morocco."

He fished some leftover nut bread from the Ground Floor out of one of his vest pockets and dropped it on the dogs' heads. They scarfed it up and went back to nipping at Riemers. Northcutt and I pleaded with him to dismount the fence but he ignored us. He dropped some more nut bread, and then he swung his other leg over the fence and slid to the ground.

The dogs struck first, shredding his pants legs and tearing at his vest. Riemers gasped as the powerful Doberman lunged into his groin. "*Platz! Platz!*" he screamed. "*Nein! Nein! Pfui!*" Northcutt was yelling too, just abstract sounds of fear. I started looking around for a stick or a stone, but when I found one and came back the tides had turned and now Riemers seemed to be the one on the dogs. I'd never seen anything like it. He grabbed the Doberman by the collar and punched it in the nose three times fast. The heeler went at his feet as heelers do and he turned around and kicked it in the neck with the steel toe of his boot. The dog let out a cry and rolled backward while the Doberman snuck around and bit Riemers on the hand, but before its teeth were sunk in too deep, Riemers yanked his hand away, throwing blood, and threw himself viciously at the Doberman's back, roaring German obscenities like a bear.

While I clung to the fence, gasping for air, Riemers seized both collars and slammed the dogs' heads together repeatedly until they began to whine and moan. "*Pass auf!*" he shouted, tossing them to the ground and giving each one an extra kick for good measure. He grabbed his camera before they could regain their composure and ran over to the rental office. Using the security bars over the windows, he swung up to the roof, where he shook out his hair with gusto and strode to and fro against the colors of the evening sky, screaming, "*Das ist's! Das ist der verdammte shot!*"

I slid down onto the sidewalk and leaned against the fence. Northcutt had vanished. Somewhere in the midst of the violence he'd turned and run, and I'd been too distracted to see which way he'd gone. I stared in stupefaction at Riemers's dramatic silhouette. The nonchalance with which he had faced the snapping canine jaws seemed to suggest a routine of such violent confrontations. What would Deborah Gallatin think? I happened to know from some of her articles that she was a dog lover, but I was starting to believe that this sort of professional ferocity was common to the higher echelons of journalism.

The sky faded around Riemers as he worked; the dogs came back to life. They stood at the base of the rental office barking and howling. Riemers hopped up and down, howling back in jubilation. Everything was going his way. Before too long Northcutt returned, riding in an El Camino with a man named Ray who worked at the yard. Ray was a fat man, sweaty and hitching up his pants. He opened the gate, quieted the Doberman and the heeler, and brought out a ladder. He and Riemers stood and talked for a while, and even though Riemers had broken and entered and left the dogs in tatters, he somehow convinced Ray to let it all go. He shot a roll of film of Ray posing with his arms crossed and a stern look on his face next to different pieces of rental equipment, and even took a few pictures of him with the dogs, who seemed confused. Back at the Hilton bar we drank two bottles of champagne on *The New Yorker*'s tab and ate shrimp cocktails as fast as they could bring them. Riemers kept proposing triumphal toasts; he toasted Midland, George Bush, Northcutt, me, the twins, Ray, Deborah Gallatin, pump jacks, J. R. Ewing, and the Petro-Pointer, at which point I thought I saw Northcutt daub at his eye with a cocktail napkin.

I couldn't share in the exultation. When Northcutt said he knew a bar that had a pretty good girl singer from Oklahoma on Thursday nights, they left to go find her in a taxi.

THAT NIGHT I had a feverish dream that Deborah Gallatin was driving the Toyota down a gaudy stretch of Nevada highway, past flashing neon signs and leering truck stop hotels. She was looking for an all-dog circus. I was riding shotgun, in charge of navigation. Some fungus was growing in the glove compartment. Worrying about it, I missed the exit for the circus, and right in the middle of the highway she threw the car in reverse. The Toyota began to bleat like a delivery truck. It's never done that before, I thought. How does she get it to do that? After a while I realized that it was the alarm clock.

I'd set it early so as to catch Mrs. Northcutt before Vasquez took her out in the truck. Even with the curtains open the room was still dark. I made another pot of bathroom coffee. This time she answered on the third ring. I explained who I was and how I knew her son, and she wasted no time in telling me what a fool she thought he was.

"That man Finley filled Willy's head with all kinds of get-rich-quick talk and scientific theories from thin air, to where he can't have a reasonable conversation anymore," she said. "It's always, 'Oh, you haven't seen Finley's charts,' or, 'Oh, you haven't watched the demonstration video.' Do you know how he bought that silly patent?"

"How?"

"With money his daddy had put aside for him. And there goes Willy, throwing it away on a bit of California pie-in-the-sky. He's about as sharp as a mashed potato."

"Does it work?"

"Are you crazy? When I was a child a man could get run out of town for one of those devices. But it fits with Willy's view of things, which is that you can get rich without working for it, just by finding it with a magic wand."

I asked if she'd heard from Deborah Gallatin.

"Sure I did! Willy sent her down here looking for the Dust Bowl. He told her we're living off armadillos and wild pigs. All he wants is to run me off so he can go hunting for oil. Did he ask you for any money?"

"No, but are you saying—"

"Good. Don't give him any. He's my own son, and I love him, but that boy has his head so far up his own behind he can see what he ate for dinner last night."

"I'm sorry. Are you saying Deborah Gallatin has already visited you?"

"Thank goodness she's gone! I couldn't do a thing with her around. Always asking me questions and following me around. I told her there wasn't much to say about hard times but she wasn't satisfied with that. No, sir. Had to keep pushing for more."

"What did you tell her?"

"Oh, I don't know. I can't even remember what I said. It was like when the police interrogate somebody and won't even let them think straight. She drug it out of me just the way they do, asking questions over and over, making me go through the whole history of the ranch and how we got here and everything. Half the time she just sat there looking at me, not even asking any questions, only not letting me relax. She wouldn't quit. I said more words to her than I believe I said to my own husband during the last year that he was alive. And I'm not the only one. Couple weeks later I saw George White, who has a place over there by Sanderson, and she had been to see him too. He said he'd told her things he had not even told his own daughter, just to get her out of the house where he could get some work done again. Can you believe that?"

I PACKED MY SUITCASE and rode the elevator down. The lobby was shiny and empty; the desk clerk hoped I had enjoyed my stay. Outside a bluish glow was beginning to illuminate the streets. The valet wasn't on duty yet, so I had to walk around and around in the echoing garage, looking for the Toyota. It was rooftop. Back on the road I drove fifty-five under a cover of clouds. The morning stayed gray. Big trucks and loaded minivans whipped shuddering past me in the fast lane, getting where they were going, but I stopped at every rest area and gas station I could find. I was in no hurry to return to Marfa.

I ate a breakfast burrito at the Town & Country in McCamey and headed down toward Interstate 10. As I came up on the Pecos River the clouds cleared and suddenly the sun was streaming. I could imagine it racing up the rest of the riverbed, northwestward all the way to Carlsbad, and racing south and west down the plains ahead of me, over the empty pastures, two-lane roads, faded flags, bald hills, and dry gullies; soon the tin roofs of the abandoned wool and mohair warehouses in Fort Stockton and Alpine and Marfa and all the other little towns would begin to creak as they expanded in the heat; the bleached timbers of the disused cattle chutes along the rail line would twist and crack; old dogs in Valentine and Van Horn would slink under benches and tables; on the ranches down south men would frown at the sky as they drove down dusty roads to check their cattle troughs; dashboards would melt in parking lots and food not set in the shade would spoil; anything that nobody had watered would perish before too long; by noon the glare would be at its height, casting a fierce eye on all the hopeless activity.

The interstate appeared. *West. East.* To the west there would never be any respite. To the west the devil was laughing. I turned east. I had no plan. It was only a detour, I told myself, as the hours and towns rolled by. Fredericksburg. San Antonio. Houston. Lake Charles. Just past midnight I drifted into New Orleans. I slept in the car.

The days became weeks. I drank coffee with chicory and tried writing poetry again. I found a job busing plates at the Palace Café, a two-story restaurant on Canal, eight blocks from the Mississippi, where the bananas Foster was flambéed tableside and the wait staff wore white formal coats. I rented a tiny place in a boardinghouse on Elysian Fields and sent a letter to my old landlords telling them to dispose of the few things I'd left behind. I sat in bars and tried not to think about the drought-stricken plains of Far West Texas. Every week, en route to the Palace, I would stop and check the table of contents of the new *New Yorker* at a newsstand down the street, apron in my back pocket, shoulders braced against the wall. It was May when Deborah Gallatin's drought story came out. I didn't read it. I didn't want to know what it said. I still don't know what it says.

Chapter III

SUMMER IN NEW ORLEANS IS A LONG SLOW THING. Day and night, a heavy heat presides. Rivulets of sweat run down the necks and arms and legs of unlucky pedestrians. Dogs retreat under houses. Waiters stand idle at outdoor cafés, fanning themselves with menus. The unreasonable weather drives off tourists, and as they go, so goes the city's main industry. Throughout town the pinch sets in. Rents are missed. Bald tires go unreplaced on cars. Couches are torn apart for loose change once, twice, even three times. It is an idle, maudlin time, a time to close up the shutters and tie streamers to your air conditioner; to lie around drinking very weak drinks while you plot ways of scraping by that involve neither exertion nor exposure.

So I was occupied one humid afternoon, when I came across a small newspaper notice that announced in large letters, "$25,000 POETRY CONTEST." "Have you written a poem?" the notice began. I had. In the nine months since the trip to Midland I'd written little else. A couple were decent, but who knew they would be worth anything? In the past, back when I was trying to become a poet, I had submitted poems to mail-in contests and lit mags all the time. The prizes they offered never amounted to much—three hundred dollars, a year's free subscription. This was a different proposition altogether. This was real money. Twenty-five thousand for the grand prize winner, five thousand for first place, three thousand for second place.

I needed a break like this. The Palace Café had been enough to keep my head above water but now that the tourists were gone it was barely even doing that. The debts I'd incurred casting around the sands of Far West Texas were no closer to being paid, and my plan to become a journalist had stalled completely. I was no longer a roving eyeball searching for truth. I was broke. If I could clear my balance sheet I thought I might move to Mexico and look for stories down there. I figured the chances of getting scooped would decrease considerably the farther I got from the "centers of power," as the new president had put it. Twenty-five grand would last for years in one of those little fishing villages along the Pacific coast. I submitted my poem that very day.

Two weeks later I had in my hands a letter from something calling itself the Famous Poets Society, based in Talent, Oregon. The Executive Committee of its distinguished Board of Directors, the letter informed me, had chosen my poem, from a multitude, to be entered in its seventh annual poetry convention, which would be held September 16–18 at John Ascuaga's Nugget Hotel and Casino in Reno, Nevada. "Poets from all over the world will be there to enjoy your renown," the letter boasted, "including film superstar Tony Curtis." A color brochure showed rollicking scenes from conventions past. Inside the brochure, an entry form listed the Nugget's room rates and the convention entry fees.

It was not exactly what I had imagined. The notice in the newspaper had said nothing about a convention in Reno, and I'd taken this for a legitimate prize and not the shadowy scheme it now appeared to be. Doubtless I was not alone. Poets, it occurred to me, must make very good marks. Even a half poet like myself was still credulous enough to get roped in. You wouldn't get nearly as far with a convention for journalists. At the first faint whiff of a racket, they'd have their notepads out and their tape recorders rolling. As Lord Macaulay once observed, "Poetry requires not an examining but a believing frame of mind." My attempt to trade the latter for the former was still a work in progress, but I was no fool. I was about to throw the letter away when it dawned on me that there was still the matter of the $25,000.

The letter was signed by Mark Schramm, the executive director of the society. He informed me that should I choose to make the trip, I would be honored with the "Jake Silverstein 2001 Poet of the Year Medallion" and the "Prometheus Muse of Fire Trophy," both of which I would find to be "unique." Schramm continued, "The fabulous Tab Hunter has asked that you personally walk with him in our Famous Poets Parade! As our Grand Marshal, he invites you to bring a poem of peace to release 'on the wings of Pegasus,' during our Famous Poets for Peace Balloonathon. Your poem is your message of love to the world. . . . I also look forward to seeing you win our poetry contest! Imagine yourself with a $25,000 check in hand and being crowned 'Famous Poet Laureate for 2001'! I can already hear the crowd cheering as the laureate crown is placed on your head! How beautiful you look!"

Clearly everyone who submitted a poem in the first place had been invited to the convention (excepting, I would later learn, an incorrigibly obscene few), and clearly Tab Hunter had never said anything to Schramm about my walking with him. But it was also a good bet that the competition at the Nugget for that $25,000 might not be so stiff. You had to figure that the crass marketing pitch would act as a deterrent to the country's best poets. Factoring in my past writing experience, I pegged it at no worse than 100 to 1 that if I went to Reno, I'd win $25,000 and get to wear a crown. Longer odds are played every day. I wrote back to say I would attend.

FIVE DAYS BEFORE the convention was to begin, terrorists flew planes into the World Trade Center and the Pentagon, killing thousands of Americans and plunging the country headlong into the age of terror, but the Famous Poets Society decided to push ahead with its program as planned. It was felt that poetry was needed now more than ever. It was also felt that there would be no full refund of the $495 registration fee, in the event of a canceled flight or a distraught flier or a sinking sensation that the timing was bad for big bets. I flew to San Francisco, rented a car, and took Interstate 80 up into the Sierra Nevadas, over Donner Pass, to John Ascuaga's Nugget in Reno.

The Nugget started off as a coffee shop, and grew, over the years, into a full-scale operation with its own dancing elephant. Now it was a double-towered stucco giant, huge and labyrinthine, with underground chambers so vast that the pillars in the Polynesian restaurant near the slot machines were actually supporting Interstate 80, or so I read somewhere. I identified myself to the bellhop as a famous poet. It had a nice ring to it, but the heavy-lidded teen was completely unimpressed. Waving a lackluster arm, he directed me to the second floor for convention registration. There I was presented with my Prometheus Muse of Fire Trophy and my Poet of the Year Medallion. My Muse of Fire Trophy was a cheap-looking wedge of plastic with an image of a man in a toga—Prometheus, I assumed—pressed into its back. A sticker personalized this gimcrack. My medallion seemed more valuable, since it was made from a metal into which my name had been irrevocably punched. Once I had the trophy and medallion in hand, I was presented with a certificate honoring me as a recipient of the trophy and medallion. I also got a red T-shirt. Stowing these laurels in my room, I made for the Champagne Reception in the Rose Ballroom.

The room was full of poets. It was difficult, scanning the crowd, to arrive at a conclusion as to what exactly I was up against. Who were my fiercest rivals for the $25,000? The brunette in the revealing blouse with the falsetto laugh? The loner with the black leather hat and the matching black fanny pack? The tan old man wearing cargo pants? The minister? What would the grand prize mean to them? How bad did they want it? My failures in Texas and all the lean months in New Orleans had honed my need. Up in my hotel room, I had a suitcase full of books from my old poet days—anthologies, copies of treatises on versification, anything that seemed like it might give me an edge.

"First time here?" a man asked me. He was wearing a jean jacket and jeans. He had a bristly brown beard and a long hawk-like nose. His name tag identified him as Doc Smith.

"Yes," I told him. "Yours?"

"Nah," he said. "I been here before."

"So you like it?"

"It's all right." He scanned the crowd with a sour expression. "Thing that gets annoying is all these thirteen-year-old girls writing about broken hearts, lost love, suicide, that sort of thing. Try going to war."

Doc's voice was gruff, and his bearing suggested a long-standing annoyance with the world. He was a Vietnam veteran. I wondered if he'd ever shared the battlefield with Professor Willeford. Before the war he had been a singer in a band called People whose song "I Love You" had traveled up the charts to number fourteen in 1968. He sang a few bars for me. It sounded like a good song for dancing close with a girl. He gave me his card, which said "Vietnam Veterans of America, Chapter 290," in big letters; and in smaller letters, "John Doc Smith, The Poet."

"This is an okay conference," he said. "But it's not as nice as the one the International Library of Poetry puts out. When they have a champagne reception, it's all the champagne you could want, plus punch and hors d'oeuvres, and top-flight entertainment. Classy." He looked disparagingly at the tables. "This one's going downhill."

It was true that the scene lacked glamour. The Rose Ballroom did not feel much like a ballroom. The walls were carpeted in institutional gray, the floor in a tacky pattern of red and blue. The stage was empty save for an off-center podium. Fluorescent tubes lit the room unkindly. On folding tables covered in red paper, the champagne was lined up in plastic glasses. The supply was sorely insufficient. Mostly, the tables were covered with empty glasses, upside down and on their sides. "They don't put enough champagne," I heard an elderly Filipino man in a three-piece suit and snappy two-tone brogues complain.

Doc seemed to know his way around the convention, so I asked if he had any tricks for winning the cash prize.

"Nah," he said. "Just do your thing. Don't get nervous. Hardest competition is going to be from the black people. They tend to be more expressive, and that impresses the judges."

Before Doc could finish his counsel, the emcee of the convention, Alisha Rodrigues, called us to order. Doc snorted. He'd seen it all before and was going to try his luck on the slots. According to the General Schedule, we were to be introduced to the poets who would be our teachers for the next three days. There was Rigg Kennedy, who had a supporting role in the 1982 film *The Slumber Party Massacre*; Joel Weiss, who played an orderly in *The Meteor Man*; and Al D'Andrea, who appeared as Lieutenant Wilkins in the short-lived television drama *Brooklyn South*.

"Please help me welcome," Alisha said, "the acclaimed author of *Riggwords*, and a true famous poet: Rigg Kennedy!"

From the front row, a man in a white turtleneck and safari-style pants rose. As he mounted the stage, I noted a strange buoyancy to his bright white hair, as if each follicle housed a tightly coiled miniature spring. He grasped the podium with both hands, leaned in to the microphone, and proclaimed, "As poets, each one of you, in your cellular structure, in your brainpower, can change the universe." His hairs trembled. "I'm going to read 'Kozmic Alley.' It was first published in *Architectural Digest*."

Rigg shuffled his papers with a dignified air, took a sip of water, and cleared his throat. He then began to wail at the top of his lungs. Across the aisle a cowboy poet who had been napping sat up like a shot had gone off. The woman in front of me covered her baby's ears. Rigg modulated his wail up and down and then started breaking up the wails with some whistles. When he'd had enough of that, he intoned solemnly:

space dust clouds spinning whirling
gushing gases dancing throbbing divinely
exploding indefinites definitely longer farer
than i dare count to kingdom come

Rigg took a dramatic pause to let the first stanza sink in. The silence was partial. Like a shopping mall, a casino is full of hundreds of tiny speakers that play soothing background music in one genre or another. At that particular moment the Nugget's system was playing a punchy jazz tune, and the piano filled Rigg's caesura with unwanted gaiety. He did his best to ignore this, then opened his mouth extremely wide and began to croak. He took a drink of water and gargled into the microphone. He did some panting, then finished with more of the wailing and whistling that had gotten him started. Across the aisle, the cowboy poet tipped back his ten-gallon hat and frowned.

I shared the cowboy's consternation. If this was the sort of poetry the judges were looking for, I might be in trouble. My poem had no sound effects. Did they expect me to gargle?

These fears were allayed somewhat by the next poet, Joel Weiss, a younger man with a thick Bronx accent. When his name was announced, he bounded onstage and began an awkward striptease. "I'm not dressed right for this poetry," he said, swinging his jacket. Women hooted and rushed the stage with cameras. Underneath his shirt and slacks Joel sported New York Mets boxer shorts and a matching Mets jersey. "I'm a lifelong baseball fan," he said with a laugh. "That explains my poetry." Joel asked that the ladies return to their seats, then recited an original composition entitled "On My Way to Shea." The poem rhymed and had a metrical structure that he regularly defied. There was a clever twist at the end when the narrator, who you think is a fan, turns out to be a player, but because of the way Joel read the poem this effect was lost. His bungled recitation suggested either that this was the first time he had seen the poem in years, or that it had been composed in haste during Rigg's bag of tricks. Still, Joel's verses were warmly received, in large measure because they reassured us that we would be expected neither to gargle nor to pant.

There followed a confused interlude in which Alisha got up onstage, walked to the podium, started to speak, then stopped and went to the edge of the stage to confer. When the conferring was done she explained that Tony Curtis had lost friends in the tragedy in New York and would not be with us today. Alisha told us to hold hands and bow our heads together as we observed a moment of silent prayer for Mr. Curtis and his family. We did, and the theme song from *Bonanza* filled the ballroom.

AFTER A SHORT BREAK, we reconvened for the Master Workshop, presented by Al D'Andrea. Al affected a professorial demeanor, repeatedly snatching off his reading glasses and gesturing philosophically with his hands. He ranged over a number of poets, from William Carlos Williams to Lucille Clifton, each one serving the overall point of his address, which was called "Saying Yes: Embracing the Life Force of Your Poem." He closed with a poem by James Scully entitled "What Is Poetry?" Having just witnessed the dramatic opposition of Rigg's experimental soundscape and Joel's corny baseball rhymes, and with $25,000 hanging somewhere in the balance, I found the question pertinent. Unfortunately, Scully offered no definitive answers. He posed instead a series of odd counter-questions, such as "if it were a crib / would you trust your baby to sleep in it?" Al added to the weight of these quandaries by chewing on his glasses.

As we filed out of the Rose Ballroom, it suddenly occurred to me that despite all the time I had spent trying to become a poet,

I'd never once tried to formulate an answer to Scully's question. What is poetry? How could I have expected to get anywhere if I'd never even tried to solve this riddle? There were twenty minutes to kill before the next activity, and I spent them upstairs, thumbing through my books, looking for someone who had. What is poetry? For that matter, what is journalism? I'd never tried to solve that one either. No wonder my plans kept foundering. The closest I got to an answer was Samuel Johnson, who had struggled with Scully's very question before concluding, "It is much easier to say what it is not. We all know what light is, but it is not so easy to tell what it is."

How would Joel Weiss field the query? To prepare our poems for the judged readings, we had been divided into ten "classes" and assigned "homeroom monitors." I'd landed in Class Six with Joel, a lucky break. He was no Dr. Johnson, to be sure, but the feeling among Class Six poets was that the chance to study under him, if only for several hours, would give us a considerable advantage over the poor slobs whose monitors had not even been deemed worthy enough to speak at the opening ceremony.

"Just to give a brief introduction to myself," Joel began, as we found seats in a gigantic room we only half filled. "I'm an actor. I've got a movie coming out in October with Wesley Snipes. I've been in forty-two films, and in most of them I get beat up or killed. I started writing poetry on trains and stuff. I never really call myself a poet. I just try to get out my frustrations. Who's got a question?"

"Do I need to cut my poem to twenty-one lines?" This came from Bertha Venson, a small black woman with a lisp from Euclid, Ohio.

"That's important," Joel said, dropping his voice an octave

to indicate that he was leveling with us. "If your poem's going over, cut the extra lines. You have one solid minute when you're up there. I know you care about your poem, but once you're up there, you're trying to win the moolah."

This was true. Whatever Dr. Johnson might think, in Reno a poem was a lottery ticket, and none of us shied from this important fact. Poetry might be "the spontaneous overflow of powerful feelings," as Wordsworth said, but what good would it do you if it flowed right over the time limit? Joel's caveat sparked an anxious discussion, in which it came out that many of the poets were in violation of the time limits and at a loss for how to prune their verses. Realizing he had caused a minor crisis, Joel hurriedly offered up the best panacea he could muster. "You know what I always say?" he said, leveling with us even more. "If it ain't broke, don't fix it." This settled things down somewhat, even though it didn't make any sense at all. A blond woman with heavy eye makeup and a German accent stood up. "I have a glittery dress," she said. "Do I wear my glittery dress before the judges?"

"What about a peach dress?" another poet cried. "Is peach a good color for the camera?"

Joel relaxed a little, sensing that he was out of the woods with having to edit all our poems and back in familiar territory. "Peach, glitters, or whatever you're gonna wear," he said. "Figure it out tonight and lay it out on your bed so you won't have to think about it tomorrow morning."

We took a dinner break after the first round of readings. I brought my books down to the Golden Rooster and, over a plate of fried chicken, reconsidered Scully's question in relation to the Class Six poets. About half the class's poems operated on the understanding that poetry was an instructive art, a pleasant way of passing along an uplifting lesson. In this they fit the neoclassical mode outlined by Sir Philip Sidney in his 1581 *Defence of Poesie*, which defined poetry as "a speaking Picture, with this end to teach and delight." There was "An Imperfect World," by Anita Jones of Cincinnati, which put forth, in list fashion, all of the things that were wrong with the world, that we might learn to accept them; "Taking Time," by Lydia Heiges of Kempner, Texas (she of the glittery dress), which reminded the reader to slow down and enjoy life; "At a Time Like This," by Myra Ann Richardson of Kernersville, North Carolina, a patriotic verse that aimed to rally our spirits; and "I Want to Know Please," by Lou Howard of Azle, Texas, which used the device of an inquisitive child to illustrate how "it takes both sunshine and rain to make rainbows." These poems relied on poetic tropes—flowers that stood for hope, sunsets that led to contemplation—and standard formats—the list, the apostrophe, the regular metrical line—to convey certain messages to the audience. They would have pleased Sir Philip, who felt that poetry's purpose was to appeal to those "hard hearted evill men who thinke vertue a schoole name, and know no other good but *indulgere genio*, and therefore despise the austere admonitions of the Philosopher." Sir Philip figured these men would swallow the uplifting message of a poem, "ere themselves be aware, as if they tooke a medicine of Cheries."

Around 1800, Sir Philip's utilitarianism gave way to the unkempt ravings of the Romantics, from whom the remaining Class Six poets seemed to take their cue. These poems were meant to convey the rawest inner emotions, most of which turned out to be gloomy. Reena Louis's poem, "The Lost Letter," matched up against the most melancholy that Keats had to offer, and Wes Dodrill's "The Last Race," an elegy for stock-car driver

Dale Earnhardt, was every bit as mournful and sad as Shelley's "Adonaïs" or Wordsworth's "Extempore Effusion upon the Death of James Hogg." For these classmates poetry was, as Lord Byron had seen it, "the lava of the imagination whose eruption prevents an earthquake."

My own poem was neither a medicine of Cheries nor a blowhole of the soul. It was called "New York, so often recorded in photographs," and so far, I hadn't heard anything I thought would beat it. I shut my books and took a stroll around the casino floor. There were famous poets everywhere, easily identifiable by their gold medallions and red T-shirts with the proclamation I'M THEIR MOST FAMOUS POET! printed in black across the back. They stuffed coins into nickel and quarter games with such names as Quartermania, Betty Boop, Blazing 7s, and I Dream of Jeannie. At their sides, cigarettes burned untouched in ashtrays. Every once in a while, a machine shouted, "Wheel! Of! Fortune!"

I made my way over to the Aquarium Bar, where in a pale blue light, surrounded by wooden tiki lanterns, plastic banana trees, and red totem poles, I ran into Doc. He was peeved.

"They don't have the alumni jacket," he said, shaking his head.

"The what?"

"The alumni jacket. If you go to one one year you're supposed to get an alumni jacket the next year. They don't have them. You know, you get your people who swear by the Famous Poets Society, but to me it's just amateur compared to the International Library."

It was hard to believe this business with the jacket alone had set him off, so I asked him if he had been losing money too.

"Nah," he said, gazing out at the casino. "I'm up eight hundred bucks. Been at Blazing 7s all day."

It turned out that what was really eating Doc was some teenage poet who had won a prize for the last three years running. The kid was back again, looking for a four-peat.

"Kid doesn't even change the poem," Doc complained. "Just keeps bringing the same one back and winning the prize."

"Well, it must be pretty good," I said.

"Nah, it's nothing special. But he does a whole Ricky Martin routine on it. Goes down on his knees for the sad parts. The judges like that crap."

The Aquarium Bar's evening entertainment—Darcy on vocals, January on keys—started in on a cover of "Captain of Her Heart." Through the banana trees I saw a woman run out of coins on a Quartermania machine and jokingly try to stuff her Poet of the Year Medallion down the slot.

"The main problem I have with poetry is this," Doc said. "It's totally subjective."

ON MONDAY MORNING I woke in a tangle of sheets and lay there turning things over in my head. The confidence I'd felt after the first homeroom session was shaken. Clearly I needed to be dramatizing my poem if I wanted to win the $25,000. This kid with the Ricky Martin routine was going to walk all over me. How would it feel to come all this way and lose to a dance routine? I ran over my poem a few times, looking for places where I might go down on a knee, but my poem did not seem to lend itself to that kind of theater. The clock was ticking. Class Six was scheduled to read before the judges at three p.m. I threw on some clothes and headed downstairs for Joel's morning lecture, "How to Be a Poet on Your Feet."

The session was under way when I arrived. Classes Five and Six were both in attendance, and rows of poets sat listening studiously to Joel's discourse. "As actors we always deal with being in the moment," he said, speaking quickly in his Bronx accent. "As famous poets, we do the same thing. When we read it, we want to make the feelings and everything happen just like when we wrote it. Just to go back to the acting thing for a minute, we do a play like ninety times, and every night we eat the same donut, and even if you like donuts it becomes repetitious. But that audience that comes in shouldn't know that you've been eating that donut every day, and that, you know, the donut's terrible, because you're still eating it like it's the first time you're ever biting into that donut and boy, that is so good, that donut! Or apple or whatever."

Joel referred to this as "In the Moment," the second of the poet's four basic tools. The others were Focus, Emotions, and Life Experiences. In the Moment, however, was the most important of the four, and to get us there Joel had devised a game he called "How to Be a Poet on Your Feet." The idea was for each famous poet to take three random words from the audience and just rattle off a poem, employing the words like verbal steppingstones. No one volunteered, and Joel had to jump-start us with a few demonstrations. By the time he'd banged out his fifth poem-on-his-feet, the Ponderosa Room was boiling with volunteers and people trying to get their words chosen. "Sex!" yelled a man in a T-shirt with FREE SPIRIT printed across the front. In a matter of minutes the whole thing had devolved into a rancorous competition between Classes Five and Six over who had the best poets. As each poet took the stage and announced his or her allegiance, the audience responded with cheers and taunts.

"Class Six! Class Six!"

"Class Five represent!"

"You're the best, Class Six!"

When Bertha Venson of Class Six took the words "strawberry," "pancake," and "nugget," and turned them into, "In the morning I love to eat pancakes / And with them, I love to eat nuggets. / But the best of all is when I eat strawberries," the crowd went wild.

"That is Class Six!" the German woman screamed.

A woman from Class Five stood up, shaking her head, and said, "Class Five is 'bout to take home the cash money, though." Pandemonium ensued. Joel was pressed for a verdict. "Enjoy your next class!" he shouted. "You're all winners!"

We headed across the hall for Rigg's talk, "The Importance of Being a Poet for Life." Today he had on a blue turtleneck, with the same safari pants as before. I recalled that he had been photographed wearing a black turtleneck for Schramm's color brochure. This run of turtlenecks seemed in keeping with the whole Rigg Kennedy persona. Perched atop a stool at the head of the Bonanza Room, he looked like some sort of eccentric zoologist, on tour to promote his unorthodox theories about natural selection. As we filed in, he stared thoughtfully at the ceiling, nodding periodically as a familiar face drifted by. The program was as different from "How to Be a Poet on Your Feet" as "Kozmic Alley" was from "On My Way to Shea." Whereas Joel's style as a lecturer had been to challenge us with fun games, Rigg's was to confound us with weird philosophical questions.

"How do you spell a sound like this?" he asked, crumpling his lecture notes into the microphone.

Silence fell.

"Crumple?" offered a woman.

"Crinkle! Crinkle!" shouted a man.

Rigg stroked his goatee meaningfully. "Crinkle, crumple. Okay. But what is the sound? The sound is not saying, 'Crinkle, crinkle, crinkle.' It's saying . . . "

"Rumble!" someone yelled from the back.

It was hard to know what Rigg was driving at. He nodded his head as if we had hit a familiar wall. "I don't know if we'll get an answer today, but I want you to think about it. You, as poets, have the godlike privilege of inventing words. I find that pretty amazing. Can you imagine the person who created the word 'peace'? Or the person who created the word 'war'?"

There followed another baffled silence. It occurred to me that baffled silence might be Rigg's primary goal as an artist. He told us about the numerous Eskimo words for snow; the possibility of using extrasensory perception to compose poetic verses; the parallels between writing poetry, acting, and doing cancer research; and aliens. "What do you think?" he asked us. "Do extraterrestrials enjoy the power and pleasure of poetry?"

The whole lecture seemed to be built around questions that caused the mind to go slack. They had the opposite effect on Rigg, however. He had worked himself up into a lather.

"Adventure awaits!" he exclaimed. "Once I let a blind person lead me to a poetry class in West Hollywood. I drove several elderly poets there, but when I parked the car the rest was up to her. She used her cane and her superior instincts, and I held her arm, with my eyes closed, trusting her to navigate the busy boulevard." Here, eyes closed, Rigg fumbled about, dramatically enacting the scene. "Tires were screeching, horns were honking. The blind leading the blind to a poetry class! It was a beautiful afternoon. And when, my colleagues, you let go and trust that a spontaneous creation is about to happen, then you will have become twenty-four-hour-a-day poets for the rest of your lives."

The lecture came to an abrupt close. It mystified me on many fronts, and I hoped he would take questions. What had he meant by "Many poets have been proven to have six senses"? But Rigg was curious to hear our poems and opened the floor of the Bonanza Room to all. A bottleneck formed instantly.

THE JUDGED READINGS had been going on since eight a.m. in the Celebrity Showroom, an old dinner theater with heavy tables and plush cocktail booths. This was the Nugget's swankiest venue. The railings were dark polished mahogany. Red velvet covered the walls. A gold lamé curtain bordered the stage, bunched in dazzling symmetrical folds around the proscenium. Tiny Tivoli lights outlined the aisles and the steps and the ample round lip of a stage that had been trod by the likes of Dick Dale, Pasquale Esposito, and Gordon Lightfoot.

I arrived in the midst of Class Five's performances. A pretty young woman with heavy eye makeup and a tight black T-shirt was reading a poem called "Aloha Blue" that made the case for Hawaiian sovereignty. Emblazoned across her shirt in rhinestones was the title of her poem. In the center of the stage, behind the poet, hung a giant movie screen, on which was projected her enormous image, as if she played to a crowd of thousands.

The three judges sat in three cocktail booths, rapidly shuffling through mountains of paper as the readings proceeded. Despite the importance our lecturers had placed on dramatization, the three barely lifted their heads to watch the action on the boards. The top judge, Mary Rudge, wore massive spectacles and a red velvet dress. She was pear-shaped, with curly white hair and big round cheeks, and reminded me a little of Mrs. Claus.

The poets of Class Five finished their readings, and Class Six formed into a line that snaked through the darkness to a door that led to the wings of the stage. I was the final poet in this line, with the best view of the readings. It was not a show I was particularly looking forward to. In the past twenty-four hours, I had witnessed most of the performances four times. When Emma Tutson Thompson of Clinton, Louisiana, began with her poem, "Our Love," I was able to recite the opening couplet along with her: "Our love is like a dream that comes true. / Really because, I love you."

I soon found that I had involuntarily committed much of Class Six's verses to memory. Kevin Banks read his poem, "You're Not Alone," which told the story of a supernatural visit from his dead grandmother. The last line was, "Grandmother's rocking chair is rocking." One of Doc's teenage girl poets, Nicole Noel Miller, stepped up to read her poem, "The Encounter," a melodramatic account of a suicide attempt averted at the crucial moment through Jesus's intervention. Extensive choreography accompanied her verse. Initially I had found the gestures rigidly theatrical, but seeing them repeated so many times in exactly the same way gave them an almost ritualistic appeal.

As the next poet's head filled the screen, it occurred to me that beyond their differences in form and content, the Class Six poems were all remarkably similar on this point. They all included at least one verbal or physical gesture that was repeated in exactly the same way at every reading. The gestures might be flamboyant, like Nicole's; or they might be as subtle as Flora Dozier's odd way of ending every line with a spondee, or Audrey Soto's practiced shrug in the midst of her final couplet. Every poet had a certain routine that she adhered to with clerical rigidity. Running through the familiar rhythms of voice and gesture put her in a trance, an eternal swoon within which the much-debated time limits were rendered irrelevant.

The anthologies in my hotel room were full of the same sort of thing. The earliest poems in English were lamentations on the theme of time. To the anonymous poets of the thirteenth century, time was organic and indifferent.

Nou goth sonne under wode—
Me reweth, Marie, thi faire rode.
("Now goes the sun under the wood—
I pity, Mary, thy fair face.")

To Shakespeare it was brutal.

O! how shall summer's honey breath hold out
Against the wrackful siege of battering days,
When rocks impregnable are not so stout,
Nor gates of steel so strong, but Time decays?

In Reno, it was incomprehensible and cruel. Most of the famous poets had begun to write their verses in the aftermath of a great pain. Some were widows. Many had lost children, parents, and friends. Yet in the chanting of their poems, time and loss were forgotten for a minute. Sunsets did not fade. Children kept their innocence. Grandmothers endured.

Some of the first poets to have read began leaving. As they swung open the glass doors I heard that machine cry, "Wheel! Of! Fortune!" It was my turn:

New York, so often recorded in photographs,
Must have trouble believing its crows can fly,
Or that when snow, in clouds
Of misdirection, is falling, it falls.

The weight in the withstanding snubs
The whitened flakes of logic, flees
Wet streets that are streets, scoffs
At routine measurements of what is there.

New York, so often recorded in photographs,
Must have trouble believing its heart can stop,
Or that as doves, in nests along the river, forever
Swept and sweeping, are hatching, they have hatched.

THAT NIGHT AT the Shakespeare banquet we hashed out the odds on the twenty-five grand. From the open field a few favorites had emerged. At my table a dental hygienist from Dallas advised that the smart money liked a man from her class. "His name is James Stelly," she said, "and he's given his whole life to going around and telling what drugs did to him. He can bring tears to anyone's eye that hears him."

We chewed on that one for a minute. A Brownsville poet

wanted to know what Mr. Stelly's poem was about. The hygienist explained, "It's about how if every time zone in the world would pray for one hour we could have a week of solid prayer. Or two weeks. I can't remember, but he had it all worked out with a chart. Some people were crying just from the chart."

A silence fell over the table as we readjusted our own hopes in light of this new information. How were we to contend with this man and his chart? No one had told us that visual aids were allowed. Charlotte Partridge, a fellow Class Sixer from Trinity, Texas, said, "I have a poem called 'You Are My Everything' that is awesome, but it was too long."

Irregularly enforced time limits had become the convention's dominant controversy. Apparently, a number of the recitations had exceeded one minute without incurring any sort of penalty, and this had troubled those honest entrants who had cut their poems or changed them entirely to comply with the rules. I myself had been well within the minute.

After dinner I ran into Doc outside the ballroom, and we stood off to the side for a while, watching the poets promenade. Many had seen the banquet as a chance to air their finest soup and fish. There were red tuxedoes, pink tuxedoes, green tuxedoes, and black tuxedoes; satin ball gowns and ruby slippers, strapless evening dresses and short skirts with red spike heels. Some poets wore Elizabethan-era costumes with bodices and billowy sleeves; some wore great African robes with matching turbans. They paraded back and forth in the hallway in front of the ballroom, admiring one another's drapes and reciting their verses aloud.

Doc was still in his jeans. He had some complaints about the banquet.

"First of all, at the International Library they bring you into the dinner with trumpets," he said. "Then they have a real fucking meal. None of this boiled chicken."

"People get pretty dressed up, though," I said.

"Nah, this is nothing. The International Library is much classier. It's got real class."

Across the hall Rigg Kennedy stood at the center of a small crowd, hawking copies of *Riggwords*. I told Doc I was going to go see what Rigg's lyrics looked like on the page.

"Yeah," he said. "I'm gonna check out the slots." He had lost about half of the $800 he won the night before.

The crowd around Rigg was mainly older women pestering him to reveal his age. Although we had never met, Rigg seemed overjoyed to see me. I asked for a copy of his book. On the front cover, there was a psychedelic drawing of a tricycle floating over a moonscape under a lunar eclipse. The back cover was entirely filled with a photograph from Rigg's second wedding, which took place on the set of *Jesus Christ Superstar*.

"She was a dentist," Rigg explained. "I didn't stick around too long. But that front cover, that is art. It's done by R. Cobb, who did the cantina scene in *Star Wars* and the national ecology logo. George here remembered it all these years and just came over here, didn't you, George?" He turned to a large oafish man with a video camera standing outside the inner circle of women. Many years ago George had been a ship's librarian in the Navy, and one of the books on his shelves was *Riggwords*.

"A couple of my shipmates came in," George said, "and they copied love poems out of this book and sent them on home to their girlfriends. Then later they got married."

Rigg's expression was beatific. "It transcends time and space," he said, turning to his tiny audience. "You all know how I believe that poets can change the world, and here George tells me that these people got married. I only hope they're still together."

"You can't be expected to control *that*," I pointed out.

"No," he said, a faraway look on his face. "But I *can* control time and space."

BY TUESDAY MORNING the Famous Poets staff had managed to fill the Rose Ballroom with hundreds of colorful balloons bearing the words FAMOUS POETS PARADE AND BALLOONATHON. Under these words was a caricature of Shakespeare looking like a Spanish fencing master. A misstep in balloon layout put the words TAB HUNTER GRAND MARSHAL directly underneath the caricature, as if it depicted Hunter. Each chair in the ballroom had one of these balloons tied to its back with a long shiny ribbon. Now and then a balloon would slip loose and float up to the ceiling.

I found balloonless Doc standing off to the side with his arms crossed, staring critically at the stage, where Annette Ackerman, one of the assistant judges, was singing "The Rose" but with her own words, which tackled the war issue. Next, Judge Rudge climbed onto the stage in her Mrs. Claus suit (some said she had been up all night deciding the winners) and launched into a wild sermon that ranged over the Big Bang and "eternal sound vibrations" and eventually got to: "Oh, you day beyond dawn mist, beyond comets and night-falling creatures, and those who even by rubbing their legs make rhythm sounds. Oh, you brilliant, rose-surrounded day of fingers and lips, of hearts, of flute . . ."

"She's gone," Doc muttered.

There was some truth to that, but spending ten hours watching more than three hundred poets recite their verses, and then staying up all night long trying to pick the best of these while around you a casino rings and dings, would likely have devastated even Doc. Frankly, it surprised me to see Judge Rudge holding it together at all. Gesticulating with her right arm, she went into a jag about "my Super Bowl" and "five billion souls." Just as she was winding up to the meat of her idea, however, a balloon popped loudly, causing a ripple of nervous laughter. She stopped to acknowledge the interruption and then continued, but had not completed more than two sentences before another balloon went off. This time she pretended not to notice. The crowd was buzzing now, and Judge Rudge had to raise her voice to be heard: "I'm gonna shine like the stars, the moon, the sun," she yelled, "which are the microphones of the gods, through which they recite their—" Two balloons burst at the same time, and we did not hear any more about the gods.

I looked up at the ceiling. The balloons up there had been heated by the light fixtures and were going off like popcorn kernels in a skillet. A quick count of the unpopped balloons revealed that there would be no respite for the judge. Because the balloons had flown up at varying times, they were all on different popping schedules, ensuring a continuous barrage. "In universal mind you can really be anything you truly want!" she hollered, as three balloons exploded above. "You are like a golden child!"

Doc shook his head. "The balloons always cause problems," he said. "Last year the hotel was right next to the airport, and when they let them go in the balloonathon a big gust of wind came and blew them straight into the flight path. Runway was full of balloons."

Judge Rudge finished to kind applause. Everyone felt bad about how her speech had gone. During the clapping, I asked Doc what his poem of peace would be.

"I'm not sending one up," he said. "That's just for the people who haven't been here before."

The program continued illogically. Alisha, decked out in a purple velveteen Renaissance gown and matching coronet, introduced the Famous Poets Society Dixieland Band. Tab Hunter appeared and gave a short forgettable speech. The band led the Famous Poets Parade through the casino. Not all of the bleary-eyed gamblers glanced up from their games. Outside the Reno sky was clear. It was a warm day. Judge Rudge formed us into a huge circle and said a prayer. Her voice was hoarse, and it was hard to make her out, but she was certainly praying for peace, and possibly sanity. In unison, we released our balloons.

"There's mine! There's mine!" poets shouted. A few of the balloons got trapped under the Nugget's eaves, but most of them made it, and for a quarter of a minute or so the bobbing, multicolored orbs filled the sky. It was something. The Dixielanders played. Tab Hunter signed autographs. High above it all our poems of peace fluttered and waved. They floated so deep into the blue that people put down their cameras and just stared, trying to keep their eyes focused on what they thought was theirs. Awe quieted the ranks. Each balloon became a minuscule dot, then disappeared entirely.

THE FAMOUS POETS SOCIETY had impressed upon us throughout the convention that we were all winners: that as far back as the first night when we had put pen to paper we had ceased to lose.

But some would leave Reno with less than others. This fact was underscored by the $6,000 in door prizes that greeted our return to the Rose Ballroom.

After this preamble, Alisha made ready to announce the names of the winning poets. Behind her, the stage was set with a winners' circle of chairs—seventeen for the $1,000 third prizes, and one each for the second, first, and grand prizes, worth $3,000, $5,000, and $25,000. We all stared hungrily at the $25,000 seat, on which lay a red fur robe with a leopard-print fringe and a twelve-foot train; a matching crown in red, leopard, and gold, inlaid with red and green jewels; and a golden scepter.

The ballroom was tense. Muscles stiffened. Nails were chewed. I saw at least one lucky charm brought out. "Extry Sarff for 'Wild and Free'!" Alisha cried, and the first winner, an old fellow from Ketchikan, Alaska, with a giant white beard, mounted the stage. He read his poem, which was about orca whales, and we gave him a short hand. There was no time to dwell on the relative merits of the verse. Fortuna's wheel was spinning.

"Saundra Young Obendorf for 'Celestial Butterflies'!" A woman seated several tables to my left let out a small scream and ran through the crowd, throwing her arms in the air and leaping. When she read the title of her poem she imitated the flight of a butterfly with her hands. "Vanessa O. Sullivan for 'Born Black'!" A white woman in a cowboy shirt rushed the stage. "This is the second time I've been here, first time I won. So to all of you: Keep trying!" Her poem was about being an oddball in a conventional family. "Robert Nielson for 'Dance'!" Over to my right, a man in a dark suit popped up and pumped his fists in the air, screaming, "Yes! Yes! Yes!"

Some of the winners let out huge sighs of relief and gazed graciously to heaven. Some were catapulted into frenzies of hugging and crying and clutching of the cheeks. One girl, whose winning poem was entitled "My Elusive Heart," immediately began to fan herself, as if she were worried she might overheat. She fanned herself all the way up to the stage and then stood speechlessly at the podium for a quarter of a minute. Finally she shrieked, "World peace!" and burst into tears.

The number of empty chairs onstage was thinning when Alisha grasped the edges of the podium and yelled a name so familiar I didn't recognize it at first. My legs, however, took her meaning immediately and propelled me into a standing position, where I believe I then exhibited all the celebratory tropes that the others had. Blushing and grinning and waving my arms in the air, I stumbled through the crowd while a trumpeter blasted out a here-comes-the-king sort of tune. Along the way I ran into various friends from Class Six, who gave me the thumbs-up sign or snapped a picture. When I got to the stage I met Alisha, who seemed much bigger up close and more freckled. She shook my hand, slipped me a check for $1,000, and led me to the podium, where I turned and looked out at the sea of famous poets.

The third prize meant that I would break even; I had failed to capture the big money. But who cared? I was at the podium, addressing a crowd of hundreds. The dusty plains of Far West Texas and the greasy streets of New Orleans were thousands of miles away. I stared at the audience, my mind as slack as it had been during Rigg Kennedy's lecture. On Sunday, I had fallen into conversation with an old man who had accompanied his poet wife to the convention. When I asked him if he thought his wife would get nervous if she had to read in front of everybody, he said, "She will most likely have to refer to her notes because she may forget who she is." This is precisely what happened to me. I seemed to slip out of my body entirely. Who was Jake Silverstein? Some made-up person? Some giant mask? My voice, when I began to read, sounded muffled and far away. It was a strange sensation, and I could see how it might work on you until you broke down and shouted, "World peace!"

My chair in the winners' circle afforded me a new perspective on Scully's question. Who gave a damn what poetry was? Poetry was the check in my hand. Poetry was the golden scepter, only five chairs away. Alisha cried out, "Gladys Ogor-Edem for 'I'm a King's Kid—Jehovah's Princess'!" A black woman in a long black dress got up and gave a stirring performance in which she sobbed, screamed, waved her hands, stamped her feet, lost her voice, and then collapsed in her chair completely spent, clutching a $3,000 check. "Calvin G. Benito for 'Apache'!" A bald Oklahoman read a somber elegy to the great tribe's warriors with their "long black hair," and sat down with $5,000. The moment was upon us. Twenty-five thousand dollars.

"Cathy L. Kaiser for 'I Choose to Dance'!"

We looked around excitedly, but no one stood up. The initial applause had begun to peter out when all at once a buzz swept through the crowd, fingers pointed, and our eyes swung to an unused corridor of the ballroom, behind a series of mirrored pillars, where with a look of grim determination Cathy L. Kaiser of Phoenix, Arizona, slowly advanced toward the stage in a motorized wheelchair.

The applause erupted with renewed vigor. Poets on the opposite side of the ballroom hopped up on their chairs to get a better look at the handicapped laureate. Some held their cameras above their heads and snapped photos. A wave of energetic disbelief passed from table to table. Short people asked their taller companions what the hell was going on. Fingers were pointed and wheelchairs pantomimed. A cowboy poet swatted his knee with his hat. Kaiser motored silently along, her chin pressed to her chest. It was not yet time for her to celebrate. There was still the matter of what she would do when she got to the stage, which had no ramp.

Try to imagine the most melodramatic scene you have ever witnessed. Now add to the tableau as many soaring eagles and galloping stallions as can be mustered. Color it in pinks and purples. Bring up the French horns. Do all of this and more and still you would have no hope of touching Cathy Kaiser's performance that day in the Rose Ballroom. As she rolled up to the foot of the stage, the trumpeter belted out his last hurrah and fell silent. Grasping Tab Hunter's suntanned arm, Kaiser took a deep breath and heaved herself up onto her feet. She was standing! Gritting her teeth, she began to struggle up the stairs, one excruciating step at a time. She was walking! Once on the stage, she shook loose of Tab's support and stood free under her own power. The crowd lost its mind. Alisha's husband, Bob, rigged out in a jewel-encrusted doublet with a white frilly collar, placed the laureate's crown upon Kaiser's head. Tab hung the robe from her shoulders and presented her with the scepter. Her coronation complete, Kaiser began to wobble across the stage toward the podium. Alisha crept along behind her, bearing aloft the leopard train.

Her poem did not disappoint. "A song leaps from my heart at the beginning of each new day," Kaiser began. "A song with a melody that never plays a sad song." At several points she appeared near collapse, but clenched her fists behind the podium and pushed on. "If I have the choice of sitting this one out, I will choose to dance!" she chanted. "If you have a choice dance, dance, dance!" As far as raking up the judges' coals was concerned, you had to admit this was hard to top.

Kaiser gave the crowd a royal nod and fell into her throne. Alisha thanked us all for coming. "See you next year!" she shouted. Poets began to file out surprisingly fast. There were planes to catch. Cathy Kaiser sat in silence, a dazed look in her eyes. Her crown was tilted. Sweat ran down her cheeks. Poets rushed forward to congratulate the prizewinners they knew from their classes, but it did not look like Kaiser had any intention of moving, perhaps for days. While the other prizewinners—her court, I suppose—bustled around the stage taking pictures and shaking hands and even signing autographs, Kaiser, whether from exultation or exhaustion, remained seated on her throne. Hers was a quiet reign.

Within twenty minutes it was over. All in all, the glory was, as the man on the balloons put it, "too like the lightning, which doth cease to be / Ere one can say, It lightens." Out in the hallway, I ran into Doc. I asked what he thought of the winners.

"Dunno," he said. "I left. As soon as I heard that crap about dolphins and butterflies I left. I could see where the judging was going."

"We feel," another man said, "furthermore, that the time limits were unfairly imposed. There were some on the stage who should not have been there."

"She could *walk*!" said a wiry little guy with a Hawaiian shirt and tattooed forearms. "We all saw her walking across the stage. I *been* to L.A. I *seen* how the panhandlers do it in their wheelchairs and with their crutches."

"Gentlemen," said a man with luxurious dreadlocks, "we have been duped."

The man with the dreadlocks proceeded to make an allegation that I had some trouble swallowing. He claimed that Cathy Kaiser was an employee of the Famous Poets Society, the idea being that by awarding her the prize money they could fold it back into their revenue, with maybe a little coming off the top for Cathy's show.

"Following the tragedy in New York," he explained, "a man whose acquaintance I have made here in Reno called in to the office. Today when Ms. Kaiser read her poem, he recognized her voice as the same one he talked to on the phone that day. We've been had."

The tattooed man let out a long low whistle. "I knew something was up," he said. "I could tell the fix was in from the way the judges were acting. They weren't even paying attention. Why not? Because they knew who was gonna get the prize. I went down for my group, just trying to wake them up. When my turn came, I says to the guy behind me, I says, 'This is for you, buddy,' and I went out and took a nosedive, yelling at them, doing my best Pee-Wee Herman routine, jumping around on the stage like a retard, you know, just to get them to open their eyes. Well, it worked, one of the guys in my group won a prize. But I got the shaft, and I got the shaft from this other society too. I came out here with just my shirt on my back, all the way from Jersey without a penny, and now I'm gonna have to ride the train cars back, which I don't mind because a freight car is a fuck of a place to write some poetry."

■ ■ ■

MY PLANE DID NOT leave until the following morning. I spent Tuesday night in the casino. The Nugget is not actually as big as I'd thought at first—a trick of mirrors—and most of my time was passed at the Aquarium Bar. The musical entertainment came in the form of a well-oiled duo known as Bobby and Ricky, whose engagement was listed as "indefinite." Bobby was a sax player with a genial smile; Ricky, a guitarist in a leisure suit with curly gray hair. When I arrived Bobby was tying up the last few bars of "Secret Agent Man." When the song was through he grabbed the microphone and shouted, "Have some more tequila!" pronouncing the last word with a lascivious sneer. The mostly geriatric crowd responded with a lusty yell. I noticed a table of famous poets, all wearing their medallions and drinking heavily. Bobby and Ricky started into "Unchained Melody." Dancers crowded the floor. An elderly couple stood in the center, barely swaying, locked in an embrace. A man wearing a cowboy hat and a shirt patterned with the American flag asked one of the poets to dance. I knew her. She had bent my ear the night before, telling me all about her unhappy marriage that fell apart a few years back and the poetry that had helped her through it. Her first poem had come to her on her birthday at the exact hour of her birth. Smiling, she gazed up at the cowboy and laid her hand on his outstretched forearm. Some of us began to sing along with Bobby. The din of the slots died away. Out of the fake thatched roof descended Apollo, god of song. The waitress stood and watched, her tray full of tequila shots, limes, salt. The muse of the lyre visited Ricky, and he strummed a lovely chord. Time and loss for us seemed distant, made-up things. At the center of the world were Bobby's lips, singing the immortal verses, and in these verses our hearts were gladdened. This was poetry.

Chapter IV

THE THIRD-PLACE FINISH IN RENO HAD DEFRAYED my expenses getting there and back, and the convention had proven surprisingly illuminating in the matter of what poetry was. But what was journalism? Cathy Kaiser could stop time; what could Deborah Gallatin do? Following Dr. Johnson's advice, I made a list of everything that journalism was not. Busing tables was near the top. I needed a new job. So long as I was stuck making the monthly payments on my drought debts, it was hard to see how I'd ever have enough time to track down another magazine story. After a month of searching, I ended up on a tiny construction crew working for a house-flipper named Trent. His crew consisted of myself and two carpenters named Leon and Earl, brothers with different fathers who were always bickering and drinking Big Red.

Leon was a very good carpenter. Since Earl's skill level was similar to mine, we were often paired together on the simpler tasks—tear-out, demolition, dump runs, cleanup, and, when that was all done, rough-framing. Earl's favorite pastime was to tell outrageously self-aggrandizing stories when we were out of earshot of Leon, who was constantly scolding me for believing everything that Earl said. When we had work, the job paid well, and over the next four months I managed to put my finances in better order; but there would often be long gaps between finishing one house and starting on the next, during which the cupboard would go bare. On January 13, 2002, I was three days into one of these stoppages, rummaging under the Toyota's backseat for loose change, when an unexpected FedEx delivery arrived. It was a chapbook from Raymond Durkee, a poet I'd met at the Nugget. Durkee had tended to lurk in the back of the room. He wore a black leather hat and a matching black fanny pack, which was stuffed with notes, receipts, loose paper money, snack food, small scissors, earplugs, and other odds and ends his experience had taught him to keep at hand.

The front cover of his book showed a grainy detail of a nature photo—two robins perched on a leafy limb. *The Tree of Life*, the book's title, ran in a curly white script over the branches below. The poems were a mishmash of styles—moralizing sonnets about the environment, melodramatic free verse on the subject of loneliness, a series of opera-influenced haiku. Before I could get very far into them, however, a letter fell from the pages:

Dear Mr. Silverstein,

Here is my book which I mentioned to you at the Famous Poets Convention. Unfortunately, it has taken me this long to get it to you since I have had troubles with the printer. Now I am sending it to you not only for your own curiosity and as a fellow lover of verse like myself, but because I have a proposition that will intrigue you I am sure. I recall that you have written some journalism in addition to your poetry. If this is right you are just right. If you call me I will explain.

Sincerely,
Ray Durkee

The letter had been written on personal stationery (ink pots, quills, scrolls down the sides) with a phone number printed at the bottom. I reached Durkee later that night. He said that not long after the trip to Reno, he had been in Baton Rouge buying old furniture for his antique store. At an estate sale he picked up a chest, which, on later examination, had a map of some kind hidden underneath the floral drawer paper in one of the drawers. The map was very old. Durkee had spent a long time studying it. There was a giant helmet-looking thing, a pelican nest, a beach guarded by alligators, and a turtle just floating in the middle of everything.

Stumped, he had eventually made contact with a renowned Arizona metal detectionist named Charlie Redman, from whom he had once bought some old jewelry. Durkee said that, naturally, Redman received inquiries about treasure maps all the time and often ignored them, but that in this case he had written back to say that he would go fifty-fifty.

"Where do I come in?" I asked him.

"I'm not in it for the money," he said. "I had some lucky gem purchases in 1998 and the store has done very well the past few years. What interests me is the adventure. Charlie thinks this map will lead us to the broken compass treasure of Jean Lafitte, the pirate. You know who that is?"

"I've heard the name."

"So had I, but after Charlie told me what this was I read some more. It's wonderful! I've already written three poems about his island kingdom where the men slept in hammocks and drank rum from seashells. This treasure we're looking for, it was buried right before the Battle of New Orleans, where Jean and his brother were such heroes. When I heard where we were going I said to myself, 'Ray, wasn't there a reporter at the poets convention who lives in New Orleans?' And that's you. Don't you work for a newspaper?"

"I used to. In Texas."

"Good enough for me."

Durkee wanted someone who would come along and document "the expedition," as he referred to it. He said he would pay me $1,000 to record the whole thing and write a proposal to send to the Discovery Channel. He was certain that the Discovery Channel would be interested in his expedition and also wondered if we wouldn't be able to sell it to a magazine like *Smithsonian* too. Either way, it would help him move copies of *The Tree of Life*. He told me about an article he had read in *Popular Mechanics* when he was a boy about divers who search for sunken ships. "Everybody loves tales of pirate booty."

I allowed that if the booty was found, his story might have legs. But that was a big if.

"Oh, no. This is the real thing. Charlie Redman is one of the best. Have you ever seen his book? It's called *Treasures Can Be Found*, and it made a believer out of me. When I read it I said to myself, 'Ray, this man is the real thing.' If I told you what he was on the trail of, even just currently, you'd be amazed. One that he mentions in the book is five hundred thousand dollars in silver taken by Pancho Villa. Now, he knows where that's buried. He's been there. He's seen the markings. They're on a cave wall inside the state of Durango, Mexico, but he can't go back because the *federales* are watching it, and the last man that came around was killed with a long-range bullet and left for the panthers."

This sort of thing held less appeal for me than it might have before my failed search for the bones of Ambrose Bierce. I already knew a little about Jean Lafitte. Everyone in Louisiana does. To suggest the bygone romance of older times, his name and aura are constantly being trotted out by seafood joints and swamp-tour operators. Streets and freeways are named for him, even a town. Considering this high level of exposure, Durkee's claim struck me as thin soup. Old maps like the one he'd jimmied out of the dresser probably turned up by the hundreds every year. Their landmarks were long gone, their codes unknown, and, most likely, whatever they led to had been unearthed ages ago. True, Charlie Redman thought it was something, but who was he? There was no mention whatsoever of his book online. No treasure-hunting blogs touted his previous expeditions and discoveries. No message boards discussed his prowess. No photos showed him brandishing ancient ducats. The only result that a search of his name turned up was a description of the Galveston Metal Detectionist League's September 2000 meeting, at which Redman had been a guest speaker on the topic of "U.S. government regulations concerning abandoned property vs. concealed property."

Durkee, however, was offering $1,000 just to write the proposal for the Discovery Channel, and he had promised to pay me the money whether they found anything or not. It didn't matter to me if they were chasing fireflies. I emailed him to sign me up.

■ ■ ■

LAFITTE, I SOON DISCOVERED, is far more mysterious—and disreputable—than the tourist bureaus would have us believe. Both the year and the place of his birth are unknown. He appeared in New Orleans full-grown around 1809. Colombia had recently declared its independence from Spain, and the city of Cartagena had authorized him and his brother, Pierre, to capture and destroy Spanish merchant ships sailing in Gulf waters. The brothers made a loose interpretation of their warrants, sacking every ship that came their way and often winding up with a stolen cargo of slaves, which they would sell off at clandestine auctions deep in the bayou. They had a brief turn as heroes after their banditti helped Andrew Jackson fend off the British during the Battle of New Orleans, in 1815; but public approbation failed to reform them and they were soon run out of Louisiana and into Texas, where their piratical ways raised the eyebrow of authority once more. In 1821 the U.S. government commanded them to abandon their bulwarks at Galveston Island. Lafitte, who was probably about forty years old at this point, found himself in no position to refuse. He burned his headquarters to the ground and sailed off into the dark Gulf seas, never to be heard from again.

There was no mention in any of the books I found at the New Orleans Public Library of a broken compass treasure, but everyone seemed to think that during his Louisiana years, Lafitte had put down countless caches in the swamplands between New Orleans and Grand Terre, few of which had ever been found. A good number of the stories contained more embellishment than fact. Like Davy Crockett or Daniel Boone, Lafitte had led the sort of life that magnetizes the public imagination, drawing from it thousands of competing versions of the truth. Buried treasure yarns were only the beginning. Following his disappearance, novelists, poets, and magazine writers had thrown themselves at his romantic and incomplete biography with abandon. Most fancied him a tormented hero, prancing around on the deck of his boat, ventilating foes with a blood-soaked rapier, until he was eventually saved from blackguardism by the love of a good woman.

This view was patently preposterous, but according to the fashion of the times, many of its proponents claimed their fictions to be based on fact, and since there were so few facts concerning the historical Lafitte, the field was gradually choked with weeds. In 1852, the Reverend Mr. Joseph H. Ingraham found himself entangled in a controversy surrounding the veracity of his novel *Lafitte: The Pirate of the Gulf*. In an open letter to his critics, the good reverend defended his book with this observation: "I found in my researches, twenty years ago, romantic legends so interwoven with facts that it was extremely difficult to separate the historical from the traditional. I am very sure that the same cause will make it impossible to arrive at the truth of his life. His only biographer at last must be the romancer."

Reverend Ingraham's difficulties would have pleased Lafitte. More than coastal navigation, swordsmanship, or rapine, Lafitte's piratical talent lay chiefly in his prodigious abilities as a deceiver. Duplicity was his art. In *Lafitte the Pirate* (1932), a biography I quickly came to trust, New Orleans folklorist Lyle Saxon makes the case that much of the confusion that later engulfed writers like Reverend Ingraham originated with their subject. "It appears that, toward the last, he lied for the sheer joy of lying, long after the time when such lies could have been of benefit to him," Saxon writes. "Many of the wild tales concerning him seem to have come from the man himself. This is probably the key to his mysteriousness. He transformed himself into a legend while he was still alive."

I decided to drive down to the Jean Lafitte National Historic Park and shake the trees. In the visitors' center a bespectacled ranger named Henry Chang gave me a dossier of photocopies of primary documents he'd compiled relating to Lafitte's smuggling activities. Chang was a historian. Before taking the job at Jean Lafitte in 2000, he'd worked at Potomac Heritage National Scenic Trail and Independence National Historic Park, "the birthplace of the nation," in downtown Philadelphia. Since relocating to the Louisiana swamps, he'd made a close study of Lafitte. I asked if he'd heard of the broken compass treasure.

"Some people call it Landingham's Folly," he told me, "because a man named Landingham looked for it. Supposedly, when Lafitte was fleeing the attack on Barataria, he came ashore somewhere in Barataria Bay and buried a chest because it was slowing him down."

"And the broken compass?"

"In those days, you marked treasure by driving a surveyor's rod into the ground over the cache. You took your bearings with a compass, and then banged the rod down so a couple inches show. That's a pretty good marker. Doesn't look like much if you don't know what it is. Only, on this one, the story is that they couldn't get the compass off. They had to bang the rod down with the compass still screwed on, and that destroyed the compass, but part of it's still there. The whole thing's not very credible, if you ask me."

Chang thought it was unlikely that anything was still buried in the vicinity. "Toward the end of his time in Louisiana, Jean

Lafitte was not in the best financial shape," he explained. "If he buried any treasure during his early years, he probably went back and dug it up."

IT WAS APRIL when the expedition finally commenced. Trent still hadn't closed on his next property, and by the time I went to meet Durkee and Charlie Redman for breakfast at a Denny's in Gretna, the work stoppage had lasted for six miserable weeks. The breakfast was awkward. Though Durkee and Redman had corresponded at length and discussed the expedition many times over the phone, they had only met in person the night before, and their fledgling bond was strained by my arrival. Apparently, Durkee had avoided telling Redman that he had invited a journalist to tag along.

"Who's this?" Redman said, when I pulled a chair up to their table. Redman was an outdoorsy-looking man, with hiking boots and a beard that came to a tiny point below his chin. The pointed beard gave him a slightly festive appearance, as if he were on his way to a community theater production, but his expression was extremely serious, like a secret agent's in an espionage movie. When Durkee told him who I was and what I was doing, he simply stood up and walked out of the restaurant. Durkee apologized and ran after him.

I sat at the table and waited for them to return. A waiter came and asked if he should take Redman's plate, which was still more than half full. He'd been eating steak and eggs and had started with the eggs. The T-bone was untouched; the potatoes were shaved in generous piles and browned on the griddle. I sent the waiter away and stared hungrily at the chow. After five minutes

Durkee came hustling back into the room with Redman strolling behind him. Durkee looked miserable. He sat down, cleared his throat, and explained that Redman had forbade him to contact the Discovery Channel.

"Those chumps will come down here with their lights and their cameras and within two weeks the place will be crawling with amateurs," Redman said, not looking up from his eggs.

Durkee blushed. He was still wearing the same outfit I'd seen in Reno—black leather hat, T-shirt, black leather fanny pack, but I noticed he'd added a feather to the band of the hat. Durkee said that the compromise he and Redman had made was that I could write about the expedition for a magazine, but only if I signed a contract outlining certain journalistic conditions. "We already signed a contract of our own, the two of us," Durkee told me. "Everything's got to be official with Charlie. He likes to say a verbal agreement isn't worth the paper it's printed on."

Redman nodded, slicing up his steak and sliding it around in the congealed yolk. He speared a nice-looking piece, lifted it into his mouth, and chewed it calmly, glancing over our heads around the restaurant until he swallowed. "First," he said, as his sharp gaze settled on a point between my eyes, "you relinquish any property claims. This is our hunt one hundred percent. Second, you don't write about any real places or identifiable landmarks, you don't use my real name, and you don't reproduce the map in any way. Third, whether we find it or not, you can't write what we're looking for."

"Even if we find it he can't mention it?" Durkee said.

"Tax burden," Redman said. "I'll be damned if I'm going to pay Washington a cent. Finders keepers. Would you tell Washington if you found a twenty-dollar bill on the ground or would you go spend the full amount?"

"Spend it, I guess," Durkee said.

"If we find this cache, no one should ever know. This will be between us and Jean Lafitte. The IRS doesn't have a part to play in it and the damn television news media definitely doesn't have a part." Redman speared another long slice of meat. I watched it disappear into his mouth and followed his jaws as they worked it back and forth. After a while I said I would sign the contract.

"Fine," he said. "There's one other thing—just to be sure, during the hunt you go blindfolded."

Durkee had been fiddling nervously with his knife, and now he dropped it on the table. "Blindfolded? You didn't say anything about that. How is he supposed to write the account of the expedition if he can't see anything?"

"He's seen more than he should already."

"Now, listen, Charlie. I found that map. I brought it to you."

"You can look for it yourself if you want. I can get up from this table and tow my boat back across four states right now. I don't mind."

"You're getting upset. Don't get upset."

"I'm not upset. I telling you a fact. You found the map. I acknowledge that. It's your map. But if you want my help, we do it my way—and let me offer the observation that without my help you are nowhere, sir."

Redman turned back to his steak. Perhaps I had been wrong to interpret his absence from the Internet as evidence of untrustworthiness. For all I knew it was the result of a meticulous scrubbing intended to preserve his anonymity. The work of a true pro.

Durkee sighed heavily and shook his head. "I do apologize," he said to me.

"Then we have a deal?" Redman said.

I nodded. "Only, if I can't write about what you're looking for, who you are, or where you go, and I can't see anything while you're doing it, what can I write about?"

He shrugged. "That's your problem."

DURKEE WAS FRETFUL the next morning, apologizing continuously for Redman's harsh demands. I picked him up at his hotel and we drove down to the rendezvous point in the town of Jean Lafitte, not far from the park headquarters where Chang worked. "I didn't know he would be so darn professional about every last thing," Durkee told me. "I thought this would be fun." To make up for it, he showed me the map. It was exactly as he had described it—a fragile, yellowed sheet of paper bisected diagonally by a wavy line that might plausibly denote a shoreline. On one side of the line was a scattering of symbols, a helmet, a bird's nest, and three alligators. On the other side was a turtle.

Redman was waiting for us at a boat launch, leaning against the grille of his truck and whittling a stick. On a trailer was one of those flat-bottomed, square-nosed dinghies often found prowling the long straight channels that cross Louisiana's highways like bog-to-market spurs. Digging tools lay in the bow; two fishing poles and a tackle box occupied the stern. On a bench by the tiller, a waterproof bag held a pocket GPS device and scale maps from the Geological Survey and the Bureau of Land Management.

"Are we planning to fish?" Durkee asked, pointing to the poles.

"Cover," Redman said, not looking up from his knife. "Case we're not alone."

"What do you mean?"

Redman tucked his sharpened stick into his belt and stood up. "People know what I do," he said, walking around to the truck bed. "Sometimes they might come around looking for an easy grab."

Durkee followed him. "You never said anything about this."

"Don't worry about it." Redman opened his jacket to reveal a handgun in a holster against his ribs.

"What? Why do you have that? Is there any chance you'll have to use it?"

"There's every chance."

"You should have told me about this."

"It's no big deal." Redman shrugged. "Treasures attract flies, so I carry a swatter."

Durkee blushed in frustration and fear while Redman went over the contract with me. He had printed it out at the hotel that morning. Long passages of legal boilerplate addressing confidentiality, financial interest, etc. He and Durkee were identified as "Seeker #1" and "Seeker #2" and I was identified as "The Journalist."

"How long have you been doing this?" I asked him.

"Fifteen years," he said. He claimed that during that time, aside from a small stream of income from his book and the occasional speaking engagement, he had made his living entirely from digging up treasure. There had been good years and bad years, but none so bad he'd had to go back to wiring office buildings, which was what he'd done before during his twenty years as a commercial electrician.

"There are treasures everywhere," he said a few minutes later, as we pushed off from shore. "There's enough buried treasure in the world to pay off the national debt of the United States with plenty of wealth left over. Lafitte alone probably put down five million."

According to Redman, Lafitte had buried more caches than any other outlaw, though it was Dutch Schultz who held the honor of the single most valuable cache, a box of gold coins, jewels, and government bonds worth some $12 million, which was buried near the village of Phoenicia in the Catskills. Lafitte's deposits were smaller, but Redman guessed that there were hundreds of them scattered around southern Louisiana and on islands in the Gulf of Mexico.

"And a lot of it he never even looked for!" Durkee interjected. "He was more interested in burying treasures than in digging them up. One of my poems is about this."

Redman snorted. "The fact is he was a busy man. He had a federation of pirates to lead. Think how difficult it would be to run a federation of pirates. Take fifty of the worst lowlifes out of any prison you like and put them on a boat and that's what you're talking about."

Durkee was silent for a minute. Then he said, "Well, I don't know. I guess he had his hands full, but I think he also just got a thrill from stealing jewels, even if he didn't need them."

"He was a businessman," Redman said. "Everyone is."

We came around a bend and the water opened up into a long bayou, bounded to the west by islands and swamps and to the right by a solid peninsula cut through with shipping canals. Past a refinery and a small commercial dock, the bayou narrowed and signs of human presence disappeared. Herons watched us from the upper limbs of cypresses that grew straight out of the water. Eddies alongshore were carpeted with floating duckweed.

"I guess Landingham was a businessman too," I said. "A pretty bad one."

"Where'd you hear about that?" Redman snapped.

"What?"

"The name you just said. Where'd you hear that?"

I told him about going to see Chang.

"Jesus! You didn't tell him about our hunt, did you? What did you say exactly?"

"I didn't say anything. I just asked him about the broken compass and he told me the story."

"Broken compass? Goddamn!" Redman tugged on his beard and looked up and down the bayou. "Put the blindfold on him." He threw a piece of black cloth to Durkee.

"But he said he didn't say anything," Durkee said.

"He's a goddamn *journalist*! He can wear the blindfold or wait here." He pointed to the shoreline.

"All right, all right." Durkee reached around my head, pulled the cloth tight over my eyes, and cinched a knot in the back.

"Put these on him too," I heard Redman say. "And this."

Durkee placed a hat and some sunglasses on my head, to keep me from looking like a prisoner, I suppose. For a while the only sound was Redman's little outboard motor growling us along. The blindfold prevented me from opening my eyes more than a sliver. All I could manage was a downward glance at the side of my own nose, and even this took some effort. The water slapped against the boat and occasional birdcalls died in the damp air. I had forgotten how wearing a blindfold always makes you feel like prey, even among familiars; despite the hat and sunglasses, it was easy to succumb to the fear that I actually was a prisoner, being taken to a hidden swamp lair to be butchered in fulfillment of some diabolical ritual.

"Landingham was the name of the first person to look for it," Durkee said. "He spent his whole life looking for it."

As we motored along, he told me the rest of the story, with Redman periodically reminding me that I couldn't write about any of it. According to Durkee, there had been two men with Lafitte when the treasure was buried. He told them that if, after three years, they returned to the site and found the treasure still unexcavated, they could keep it for themselves. Only two months later, however, one of these men was killed in the Battle of New Orleans. (Redman claimed it had been by his greedy compatriot's own hand; "like I said," he said, "everyone's a businessman.") The other man waited and waited until finally his curiosity got the better of him. Only two and a half years had elapsed, but he decided to go back and check the status of the cache. The rod with the broken compass was still there, untouched. Afraid of what might happen if he disobeyed Lafitte, however, the man declined to dig it up. Instead, he returned to New Orleans, convinced that in six months' time he would be a rich man.

From there the story took a tragic turn. While he was waiting, the man caught yellow fever. On his deathbed, he told his story to his trusted friend Landingham and gave him the map he had drawn. Landingham dutifully waited the remaining sixty days until the three-year mark had passed, then went to claim the treasure. Only he couldn't find it. Convinced he had made a simple navigational error, he continued to go back to the salt marsh for the rest of his life. When he died, the map was his only inheritance. Over the ensuing decades the story became one of the romantic legends of the Gulf, and it might have eventually been forgotten, except that in the 1950s, a moss-gatherer came into a bait store near Lake Judge Perez asking for a bandage to wrap his foot. He had split it open that morning, he said, tripping over a short iron rod. The storekeeper, a man named Hood, was well aware of the potential significance of a short iron rod in those parts. He asked the moss-gatherer to draw a picture of his toe's aggressor, and the man produced a neat little drawing of a vertical rod with a mangled cap. Hood immediately dragged him back out to the bayous and rode him around the rest of the day, but the man could not find his way back to the rod and finally, confused by Hood's mounting frustration, began to deny that he had seen it at all.

"Those freaks were never going to find it anyway," Redman said.

"What do you mean?"

"They didn't have the technology. It's one thing to hunt for a mine in the mountains of Arizona. Those mountains don't change. It's a whole other thing to go looking for a cache in the bayou where the topography doesn't look anything like it did one hundred years ago."

"That's right," I said.

"The terrain down here is in constant flux."

"The whole coastline is eroding," I said. "The sea levels are going up."

Redman paused. "And why do you think that is?" he said.

"Global warming, destruction of wet—"

"Global warming is the biggest hoax ever perpetrated on American soil. There's no proof for it. If you look at the science, the science says the earth has cooling cycles and warming cycles.

That's all it is. But now you have these idiots in Congress thinking they know better than Dr. George Rutland, a man who has personally taken the Antarctic sea ice measurements and testified, *before Congress itself*, that they're no lower today than they were in 1970!"

After that the conversation fell away for a while. I had no sense of our whereabouts. Redman kept a steady pace and his maneuvers were gentle. Sun and shade alternated. Birdcalls pierced the motor's drone from time to time. Twice, Redman stopped the boat and Durkee told me he was taking a reading with a GPS, but both times his comments were vague. "We need to cut through here," he said the first time, and, "That could've been our turn back there," the second. I asked Redman how he knew where to go.

"I do research," he said. "This is a historical science. It's not just digging in the dirt."

A period of time that felt like a half hour passed. "Okay," I heard Redman say. "Up around this bend." The boat leaned gently to the right and seemed to speed up a little bit. Then all of a sudden the motor dropped to an idle and we began drifting until we glided to a stop. I heard them unload the tools. Durkee pulled the boat out, dropped anchor, stuck a fishing pole in my hands, and waded back to shore. Before he left he threatened to leave me in the swamp without food or water if I took off the blindfold.

For a while I could hear them talking. Redman was bossing Durkee around, telling him to walk a straight line toward a certain tree and not miss an inch of ground. The rest of their discussion was hard to make out. Soon their voices disappeared. I took off the blindfold and looked around.

The boat was parked about twenty feet off the shore of a sizable island, maybe 150 yards long, from the center of which rose an enormous oak tree. From a distance its dark green canopy looked a little bit like a helmet. Elsewhere the bayou was a labyrinth of land scraps no bigger than city blocks and still, green-glazed water. This was the intricate wetland on which Jean Lafitte had depended for his many escapes. Gazing out at its endlessly winding streams and marshes, I recalled a passage from Saxon's book: "These lagoons lie in serpentine coils, turning back upon themselves; many of them end at last in culs-de-sac. A boatman must be skilled indeed to find his way. Hundreds of men have lost themselves forever in this reedy marshland."

The sound of voices approaching roused me, and I hurriedly put back on the blindfold, hat, and glasses. Just as I'd finished, though, the sound of a motor became audible as well. Another boat was passing. It was too late for me to remove the blindfold. I tossed out the fishing line and waited. The sound grew louder.

"Catching anything?" a man said. The motor dropped to an idle.

I couldn't tell exactly where to direct my reply, so I just kept staring at the water. "Doing all right," I said.

"What ya gettin'?"

"Redfish."

"Catchin' 'em with the quarter-inch jigheads?"

"Beetle tails, mostly."

He thanked me and moved on. I was reasonably confident that he hadn't noticed the blindfold. Even if he had, he might have assumed it was no more than an unconventional angling technique, some bit of piscatorial superstition he'd not yet run across in his travels with a rod. Fishermen will try almost anything. I dozed off then and slept through the rest of the afternoon, slumping down onto some life jackets. The heat was stultifying. I woke up when I heard Redman shouting at me to sit up.

They were empty-handed. None of the spots they'd scanned with the detector had even delivered a signal. Redman was frustrated, but not yet ready to quit the island. In the center of it there was a large marsh, which he wanted to scan with a special detector that was back in the truck.

"Anyone pass by?" he asked me, as we motored back to the launch.

I told him about the fishermen.

"Goddamn! They seem suspicious?"

"Not really."

Redman was unconvinced. He gave Durkee a pair of binoculars and made him keep a lookout, but Durkee's eyesight was not very good and he kept mistaking tiny islands for boats on our tail. The one time he spotted an actual boat, Redman turned around and gunned for it. The harmless occupants were five buddies from Biloxi, Mississippi, who'd been drinking all afternoon. Their spirits were high and sloppy. They offered to pay Durkee ten dollars for his leather hat and told Redman that his beard made him look like Peter Pan. After that we put away the binoculars and headed home.

BY MIDAFTERNOON the next day Redman and Durkee had been up on the island for four hours and I was beginning to think it had been a mistake for me to return at all. I'd had a message from Trent the night before—he'd finally closed on a two-bedroom in midtown. It was Friday but he was ready to get started. Wouldn't that have been a more valuable way to spend the day? Once again, I'd been left in the boat as a decoy, only this time I hadn't even bothered to remove the blindfold. What was the point? I knew what I'd see—a vast terrain of shifting tides and numberless islands, within which a paranoid metal detectionist and an amateur poet had proposed to exhume a pirate treasure that may or may not have existed in the first place.

No journalism was going to come of this. In fact, it was time to admit that no journalism had come of anything since I'd left the newspaper. Two years had passed since my last byline; I'd had more success as a poet. Maybe I lacked the necessary professional ferocity. I was no Deborah Gallatin or Jonas Riemers. I wasn't even a Cathy Kaiser. Maybe journalism required a piratical mind-set, like Lafitte's, a willingness to pillage and deceive and do anything whatsoever to get the story. The boat knocked hard against something and I toppled backward off my perch, dropping the fishing pole and whacking my head on the gunwale. I pulled off the blindfold and looked around: Redman had forgotten to drop the anchor. I'd been drifting for hours. The water had been still for most of the time, but in the last hour or so the wind had picked up. There was no telling how far I'd gone. I had banged against the roots of a giant cypress tree along the shoreline of a lake with several wide passages leading to other lakes. Saxon's line ran through my mind: "Hundreds of men have lost themselves forever in this reedy marshland."

Panic was beginning to stir in my gullet when I saw the giant oak tree that looked like a helmet. It was about a mile off, a clear shot through one of the channels out of the lake. No wonder Landingham had put it on his map. It towered over everything. The fishing line had floated off and gotten caught on some rocks or roots where the bobber had drifted toward shore. I yanked it a few times to no avail and then paddled over to free it. If Redman came back to shore and found me gone, he would never believe that I'd simply drifted away. Who knew what he'd do? I followed the line into the brush along the shore, and a jolt of electricity went through me as I saw that right at the water's edge, the lure and hook had fastened onto something shiny. Something sticking up about two inches above the mud. I stared at it, waiting for my brain to articulate what my eyes already knew was a broken compass.

Time stopped. I peered at the island. I scanned the lake. I looked at the compass. I looked at my hands. I scanned the lake. I looked back at the compass. Some kind of historical vertigo rippled up through my legs and spine, and I had to drop to my knees in the bottom of the boat to keep from falling over. I wasn't thinking of money. I was thinking of time. It was as if the present had suddenly ceased to move forward and now the past was hurtling toward me. In seconds the decades diminished; I saw the compass and then I saw a man, dark-haired and sweating, laboring in vain to unscrew it from the rod. He curses the threads that have crossed and locked up. He uses his shirttail for a better grip. I could see him. I had jumped all the romantic fictions and dubious legends that caused men like Reverend Ingraham to throw up their hands. I was in the past.

Without fully understanding what I was doing, I began to act. I yanked the fishing line free and tied the red-and-white bobber to a tree root protruding from the bank about five feet away from the compass. Then I flipped open my notepad and drew a picture of the compass, a detailed map of the scene, and a larger map showing the relative positions of landmarks leading back to the island where Redman and Durkee were digging in vain, a mile away. I took one more look at the compass and then steered the boat out across the lake and down the channel toward the tree. Near the island, I cut the motor and paddled along quietly to the spot where Redman had likely left me. About forty-five minutes later, Redman and Durkee came clanking back to the boat.

"What happened?" I asked them.

Redman didn't say anything. He threw his gear down, fired up the motor, headed out. "It wasn't there," Durkee said to me. "We looked all over that island. It wasn't there. He thinks maybe the map is wrong."

Redman wouldn't say a word. We droned back to the truck and loaded the boat. Everyone was hungry, so we stopped on the way back up to New Orleans and ate hamburgers at a highway café full of old folks and high school students. I waited until Redman was about halfway through his burger.

"The map's not wrong," I said.

"Huh?"

"The treasure's back there."

Redman laid his burger down bottom-bun-up and silently studied my face for a long while. "Explain," he finally said.

"You forgot to drop my anchor this morning, and the boat was drifting for hours. I didn't realize until it finally knocked against something, miles from where you left me. I had to take off the blindfold to find my way back. That's where I saw the compass."

"Bullshit," Redman said.

"It was right there, just below the surface of the water, sticking up about two inches from the mud."

"This is bullshit."

"The map isn't wrong, it's just incomplete. The treasure is not on the island. You need to know how to get from the island to the treasure. Look." I flashed them my drawing of the compass. "The ink's still wet. I was staring right at the compass."

Redman banged the table and yelled at me. "You pulled that anchor up yourself and took off your blindfold and went exploring, didn't you?"

"No."

"Wow," Durkee mumbled.

"What have I said all along? You can't ever trust a journalist." Redman balled up his paper napkin and threw it hard at his plate. It bounced off his french fries and landed in Durkee's ketchup. He pointed a fork at me. "You signed a contract!" he shouted. "You got no legal claim on that cache. Recall, sir, that I intend to protect my claim." He was causing a scene now; the high schoolers glanced nervously in our direction and the church ladies frowned over their iced teas.

"Relax. I don't want the treasure. That's yours."

"My gosh, are we going to be rich?" Durkee whispered to no one.

"What do you want?"

"I made a map that will take you from the island to the treasure. It's for sale."

Redman grinned ruefully and laughed once with his nose.

"I'm not asking for a lot. Ten now and fifteen when you dig it up. You said it was worth three hundred thousand at least. This is less than ten percent."

Redman leaned back from the table, shaking his head. Durkee turned to him. "Well, that seems awfully fair to me. If it wasn't for him, we wouldn't of ever known about this."

The deal worked much more simply than I had hoped, so simply, in fact, that I began to wonder if I'd asked for too little. Maybe the treasure was worth much more than three hundred grand. After discussing it for a few minutes, Redman and Durkee agreed to give me the money, provided I accepted a new confidentiality provision—not to write anything about the hunt at all. In fact, never to mention it to anyone. Redman wrote a personal check for ten thousand dollars drawn on his account at a bank in Tuscon and held it in the air until I said yes. We shook hands and I handed over the map. The next day they took me back, no blindfold, and we motored to the island. From there I guided us to the spot. Everything was exactly as I'd left it—the bobber still tied to the tree root, the compass still protruding a couple inches above the mud. Durkee's initial reaction was similar to mine. He jumped out of the boat and stood stock-still, gripping his hat brim and mumbling to himself, "Oh my gosh, Ray, oh my gosh." Redman was more professional. He squatted down and inspected the compass as best he could through the murky water. After a few minutes he stood up and said, "It's real."

"Oh my gosh, oh my gosh."

"Get a hold of yourself, Raymond. We have work to do."

He posted Durkee as a lookout and brought out a metal detector, which rang out loudly before the search coil had even touched the surface of the water. Redman changed the mode on the detector to a more discriminate setting, turned way down his audio threshold, put on some earphones, and checked again. Almost immediately his eyebrows went up. "Nearly blew out my speaker cone," he said. "Let's get back to the truck."

"You're not digging it up now?" I asked him.

He shook his head. "Better to do that at night."

They left the bobber on the tree root and we cruised through the swamp. Durkee hummed "I'm In the Mood for Love" and "Begin the Beguine" and "You've Lost That Lovin' Feelin'," just any old song that came into his head. On the way back to the hotel in Gretna he made Redman stop at a liquor store so he could buy a bottle of cognac. We sat in the hotel lobby and discussed the rest of the plan in hushed tones. Redman and Durkee would finish the job without me that very night. If everything went well, they'd wire the fifteen to my bank account within a week.

"Oh, we'll send it," Durkee said, grinning broadly. "We'll be happy to send it." He was drinking cognac from a plastic cup. "And it was a pleasure getting to know you for sure. To think that we almost didn't bring you along!"

I left them there, readying to return to the swamp in the dead of night and claim the treasure. It had to be more than $300,000. It had nearly blown out Redman's speaker cone! It had caused Durkee to sing and drink liquor! No question it was at least half a million. I steered the Toyota onto the Pontchartrain Expressway and over the bridge back to New Orleans. The next morning I told my bank that I was expecting a large wire deposit. A week later a teller called. I was standing in the middle of my kitchen, shaking the dregs of a potato chip bag into my open mouth. "A deposit of this magnitude will take a short while to clear," he warned me. I wanted to ask him who made the deposit, how did they look, and what else did they find, but of course he knew nothing. Neither do I.

Chapter V

ONE DAY I UNFOLDED A MAP OF MEXICO AND LOOKED for a place to live. Along the coast would be nice, but it was the northern central highlands that appealed to me, the silver mining country. I had the notion that it would be good, both financially and journalistically, to live someplace where there was nothing happening. That way, when something did happen, there would be no one but me to write about it. Mérida, Oaxaca, Veracruz, Guadalajara, Mazatlán, Mexico City—these places would be crawling with expats, foreign correspondents, yoga studios, environmentalists, novelists, and backpackers. The minute that anything of note transpired, a flock of gringos would descend, all trying to claim the story for themselves. There was no way to ensure that I'd have the kind of time I needed to complete an article without getting scooped. But how many Americans were on the loose in a dusty old desert crossroads like Gómez Palacio? In colonial times the whole northern plateau, with its cold mountains, dry valleys, and unimpressive nomads, was considered a barbaric wasteland, and this prejudice had persisted in one form or another down to the present day. Few foreigners visited; few natives stayed. The city I finally settled on,

Zacatecas, was the capital of one of the least populated states in Mexico. Per capita, it sent more immigrants to the U.S. than any other Mexican state, and many more Zacatecans lived outside of Zacatecas than inside. Located smack in the geographic center of Mexico, far from the coasts, far from Mexico City, and far from the U.S., Zacatecas was guaranteed to be a place where nothing was happening.

I took a year's lease on a cheap apartment in an empty brick building. If I spent money on nothing else, I could live in this frigid, echoey box for a decade without working. Surely I'd have journalism figured out by then. The lease was handled by a real estate agent named Juan Carlos Sigg, who wore his hair slicked straight back and always, indoors or out, sported a pair of dark aviator sunglasses. On our first trip to look at apartments in his VW Bug, he took the turns so hard that only two blocks from his office I ended up in his lap. I apologized but Sigg just scowled at the road ahead and downshifted. It was his opinion that there wasn't much to do in Zacatecas. His favorite thing about the city was a road race that tore through once a year, engines roaring and backfiring up and down the cobblestone streets. He said he was the local organizer. When we got back to the office he showed me photos of garishly painted race cars brightening the drab Zacatecan terrain.

Over the next couple months I settled into a pleasant routine, reading in bed, exploring the old churches and convents, subsisting on gorditas and Pollo Feliz. Sigg was right, there was unquestionably a dearth of action in Zacatecas. It wasn't long before my strolls around town began to lead back to the same old bars, the same cafés, the same subpar troupe of actors playing *Romeo y Julieta* in the *plaza mayor*. The nights were cold and the days were hot. The local food was *birria*, a plain dish of baked goat that does not woo the eye. You could take a cable car to the top of La Bufa, the red rock hill where Pancho Villa's Division del Norte routed Victoriano Huerta's federal troops in 1914, but there wasn't much happening up there. It wasn't unusual for me to pass the day on my roof, staring downhill at the cathedral's façade of carved pink stone, waiting for the broken clock on the belfry to hit its twice-a-day mark. In Zacatecas there was no rush to repair inaccurate public timepieces.

It had once been the second richest city in Mexico. After the first enormous silver vein was hit in 1548, prospectors flooded in from all over New Spain, and Zacatecas quickly became one of the most rollicking towns in the New World. One local silver mine was said to have produced $800 million between 1548 and 1867. Then the veins tapered and the price sank. Some of the mines shut down, some of the miners went broke, and in time the city drifted into unimportance and disregard, the small capital of a poor state in the infertile northern desert. In the center of town, beautiful stone buildings from the Spanish times lined the streets, but not much went on inside them. As a civic leader once wrote, "In this city we have no scorpions, we have no flies, we have no mosquitoes, we have no earthquakes, we have no floods, and we have no money. Therefore, we have no problems."

I soon added another item to his list: no McDonald's. The nearest Big Mac was one state over, in Aguascalientes. I had made the trip several times myself. Zacatecas, it turned out, was the only state in Mexico without a McDonald's. This came as no surprise. "Zacatecas is last in everything," a local saying went, "even the alphabet." Throughout the member nations of the North American Free Trade Agreement, there was only one other McDonald's-free zone, the Arctic territory of Nunavut, home of the Inuit.

Despite my own personal taste for the famous fast food, this seemed to me a distinction worthy of preservation. To be the only non-Eskimo state in Canada, the U.S., or Mexico where the golden arches had not yet risen was a heroic accomplishment, even if all it meant was that the profitability study the rapacious corporation had almost certainly conducted had concluded that Zacatecas was too insignificant to warrant a constant supply of Filets-O-Fish. Victory must be taken where it can be found. For my journalistic purposes, the fact that entire state of Zacatecas had been deemed an unworthy market by a fast-food chain that operates thirty-one thousand restaurants in 120 countries worldwide seemed to indicate that I had chosen wisely. There probably weren't any American journalists in Nunavut either.

Then in November the rumors began to swirl. Construction of a new McDonald's would begin in January; it was going to have three levels; it was going to be owned by the governor; it was going to be owned by the man who owned the McDonald's in Aguascalientes; it was going to be involved in a complicated drug-trafficking scheme; it would have two play palaces; it would have three; it would have a tunnel connecting it to the Wal-Mart through which sacks of dollars would be hurried.

I decided to pay a visit to Secretary of Economic Development Carlos Lozano de la Torre, and see if there was any merit to this depressing chitchat. Anywhere else, directing my inquiry to such a high office would have seemed presumptuous, but in Zacatecas it was as simple as walking into a modest, low-ceilinged building off the frontage road and saying, "*Me gustaría hablar con Señor Lozano de la Torre.*" The secretary happened to be indisposed when I called, but a subordinate wearing an enormous mustache agreed to see me. This was Guillermo Escarcega, the director of interior commerce. The walls of his office displayed the triumphs of his post—photographs of a new multiplex cinema under construction, the Wal-Mart on day one, an empty lot on its way to becoming a mini-mart. It was his pleasure to meet an American; there were so very few in Zacatecas. He suggested we smoke and produced a pack of Faros, an unfiltered Mexican cigarette rolled in rice paper. The Faro, he said, leaning back in his chair and taking a deep drag, was vastly superior to the American cigarette, because of the rice paper. Consider: if you were dying of hunger and had only your cigarettes, you could eat the paper and live for some time, without, however, being able to smoke. With the Marlboro, you would starve. He hunched forward and used the ashtray. It was true what I had heard. A McDonald's was indeed coming to Zacatecas. Construction would begin any day now, any day. In fact, the McDonald's architects were arriving from Monterrey on Tuesday.

Tuesday morning I dropped in on Escarcega's secretary, Teresa. She poured me a gritty cup of Nescafé and explained that the director was out and the project held up. We performed this routine two more times before I began to suspect that the entire forecast had been stretched. Where were the architects? Teresa had no idea. They always seemed to be on their way. Weeks passed and Escarcega was never in. It appeared he was giving me the dodge.

THIS ALL HAPPENED during a rough patch for McDonald's. A few trips to the Internet café shed some light on the matter. The company had opened its first Mexican restaurant in 1985, the same year they served their fifty-five billionth hamburger, and since then things had continued to go well. But shortly before I'd arrived in Zacatecas, there had been a rare setback. Plans to open a restaurant in the historic *plaza mayor* of Oaxaca, one of Mexico's most celebrated cities, had met with fierce resistance and dramatic protests. Led by the artist Francisco Toledo, the discontented had filled the plaza, shouting and stamping and sitting at wooden tables eating tamales and *atole*, a thin Aztec porridge. The defiant feast had garnered considerable attention from the press, and although the fuss was about the restaurant's proposed location (Oaxaca already had a McDonald's, outside the *centro*), it soon engaged the larger qualm. "Why put a wart of ground beef right on our plaza?" Toledo had asked. He called the McDonald's "an ominous sign of our loss of values." The protest petition overflowed with irate signatures, and the restaurant was forced to withdraw.

The menu made it clear that the values Toledo and his supporters had in mind were the indigenous ones, and so I turned to my books. Pre-Hispanic civilization was about as rich and varied as they come, but where the Aztecs in particular were concerned it seemed he had a point. You hear a lot about the Emperor Montezuma, but one thing is for sure: he knew how to spread his board. This is from the *Verdadera Historia de la Conquista de Nueva España* (*The True History of the Conquest of New Spain*), by the Spanish soldier Bernal Díaz del Castillo: "For each meal his servants prepared him more than thirty dishes cooked in their native style, which they put over small earthenware braziers to prevent them from getting cold. I have heard that they used to cook for him the flesh of young boys. But as he had such a variety of dishes, made of so many different ingredients, we could not tell whether a dish was of human flesh or anything else, since every day they cooked fowls, turkeys, pheasants, local partridges, quail, tame and wild duck, venison, wild boar, marsh birds, pigeons, hares, and rabbits, also many other kinds of birds and beasts native to their country, so numerous that I cannot quickly name them all."

Nor were these plates roughly consumed. Never outstripped in matters of style, Montezuma put away his meats with keen attention to ambience and presentation. "When he began his meal," Díaz del Castillo tells us, "they placed in front of him a sort of wooden screen, richly decorated with gold, so that no one should see him eat . . . Montezuma's food was served on Cholula ware, some red and some black. While he was dining, the guards in the adjoining rooms did not dare to speak or make a noise above a whisper." Cortés, in a letter home to Charles V, adds to the picture: "Before and after the meal, they gave him water for his hands and a towel which once used was never used again, and likewise with the plates and bowls, for when they brought more food they always used new ones, and the same with the braziers."

I was convinced. Aside from his throwaway Cholula ware, there was nothing in Montezuma's routines that would have favored the culture of fast food. It seemed unlikely that the pampered king could have withstood the bustle of a McDonald's even long enough to count the meats.

The conquistadores were of a different stripe. It was a safe bet that had such a thing existed during their march through the hostile country, those soldiers of fortune would have been enthusiastic patrons of the drive-thru. Cortés and his men ate and ran and often just ran. Recalling the period later on in a letter to the king, Cortés simply wrote, "Bad food." They made do with unsalted fowl, moldy cassava bread, dead dogs, and whatever else they could scavenge from the countryside. Following their defeat at the infamous Noche Triste, they wandered for days deprived of even these modest victuals. "Their principal food was the wild cherry," notes William H. Prescott, in his masterful *History of the Conquest of Mexico*, a book that was never far from my hands in Zacatecas. "Fortunate were they, if they found a few ears of corn unplucked. More frequently nothing was left but the stalks; and with them, and the like unwholesome fare, they were fain to supply the cravings of appetite. When a horse happened to be killed, it furnished an extraordinary banquet; and Cortés himself records the fact of his having made one of a party who thus sumptuously regaled themselves, devouring the animal even to his hide."

The overlap of these habits with the alimentary culture of McDonald's made me wonder how well Toledo's dispute would travel. It had held water down in Oaxaca, where the Indian presence is strong, but I feared it would leak up north. Oaxaca is a graveyard of the antique glories. You can't throw your hat in that state without hitting an archaeologist. Zacatecas had a few pre-Hispanic monuments, but nobody was visiting them, or excavating them. Before the Spanish the state was as empty as it is today. Worse, the regional gastronomies defied comparisons. Oaxaca had its tamales and its seven *moles*; all Zacatecas had was *birria*. And while the table talk in Oaxaca included the names of celebrity chefs in town to learn the ancient secrets, in Zacatecas it was more likely to concern a local burrito shop with a dented fleet of delivery bikes, whose owner was rumored to have appeared one night in a local emergency room, trench-coated, with a dead cat stuck in a compromising position.

I suspected too that the appreciation shown by the *oaxaquenses* for their rustic past had been at least in part related to the prior existence of the other Oaxacan McDonald's, since this went hand in hand with the well-to-do local economy, and that fed the sophistication and education of a citizenry who knew their history and would not stand to see their plaza defiled. Zacatecas might need to get a McDonald's to become the sort of place where one didn't belong.

BY THE TIME the job broke ground in spring, my visa was about to expire. This required me to return to the United States for at least a short stay. My theory was a bust. I'd found a place where nothing was happening and lived there for nearly a year and, not surprisingly, nothing had happened. Nothing except this business with the McDonald's, which didn't amount to much. The restaurant would not be elbowing its way into the historic plaza, or displacing a colonial church. Toledo and his protesters would have trouble working their hackles up this time around. The site that had been chosen was on the freeway at the edge of town, along the far side of the giant parking lot of Soriana, a Mexican superstore. There wasn't much to object to. If you had to put a wart of ground beef someplace, this seemed like the place. The only possible source of opposition was a *birria* joint about fifty feet away called Birrieria Jaramillo. Jaramillo was itself a chain, with about eight locations citywide, and its own dreadful rumors about employees being sent out to the airport at dawn to retrieve giant frozen bags of horse meat for the goat grill. Not the sort of place whose demise inspires a petition.

Still, Director Escarcega had been kind enough to keep me

informed of the project's start day, and when April 4, 2003, rolled around, I decided to go have a look. When I arrived at the site, four men were laying out the property lines and spray-painting tiny X's on the ground. History had chosen Jesús Huerta, a pudgy engineer, to bring McDonald's to the desolate Zacatecan plain. From his thin, taut mouth, the worries of the post were easily inferred. One of his hands massaged his forehead constantly, as though there were an incubator of the building's plans inside that had to be monitored closely in order to function properly. This McDonald's would be his eighth. In the past five years alone he'd built three in Guadalajara (his home), one in Puerto Vallarta, and two in Tampico. They were nice, he assured me, but nothing like the McDonald's on Avenida Mariano Ortero in Guadalajara's Plaza del Sol. Though he hadn't built this one, it was his favorite: "It is the most beautiful," he told me, shaking his head in wonder.

Along with Engineer Jesús, as he was called, the crew consisted of a foreman, Maestro José Ascención Enriquez Torres, and two others. The workers, they told me, were yet to be hired.

"So where does the name McDonald come from?" the Maestro asked me, rattling his aerosol can. His large belly, pointy nose, and prescription sunglasses gave him a considerably more jocular air than Engineer Jesús. "Is it the name of the hometown of the business?"

"It's the name of the man who started the business," I told him. "I think he started out in a cart."

The Maestro nodded. "That's how all the best places start out," he said, grinning. "In carts. If I was going to start a restaurant, that's where I would start out." He tried to name the Guadalajara eateries that had begun in carts. (Some months after this, I read a very popular and well-researched nonfiction book about fast food and realized I'd been completely wrong about the cart.)

When I visited the site a few days later, the Maestro was standing at the ragged edge of a pit, gesturing to the men who were down in it with shovels, digging the footings. Red rock, sand, and cement were heaped up in scattered piles. The work had begun. A backhoe lurched forward, and a pigeon with a battered wing groped along the ground. The man in the backhoe hammered the pavement with his bucket. Someday soon the first Zacatecan McDonald's would be resting on all this. I tried to imagine it and then I left.

THE TRIP FROM ZACATECAS to the U.S. crosses a burning desert into which isolated crossroads towns have been sparsely scattered as if to punish their inhabitants for ancient misdeeds. In summer the temperature hangs around a hundred degrees. Hours pass in silence, stillness, and heat. Whining back across that barren in the Toyota, I was reminded of Sebastián Lerdo de Tejada, president of Mexico from 1872 to 1876, who took some comfort in the protection afforded by his country's forbidding northern wastes, and was known to say, "Between weakness and power—the desert."

I thought of his words often over the next few weeks, as I fit myself back into life on the other side. In Texas the well-paved roads, verdant lawns, and ample homes were an impressive testament to the "power" that Lerdo de Tejada had feared, but what really drove home the point were all the McDonald's. They were everywhere, constantly reminding me of Engineer Jesús, the Maestro, and the Zacatecas job. Down every street, in every mall—there was no peace from these restaurants. On freeways I sometimes saw two, staring at me from the opposite sides of an exit.

It wore me down, and before too long I found myself out on the road again, rattling through the desert for the third time. I didn't know what I was looking for. It was still unlikely that anti-American protests would erupt in Zacatecas, but returning to the land of McDonald's had given me a clear sense of what precisely the Zacatecans were sacrificing on the altar of modernity, and I wanted at least to see the offering made. At fifty-five, beyond which the steering wheel threatened to rip loose, the drive took about fourteen hours. I reached the site the following morning. The distinctive red tile roof now towered over the hammered privacy wall and the cylindrical hall where the playground would go rose high in one corner. After a round of jokes from Engineer Jesús and the Maestro about my absenteeism, I was free to wander the work site. With the ninety-day mark in sight, everyone was working hard, but I managed to pull a man aside every few minutes and see what he thought. "Mexico will always be Mexico," a vegetarian drywaller told me. Another man said it would be nice to not have to go to Aguascalientes anymore. No one seemed truly excited about the McDonald's until I met José Guadalupe Villanueva, a twenty-four-year-old who'd crossed the river eight times to work in the United States, where his usual trade was laying bricks. He was very tall, with a thin mustache and pair of green jeans. A surf cap sat on his head. I'd barely put my question when he blurted out, "Having a McDonald's here will be a beautiful thing because it'll remind me of the United States."

He told me about the values he'd learned in the United States and how kind the gringos were. He described the way he got there. It was the route I'd followed down. "I go up there as an *indocumentado*," he said. "But I feel American in my heart."

He grinned. "Here in Mexico it is just ugly. I mean, it's beautiful because it has a lot of tourism, but I really like the United States. My dreams really belong to the United States, not Mexico. If there was some way to transform yourself into a U.S. citizen, I'd do it. I can't even buy clothes here." He gestured at his unusual height. "I either have to go someplace where they got American shoes, or my mother-in-law has to bring me them from Dallas." It made him an expert. None of the men he'd befriended at the site had ever been *allá*, or "up there." I sat with them during lunch and listened as José held forth.

"*Allá*," he said, "the blacks go around wearing yellow from head to toe, with big purple shoes and Vaseline on their heads, and they carry huge cigars. They're very distinctive, sort of like the Hindus. You know about the Hindus? I have some Hindu friends and they have a little spot right here"—he pointed to his forehead—"and dresses down to here"—he held a hand to his ankles.

The group stared at him, bug-eyed, El Chaco and El Chaco's brother Fernando and Lopez the born-again and a kid and the older guy named Balzantes. El Chaco spoke first, a wide, puzzled grin on his face. "Ah! What's that for?"

"That's just how they are," José said.

"Really? Nah."

"Yep. And the ones that dress almost alike, the Japanese, they have one too. The Chinese and the Koreans have different styles of dress."

"Really?"

"They're the ones that work on floors *allá*, the Japanese and the Chinese. Mexicans don't get any floor work, they don't put in any floors."

It was clear that José had developed a skewed view of the country, although he claimed to know it better than his native land. In Mexico, he said, he couldn't go anywhere without getting hopelessly turned around. The road signs made no sense.

"You get lost here!" El Chaco cried, laughing heartily.

José went on, a dreamy look in his eye. Up there, the money was better, the people were nicer, the women were liberated, the cops were honest, society didn't degrade the poor, and McDonald's were everywhere. It was everything Mexico wasn't, and Mexico could hope for nothing better than to be remade in its image as soon as possible.

El Chaco's brother Fernando listened absently, as if he'd heard about this fairyland before. He held a different view, as I learned when we had a chance to talk alone. "Every head is a world," his philosophy went. "There's the head of McDonald, the head of Soriana, and the head of Jaramillo over here; the head of the guy who invented cars, the guy who invented airplanes, and the guy that invented televisions. No one is the same. No one does the same thing in the same way." But nowadays, he said, "the whole world is coming out of one head, and from that head you're getting everything. It's happening all over Mexico with these stores like Wal-Mart and McDonald's, stores that came out of the head of *allá*. Down here, in Mexico, that head is developing all its thoughts."

We stood in a corner of the unfinished building and discussed these developments. Fernando pointed a finger northward. "After work, they go out and play tennis; they go out and play basketball. Their routine is work, play sports, sleep. Not here."

He shook his head, wagged the finger, and tipped it toward the ground. "Here in Mexico, the Mexican gets home to his family and he wants some *chaca-chaca*."

"*Chaca-chaca?*"

"Sex. He wants to have sex. And that's why the family here is so much more united than up there. Many, many, many children. From just one couple you could have eighteen, twenty children." He considered the ample room where the McDonald's play structure would soon be installed. "Two *familias*. With two *familias* you'd fill that room. And if you kept following the branches of what is known as the family tree, you'd fill this whole commercial plaza with just one *familia*. Grandchildren, children, great-grandchildren. *Pura familia! Pura sangre!*" His eyes blazed. "Here's my brother right here. There's my cousin in the parking lot."

He paused to contemplate them and then he blinked and looked at the floor.

"It's changing, though. There's already so many American stores here, and more coming . . . You're not going to see much sex anymore, not like it was before. The woman's gonna go to work, and the man's gonna go to work, and when that happens, here in Mexico, you won't see any more sex. No more sex, because they're both gonna get home tired, like *allá*. You won't see the big families anymore. Just one little girl here, another there." He pointed them out and shook his head. "Things have changed a lot, and they'll keep changing, and we can only fight and struggle for life until we are touched by *la calaca*."

"*Laca-laca?*"

"Death."

▪ ▪ ▪

I KNEW SEVERAL PEOPLE at the university in Zacatecas and had heard about an economics professor known as El Güero (The Whitey), whose opinion of the city's new stores ran counter to what I'd heard at the offices of the secretary for economic development. It was said El Güero took a dim view of the Yankee commerce. Perhaps, just below the placid surface, a great anticolonial showdown was brewing in this desert town. All the best *resistencias* start in the universities. I made an appointment to see him right away.

El Güero met me in the department lounge and led me to his office, a tiny room piled high with student papers, books, and journals. He was pale-skinned. Seating himself behind his desk and brushing aside his thick white hair, he began what was clearly a familiar ventilation.

"In the old days," he said, leaning back in his chair, "it was very common for blue-collar workers, at eleven in the morning, to stop their work, light a small wood fire, and reheat the tacos or gorditas their wives had made for them. Nowadays this has practically disappeared, and what they do instead is buy a bag of potato chips and a Coca-Cola. This is their diet, and it speaks to us of the process of the North Americanization of the Mexican diet. The arrival of McDonald's in Zacatecas signifies that although we are a small city of two hundred thousand inhabitants, the study of our market that they have surely done shows that in the lower middle classes, the middle middle classes, and the upper middle classes, there are people who desire this trash food."

This new McDonald's would simply be "the cherry on the cake" of state policies adopted under Governor Ricardo Monreal to modernize Zacatecas through the establishment of *centros comerciales*, or strip malls. "Monreal pledged to modernize the state," he told me. "The only thing he's modernized are the strip malls. The face of modernization in Zacatecas begins and ends with the malls. Recall that he brought over Lozano de la Torre from Aguascalientes to be his secretary of economic development, a man who *specializes* in the promotion of strip malls and *maquiladoras*."

I soon discovered that the professor's interest in these matters was not entirely academic. Though a native of Zacatecas, he had studied in Spain, where he had grown fond of the tapa. Returning to find himself in a city ignorant of this cuisine, he'd opened up a small tapas restaurant in the *centro*. I knew the place; its dry *bocadillos* had clogged my pipes on several occasions. Now, El Güero explained, he intended to open another branch, nearby the McDonald's. I asked him if he wasn't mad.

"*Sí, sí*," he said, barely raising his voice, "we will have to compete with them. The kids will have to decide—do we eat fast-food burgers over there, or do we go here and have a sandwich with a nice salad and fruit?" I wished the professor luck. His salads and fruit seemed doomed, but his views were convincing, and I wanted to try them on the street.

Without exception, the taxi drivers, security guards, grocery baggers, and shoppers I flagged down in front of Soriana seemed to think I was insane to suggest that it might be preferable to build a small wood fire and reheat a taco when there was the possibility of visiting McDonald's for a burger and fries. My Spanish was not up to the task of elaborating the professor's arguments with his scholarly grace, but I doubted this would've made any difference.

I sat on the hood of my car and watched the sun set over the red rock hills. Who was El Güero to deny the Zacatecans their modern city? Then again, why should Zacatecas have to build a McDonald's to be modern? To modernize a Mexican city is to make it more like an American city, which is more and more a city that is built and cleaned and staffed by Mexicans. More migrants go *allá* from Zacatecas than from any other Mexican state, and while they toil in California and Texas, Kansas and Illinois, Florida and the Carolinas, the cities they've left behind are filled in with restaurants and stores that symbolize the lifestyle they are laboring to maintain, thousands of miles from home. Where was the sense in that?

I bought some beer and pork rinds and headed to the site. The workday was over, but Engineer Jesús and the men would still be around. We sat in the great round hall on empty buckets and boxes of tile. The Modelo began to flow and the friendly arguments bloomed. Exactly how is pulque made? Is there a difference between having a good voice and knowing how to sing? What region of Mexico has the best food? Can the chemically generated mescal of Japan truly be considered mescal? Where are the best places to dance in Guadalajara? Who grows the best mangoes? The Maestro finished a beer and slapped me on the shoulder. "The thing about gringos," he said, "is that their apples are always red."

After a few cans the Maestro started to sing. He sang "La Valentina" and "Cielito Lindo" and "La Malagueña." It was night by then. Outside the privacy wall, sounds rose to mingle with his baritone—the whine of bus brakes, the zoom of a taxi. "If they are going to kill me tomorrow," he crooned, "let them kill me today."

In the empty building, the evening's questions seemed to drift away on the Maestro's serenade. What could modernity have to do with this masonry box? The walls weren't drywalled; the windows and doors hadn't even arrived; there was no electricity, no plumbing; the trash was in piles. It was just an unfinished building where you had to step through a window and walk on a small plank over a trench to reach the porta-potty. Like everyone else on Earth, I'd been inside a lot of McDonald's over the years, but it had never occurred to me until that moment that they do not arrive whole, that they are built just the same as everything else. This innocent frame was in them all.

AT THE END of my next trip down to Zacatecas a few weeks later, the Toyota finally faltered. I had by then asked it to cross Lerdo de Tejada's impregnable desert five times. A few miles past the graffiti-covered cement ball on the roadside that marks the Tropic of Cancer, the engine started to clank irregularly. We sputtered into town, lurched off the highway, and stalled. There was no time to lose under the hood. Today was Family Day, a chance for the parents of the new McDonald's employees to acquaint themselves with the restaurant on the eve of its inauguration. Luckily, I wasn't far from the site. I arrived just as the sun was starting to dim. A stirring sight confronted my road-weary eyes.

High in the desert sky the golden arches towered, glowing against the somber hues of dusk. Pains had been taken to bring them level with the torn ticket of the Blockbuster and the rectangle board of the Soriana, but they lofted above those mundane signs. The feelings of reverence and fear they inspired put me in mind of a passage I had just read in Prescott's book describing the sacrificial altars of the Aztec capital, "on which fires were kept, as inextinguishable as those in the temple of Vesta." These altars were located atop towering pyramidal structures, where, stretched on a block of jasper stone, the victim met his doom. "There were said to be six hundred of these altars," Prescott wrote, "which, with those on the sacred edifices in other parts of the city, shed a brilliant illumination over its streets, through the darkest night . . . and the dismal rites of sacrifice performed there, were all visible from the remotest corners of the capital, impressing on the spectator's mind superstitious veneration for the mysteries of his religion, and for the dread ministers by whom they were interpreted."

The dread ministers had come along too. Pulling up to the fully assembled restaurant, I discovered a new breed inside. Dressed in slacks and polo shirts, with cell phones clipped to their hips, they strode the polished tile floors, barking orders at the rookie staff. The young trainees hustled around behind the gleaming counter with that buzz attending dress rehearsals of high school plays. They hopped from foot to foot, poking the high-tech registers. Their parents looked on from booths, nursing sodas and waiting for another visit from the kids, who periodically swung by with fries or ice cream. These young people made a sharp contrast to their well-dressed superiors, on whose ponderous brows the restaurant's readiness hung heavy.

I banged on the door. No one paid me any mind, so I did it again. Heads turned. Eyes regarded me coldly. An index finger waggled. I tried in vain to communicate that I'd come from the land of McDonald's, that I was part of the "family." Heads shook and turned away. The hot drive had not left me looking my best. To my right, a plastic effigy of Ronald McDonald sat on a bench, his arms spread wide. The fixed red grin on his painted face offered little consolation. Two boys ran up and leapt into his arms. "Amigo!" said the first boy. "Hi-*ya*!" said the second, chopping the hardened groin.

I took a walk. The Maestro and his crew sat in the drive-thru on the other side of the building, their mood not so different from my own. Though the Family Day invitation had been extended, they chose to sit outside. The restaurant was no longer a building in which they felt at home. They crouched on the freshly cured cement cracking pumpkin seeds in their teeth. The electrician looked at the crowd inside and said, "We're the anonymous heroes out here, like the workers that built the pyramids at Tenochtitlan." It was the twentieth McDonald's he'd wired.

His comment sparked a debate about architects and builders. "Since the architect has the idea, and the builder just figures out how to do it," the Maestro said, "the architect must have come first." Some disagreed. They said that when the first buildings were built, there had been no difference. The aqueducts in Zacatecas and Querétaro were structures where the architect and builder had fused in the person of a visionary engineer. "At least since Aristotle we've had architects," the electrician said.

A family with a beaming boy walked up and shook the bolted door. "*Mañana*," the Maestro said. The boy began to sob. His parents took the blow with greater fortitude. They steered him over to Birrieria Jaramillo, where a staff of two had been nervously monitoring the commotion all afternoon. Many families ate the Jaramillo goat that afternoon. The Maestro said that when the privacy wall came down on Wednesday, hundreds of people had immediately tried to force their way inside.

A worker struck a philosophical pose and said, "Their hunger for a Big Mac blinds them to the fact that the restaurant has not yet opened."

■ ■ ■

EVERY DAY AROUND the world a new McDonald's opens. June 30, 2003, belonged to the people of Zacatecas. I got there early. Out front, management had built an enormous M with yellow balloons. Around this majuscule a crowd of children agitated. I wondered why they weren't in school. Some had flattened themselves to the plate glass for a better look at the pep rally. Inside, employees and managers stood in a large circle with their hands clasped, as a pale-skinned, silver-haired gentleman in a crisp blue suit gave a speech. It was the man from Aguascalientes, whose assets would soon bracket an alphabetized list of the 268 McDonald's in Mexico.

His new franchise was in top shape, looking even better than the one back home. The exterior was painted a white so ultrabright I couldn't stare at it directly. Healthy-looking flowers now grew at the base of the walls; indoors, a festive play-maze of colored plastic tubes twisted through the *patio de juegos*. Promotional decorations twirled in the air-conditioning, proclaiming that a mechanical fish from *Buscando a Nemo* was the Happy Meal booty. The walls were hung with portraits of Ronald and his cronies. In one frame Ronald sat cross-legged with his hands resting on his knees, while his upturned, white-gloved palms emitted streams of multicolored stars in an arc above his 'fro.

Waiting outside, I fell into conversation with several of the parents. Their stories all matched up: the children had been invited to the grand opening by their schoolteachers, who on behalf of McDonald's had selected only the most outstanding students to be present when the doors were opened. It gave the scene a different air to know the children were gifted. I hadn't guessed it from their glassy eyes. Reporters from the major local papers and television stations milled among the future's hope, testing their microphones. Only several minutes remained. History and mayhem were at hand. I took up a place in the line. Ahead of me the Ronald idol smiled as fans of all ages tried out his rigid lap. Carlos Lozano de la Torre, secretary of economic development and strip mall specialist, arrived and was ushered past the roiling crowd. "Zacatecas! Zacatecas! Rah! Rah! Rah!" shouted the staff inside the restaurant. Through a sea of shoulders, I spotted the Maestro sitting on a stump and looking at the sky. The previous day he'd told me, "When you've done as much work as I have, one restaurant won't impress you."

He was alone in his numbness. It was nine o'clock. Watch alarms sounded. The line surged forward against the locked front door. Cries filled the air. I girded for a struggle. The staff inside began a muffled countdown: "*Diez! Nueve! Ocho! Siete! Seis! Cinco! Cuatro! Tres!* DOS! UNO!"

Such a thrust was then made as to recall the Spanish storming of the great pyramidal mound of Huitzilopochtli. Kids sprang through the door. Men rode full tilt against each other. Women waded in. All of this was accompanied with the yelling of a military advance. As we made our object, the seizing of territory commenced. Small bands staked tables and dispatched parties to rush the counter. A mob of gifted children tore off their shoes and scaled the plastic tubes, screaming with glee. Bedlam reigned. The kitchen oil roared as new fries were introduced. Over by the ketchup, the economic secretary wept into a blue hankie. "*Perdón!*" he cried, dabbing at his cheeks. "*Perdón!*" Within five minutes the place was crammed, and a long hungry line curled through the lot. Forty rookies scuttled to fill orders. As the first customers turned with their food and struggled to regain their families, sodas began to tumble from trays, perfuming the air with a sugary bouquet. "Oh! It's so very elegant," I heard someone shout to the man from Aguascalientes.

The fray lined me up, I couldn't help thinking, in the same spot where, just weeks ago, José had told me about his wife's poor health as he swept the floor, or where Lopez the born-again had shared the story of his wayward youth as he cleaned a plaster-spattered recessed light fixture. I studied the menu. The only breakfast on the boards was the McBurrito, which fooled no one. Hamburgers were the morning fare. Tight quarters and a long wait fostered discussion. The man ahead of me had lived in San Jose, California, for twenty-six years, doing machine work. "I still remember the first McDonald's I ever went to up there," he said wistfully. "The year was '74, and it was at the corner of San Fernando and Third Avenue."

I ordered a Big Mac, to go. The clangor had grown, as Happy Meals were torn into and relieved of the prize fish, which giggled when their fins were depressed. One of these gewgaws made a fine sort of toy, but multiplied by the forty or fifty children in attendance they soon became the devil's own plaything. No youth tired of provoking the canned laugh. The toys affected them in much the same manner as the presents of wrought gold and feather-work sent by Montezuma to Cortés along his march, "all calculated to inspire the Spaniards with high ideas of the wealth and mechanical ingenuity of the Mexicans." Montezuma hoped his gifts would dissuade the Spaniards from seeking a personal interview, but the opposite end was achieved. It went the same with the kids, who scraped through to the counter, demanding to exchange an unwrapped Nemo for another of the crawdads on the Happy Meal box, all the time mashing their fins and adding to the tinny giggles with their own howls of delight. Their time had finally come and they would not stand for less than the full array. Throughout Canada, the United States, and Mexico, only the Inuit children had been made to wait longer.

A van of the disabled had arrived and gridlocked the crowd with a half dozen wheelchairs, but I managed to get my bag outside. I sat on a curb. This hamburger had been a long time coming, and the first few bites were good enough to make me forget about anything else. I washed down the burger with some Coke. As the flavors mingled, a dull sense of the familiar entered my blood. Before me, on the high desert plateau, I saw the many McDonald's I'd known: on Telegraph in Oakland, California, by the state university in Alpine and the state capitol in Austin; on Broadway in New York and on St. Claude in New Orleans; near the cemetery in Middletown, Connecticut, and the Port of Entry in Laredo; in El Paso, Chicago, Rapid City, Orange County, Roanoke, and in the nameless all-night truck stops on the highways in between.

I put my Big Mac down. This was not food but the heraldry of a foreign king. Those arches were a cross hacked on a tree. Where were the protesters? I had come for a fight and found a jamboree. The governor arrived and the speeches kicked off. The man from Aguascalientes gathered his family behind a ceremonial ribbon. "This day," he proclaimed, "this thirtieth of June, is of great importance for all Zacatecans, and for all of us who form the great McDonald's family, nationally and internationally." Flashbulbs popped. The governor raised his scissors. He opened the blades. "With Zacatecas, we now have . . . total coverage of the nation."

"There was something deeply touching in the ceremony by

which an independent and absolute monarch, in obedience less to the dictates of fear than of conscience, thus relinquished his hereditary rights in favor of an unknown and mysterious power." So Prescott characterizes the assembly where Montezuma finally swore allegiance to the crown of Castile. As the economic secretary looked on through wet eyes, the governor cut the ribbon.

THE NEXT DAY I was back on the highway. The Toyota was running again, and I did not intend to hang around waiting for a wave of McDonald's opposition that would never come. A summer storm covered the valleys and gave me respite from the heat. The sky was gray and darker gray, the plains dotted with mesquite trees, nopales, and outcrops of red rock. I knew the road well by now, the Tropic of Cancer ball, the cinderblock altar to the Virgin of Guadalupe, the house on the outskirts of Concepción del Oro, where I'd watched a man feed a dog with handfuls of raw meat. The sea of ocotillos after Ciénega de Rocamontes, where the road curves up and to the right. The empty boxcars at Carneros. The century plants waiting to bloom in the dust from the Cemex cement plant. The sleeping tollbooth dogs. The place between the pine trees where the road straightens out and gets fast. From there it was only three thousand more miles to Nunavut.

Chapter VI

THE JOURNALIST IS A CIPHER. HE HAS NO NATION, no family, no future, no past. To his subjects he is a stranger with a pen; to his readers, if he is lucky enough to have any, he is a stranger with an editor. He is a ghost trying to see through a fog from which he is often indistinguishable, and to be successful he must spend his life going from one fog to another, unknown to everyone. Such were my gloomy thoughts as I traversed the sea of ocotillos and rattled past the empty boxcars at Carneros. Why had there been no protests? What good had it done to have so closely observed the construction of a restaurant everyone was happy to have? The Toyota had started to clank again, and the prospect of a breakdown in this unpopulated plain fueled my dark outlook. If the car died, and I hiked up into the hills to live on ketchup packets and prairie dogs, would anyone even know I was missing?

The clanking developed into a steady thwacking, and shortly after that I glanced in the rearview mirror and spied an alarming number of nuts and bolts clattering down the highway behind me. Suddenly the gas pedal plunged to the floor, and I drifted to a stop on the shoulder. Revving the motor up to a hot, high-pitched whine had no effect whatsoever on the wheels. The problem defied both my rudimentary mechanical skills and those of the Green Angels service truck driver who pulled off the highway an hour later when he spotted my open hood. We were much closer to Saltillo than Zacatecas, but for reasons that were never fully explained he towed me back down south, past the boxcars and the ocotillos and the Tropic of Cancer ball, to a mechanic on the city's western outskirts. Zacatecas was apparently not done with me yet. A pudgy repairman named Edison put the Toyota on a lift, free-handed the wheels, and proclaimed it to be the constant velocity joint. He did not have the part himself and would have to order it. This would take three days.

I called Sigg and asked if he had any vacant furnished places I could rent by the day for less than I'd pay at a hotel. He was very busy, he said, preparing for the road race. It would start in Tuxtla Gutiérrez, the capital of Chiapas, and run north to the border. One hundred cars were coming! Four hundred hotel guests! There were only several months left to make all the arrangements. The best he could do was a house that was still under construction near the bus station. There was no running water, but he wouldn't charge me anything.

This area of town was unfamiliar to me, outside my normal circuit. I waited for my constant velocity joint in a cantina called Las Siete Letras, a small, white-tiled place with tin tables, a red plastic bar, and well-worn plastic turf grass on the two small steps up to the door. Sigg explained that the name, which means The Seven Letters, was a reference to the seven letters in the name of the barman's wife, who had gone across the border many years ago and never returned. This sounded like the sort of thing they tell gringos and schoolkids, but the first time I went in there the barman told me the story himself. His name was Luis. His wife was Rosario.

I took a booth in the corner and spent the afternoon and most of the next day nursing Indios and reading *The Labyrinth of Solitude*, the great poet Octavio Paz's prose meditation on Mexican identity. For months I'd carried it around like a guidebook, marking lines like: "Our hermeticism is baffling or even offensive to strangers, and it has created the legend of the Mexican as an inscrutable being." I was studying Luis for signs of inscrutability when a man in painter's pants and a white painter's hat came in. Luis waved him over and I went back to my book. "The history of Mexico is the history of a man seeking his parentage," I read. Some fireworks went off in the street outside and a dog barked. "Jacobo?" I heard the painter ask Luis. He was looking at me. He had a dark black mustache that reached to his jawbone. "Jacobo *Zabludovsky*?" He laughed uncontrollably for a quarter of a minute, slapping at the bar to keep from falling over. It wasn't anything I hadn't heard before. Jacobo Zabludovsky had been a white-haired Televisa newsman back in the Salinas days, the Mexican Walter Cronkite. He wore thick-paned glasses and was probably about seventy-five years old but it didn't matter. Whenever I introduced myself someone was bound to feign surprise and say, "Jacobo *Zabludovsky*?"

A few minutes later the painter had forgotten all about Zabludovsky and was ranting to Luis and jabbing his index finger at a newspaper on the bar. "*Abandonó a su país!*" he shouted. Luis shook his head. I could only make out the very general parameters of their argument, something to do with the *gobierno* and a person known as "El Rey de las Tarimas." For a man who has abandoned his country, the painter was saying, even if he was the Rey de las Tarimas, certain things must be *prohibido*. "Without even living here!" he shouted. Luis shrugged. I went up for another Indio and some Japanese peanuts, but the painter was still agitated.

"Do you know of this Rey de las Tarimas?" he asked me.

I shook my head. The painter evidently thought this was funny. He rolled his eyes and laughed and said that Rey de las Tarimas was *americano-mexicano* and he was very *listo*, very clever. He lived in California.

"He own a factory for making the . . . *tarimas*," Luis explained in his choppy English.

"*Tarimas?*"

"*Son paletas*."

"He makes popsicles?" I mimed eating one.

"No, no. *Paletas de madera*. Pallets for the trucks. For the shipping. Very much money." He made the shape of a coin with his thumb and index finger.

"But he abandoned his country," the painter said. "What do his millions matter to me?"

"Perhaps in his heart," Luis said, "he never left."

The painter sneered. "Don't you believe that, man. It's what they all say."

The conversation died after that. The painter left and I wandered down the street to an Internet café, where I Googled "El Rey de las Tarimas" and got 3,460 results. The man's given name was Andrés Pasillas. He was from Antequera, a small town about an hour south of Zacatecas. I knew the place. Like most of the small towns in that area it was very poor, and most everyone who lived there ended up going to work in the United States. According to a story from *El Siglo de Torreón*, Pasillas had crossed in 1972, hidden in the trunk of a forest-green Buick Riviera, carrying nothing but a pair of work boots and a framing hammer. In California he found work as a carpenter. Then he went into fencing. From fencing into pallets. He had become an American citizen and a member of the National Wooden Pallet and Container Association. *El Siglo* reported that he now lived in a "palace" in Coalinga, California, near Fresno, and was "considered by many to be the King of Pallets."

What had bothered the painter, I guessed, was that Pasillas had been elected mayor of Antequera, despite the fact that he had not lived there, or anywhere else in Mexico, for more than thirty years. It was a fascinating story. An editorial from *La Voz de Michoacán* explained that the victory was due to the power of the migrant vote. Mexicans cast more absentee ballots than any other people in the world. In every election, from municipal contests to the federal level, ballots pour in from all over the United States. Sooner or later, *La Voz* hypothesized, this constituency was inevitably going to choose one of its own for public office. I scanned a few more stories. Though the consensus seemed to be that the Pallet King was no statesman, and that he had become excessively fond of Thousand Island dressing and other American tastes, a wave of migrant support had easily carried him past his opponent, making him the country's first elected official who was a full-time resident and citizen of another nation.

How could I have failed to notice Pasillas's story during my ten months in Zacatecas? It was exactly the sort of thing I had hoped to find. I was ready to add this to my growing list of journalistic failures when I discovered that I was not alone. Inexplicably, there was almost no mention of the Pallet King in the American press, aside from a few news briefs. How could this character have failed to rate a magazine profile? The Mexican newspapers, naturally, had been all over Pasillas, and their reports gave the impression of a real character, a swaggering populist, rough around the edges, as bold and visionary as he was crass and untutored.

I lay awake that night on a pile of clothes in Sigg's freezing flophouse, mulling the strange twists of my journey. Had the McDonald's never drawn me back to Zacatecas I never would have been on the road to begin with; had the Toyota run smooth I never would have been sitting at Las Siete Letras when the painter started ranting. Perhaps my luck was turning. Perhaps the maleficent spirit of the desert, which had thwarted my plans so often before, had finally seen fit to grant me some favors. In the morning I placed a call to the City Hall in Antequera and asked for Pasillas. A woman said, "*Eh?*" a few times before giving me the telephone number of a man named Gutierrez, who answered on the first ring. I explained who I was, and Gutierrez kept saying, "*Excelente, excelente,*" in a grave and sonorous voice. He gave me a direct line to Pasillas, who was in California at the moment. I reached him about twenty minutes later on the floor of his pallet mill. Saws roared and whined in the background, periodically drowning him out. I said I was calling from Mexico. He shouted, "Nobody down there knows shit about what's going on. They don't know shit about shit."

He went on for another thirty seconds or so, but the screech of a table saw smothered his reply. ". . . why things have always been that way," he finished. "Because they don't know shit. If you get your ass up here before Monday you can ride back to Mexico with us, and I'll tell you all about it."

■ ■ ■

THUS IT WAS that I found myself, with very little time to contemplate how it had happened, on the July 3, 2003, red-eye to Fresno. The plane was full of young Mexican men. A couple hours into the flight, the captain announced that we were passing over the border and that on the American side it was "*día de independencia.*" At the captain's announcement, the men in window seats cupped their hands to the double-pane plastic and gazed down, looking for the line and possibly some visual cue to the holiday, faint explosions. At the airport I rented a Geo Metro and headed south down the smooth California highway toward Coalinga. I knew a little bit about the town from a school trip I'd taken in high school. I knew that the town had once been the first of two fueling stops on the Southern Pacific line through California's Pleasant Valley, and when it started to grow into a settlement, the name had been derived by simply dropping the STATION from COALING STATION A.

The plane arrived early enough that when I reached Coalinga the dew still shone and the odor of manure from the Harris Feeding Company's eight-hundred-acre feedlot was still no more than a faint musky note. Coalinga is a feedlot town, and as the day heats up, the stench of the doomed beasts' crap builds like a thick cloud over Pleasant Valley. During peak periods at the Harris operation, the West Coast's largest, some one hundred thousand head of cattle fill the yards. I checked into a Ramada, took a Danish and cup of weak coffee back to my room, and looked over the list of questions I'd drawn up on the plane. How do you plan to govern? Where do you feel more at home? Why did you leave in the first place? A painter I met in a bar said you abandoned your country. How would you respond to that? Can you elaborate? What is your favorite food?

I gave Pasillas a call and went down to the lobby with a steno pad. Twenty minutes later a red GMC Sierra with tinted windows and tongues of flames painted over the wheel wells pulled up to the door. Ornate white letters on the back window of the cab read EL REY DE LAS TARIMAS—ANTEQUERA. The door swung open and the King climbed out. He had on pressed jeans, a black shirt, an open black vest, and a black felt Stetson.

"*Buenos días, señor,*" I said. "*Soy Jacobo.*"

The King grasped my hand firmly. He was surprisingly rough around the edges for a mayor. Sweat beaded his neck and tufts of disobedient hair flared from his ears and nostrils. His face was pocked and pallid, as if it had been left out in bad weather too long. A smile revealed crooked teeth.

"Jacobo Zablu*dovsky*?"

He took me to his house by a circuitous route, bumping down alleyways behind stores to see if he could find some of his pallets stacked up against the walls. He said the U.S. economy could not last one hour without pallets. We passed a hardware store where a few Mexicans stood around in the parking lot, waiting for a builder working through the holiday. The King slowed to look them over. "I pay five dollars to the handnail machine operators plus seven cents a pallet," he told me. He said that was good.

"These Mexicans, they never heard of anything that good. But I pay like that because it is a way I can give help to the people who are starting out. Maybe they are like me, they come from some *pueblito*, they have a dream, they want to provide something for their family."

I asked if that was why he had decided to run for office.

"You know why that was?" the King said. "Because those politicians they got down there are all *corrupto*, they're all full of it.

They get some money for a road or something and they make a big press conference and then they don't finish it because they take all the money for themselves and go get a new bathroom, with a Jacuzzi." It was true that in Zacatecas you saw a lot of half-done roads. "Me, I already got a Jacuzzi. I got two Jacuzzis."

We headed up into a residential area, where the houses were big and brand-new, with gold lanterns hanging over columned entries, and pools in the rear. Behind brass gates, spotless white driveways split impeccable lawns.

"People like me," the King said, "when they're young and they want to make some money, they have to come up here. Up here you can make some money because the *gobierno* isn't so *corrupto*. It's very sad what I see down there."

I was scribbling down everything he said onto my steno pad and he seemed to like it. He kept glancing at the scribbled notes, and whenever he had something new to say he would lean over and say it in the direction of the pad.

"This is the problem for Mexico. It is *corrupto* and in a land that is *corrupto* every man must be for himself. The farmer, he is for himself. The businessman, he is for himself. And the politician, when he gets to be in office, he is for himself too."

I suggested that perhaps he would be able to change this from inside the mayor's office.

He pulled up to a wrought-iron gate and tapped a button clipped to his sun visor. The gate responded by cracking down the middle. Up at the top of the driveway two stone cats peered downhill.

"Yeah, but I ain't the mayor no more," the King said, easing through the opening and up to the top of the drive. "They threw me out last year on the residency law."

"What?"

"The City Hall *chingasos*. They threw me out. Like I say, they're all *corrupto*."

He turned off the truck and headed for the house. "You like *lengua*?" he shouted, turning from the front door and shielding his eyes against the sun.

Residency law? Last year? The front hallway was a blur of white tile floors and gold trim. A small person descended a curving staircase and stood before me. The King said it was his son, Andresito. The kid had a weak handshake and stiff hair. A baggy sweatshirt hung past his waist. Mrs. Pasillas was in Antequera, the King said, setting up the house down there. They weren't going to let the court throw them out again. He and Andresito were driving down in three days and they were going to stay there until the next election, in two years.

"But I don't wanna go," the kid whined desperately.

The King turned to me. "He don't know anything about Mexico." He walked on through a gleaming kitchen into a shiny den and went to a glass bookshelf. I groped along behind, stumbling over packed-up boxes and suitcases. "He's scared to go down there," he said, shaking his head. He pulled down what looked like a photo album from the shelf and dropped it on the kitchen table. "That's the newspaper stories," he said. "All the newspaper stories from the campaign. My wife put them in a book."

The kid brought me a soda and a glass of ice and then went and sat on a suitcase. "I wanna go to the fireworks tonight," he said. Most of the clippings described events I was already familiar with, but now, for the first time, I began to notice the dates. The King had first been elected on March 4, 2002, back when I was sitting in the New Orleans Public Library reading about

Jean Lafitte. Just two months later, however, while I was still in the swamps, a Mexican court had thrown out his victory on the grounds that he had not been residing in Mexico for one year prior to assuming office. Toward the end of the King's clip book were a number of articles about the court's decision, articles that my half-drunk research at the Internet café had failed to locate. The whole thing had begun and ended before I'd even arrived in Zacatecas. It had probably been no more than a passing mention of the year-old controversy that sparked the barman's ire at Las Siete Letras.

"Look at my picture on the last one," the kid said. "I don't look like that, do I?"

I flipped to the last page to find a giant photo of the King and his family standing on the lawn in front of the house under the headline: "The King Who Would Be Mayor." It was from the May 19, 2002, issue of *The New Yorker*. I had evidently missed this too. It was by Joe Tolen, a name I recognized. I slumped down a little lower and stared out the window at a distant bluff.

"Only thing they didn't get right in that one was about the salad dressing," the King said. "That's only a rumor. You make sure you put it in your article that I like to eat Mexican food."

"He's writing an article too?" the kid asked.

"Is there a bathroom?" I said, jerking up out of my chair and banging into the edge of the table.

Gold rimmed the mirror and a porcelain swan stood beside the sink. I stared at a brass toilet paper holder. It was the vertical variety, the kind from which the toilet paper always hangs down slightly, folding backward over itself. My heart was racing but my mind was blank. All I could do was take inventory. There were Jacuzzi jets on the walls of the bathtub. There was a painting of a dog on the wall. I paced the tiny floor and flushed the toilet again and again, trying to smother with white noise the thoughts forming in my skull. How could it be? Why had it happened?

There was a knock on the bathroom door. "My dad wants to know how many tacos do you want," came the kid's muffled voice.

"Two!" I said. "Just two!"

I heard him go off down the hallway yelling, "Two!" Once had been coincidence, twice was something else. Either the editors at *The New Yorker* were trying to destroy me, or some sinister, unseen hand was at work. How else to explain my being stymied again and again by the same outfit? I turned on the faucet and let the water run down the drain. There was no other way to make sense of it. *The New Yorker* was a tool of the devil. I washed my hands and dried them in a puffy yellow towel. Soon the King and Andresito would start to wonder why I was taking so long in the bathroom, so I went back to the kitchen and ate one of the *tacos de lengua* on my plate without saying anything to anybody. The kid took birdlike bites of a ham sandwich. He had extremely delicate features and a gaze of sullen despair.

"Are you gonna take me to the fireworks?" he asked the King.

"I got a lot on my plate," the King grumbled.

The kid frowned. He looked at me. "Do you know what that is that you're eating?" he said.

"Tongue."

"That's gross. That's a cow's tongue, that he used for licking things."

"*Lengua*," said the King. "It's called *lengua*. You gotta start using Spanish."

"No, I don't."

"You won't be able to talk to anyone back home."

"Good. I don't want to talk to them."

The King sighed and looked at me. "You could teach him a thing or two about Mexico," he said.

"I don't wanna learn about Mexico," the kid said. "I just wanna go to the fireworks." He opened his sandwich and squirted some yellow mustard inside and then closed it and pulled off a tiny portion of the bread with his two front teeth.

"Well," the King said, "he's been living down there. He knows what it's like to live down there when you ain't from there."

I gave the kid a tight grin. My mind had already leapt ahead to the moment when I would return to Sigg's vacant apartment, buy a very large bottle of tequila, and drink until I passed out on the cold tile floor. The King, however, seemed to expect some bit of expat wisdom. "You know what Ambrose Bierce said about Mexico?" I said to Andresito. "He said, 'To be a Gringo in Mexico—ah, that is euthanasia.'"

"What's euthanasia?" he asked.

"When a doctor kills somebody."

He frowned. "Why doesn't he make them better?"

"He can't. They're going to die anyway."

"Like a horse," the King offered.

The kid thought about it for a minute, furrowing his small brow. Lucky for him, he had not inherited many of his father's physical characteristics. His neck was skinny, his skin smooth as sand, and his dark brown, almost black eyes looked like wet stones. There didn't seem to be any of the King's snorting bullishness in Andresito. He looked like he might grow up to be an underwear model.

"I bet if it was *here*, the doctor could make them better," he said. "What kind of doctors do they have in Mexico?"

"That's not the point," I said.

"How do you know they're not going to kill you too?"

"These people want to die."

"But *I* don't want to die!"

"That's fine. You just tell the doctor that and everything will be fine."

The kid's eyes reddened and his lip trembled. "But I can't speak Spanish!"

"Oh, quit that," the King said. "No one's gonna die. What are you crying about?"

But he just pushed back his chair and ran out of the room. The King sat in silence, staring at his food and shaking his head. He looked depressed. The futility of the situation was overwhelming. What was I doing here? A motor whirred to life inside the fridge. I apologized for bringing up euthanasia, but the King said it wasn't my fault. He said the kid was too touchy.

"Can you take him to the fireworks?" he said. "I gotta pack."

I PICKED UP ANDRESITO at eight and drove him to the municipal park where the show was. He had spiked his hair, drenched himself in some awful cologne, and put on an oversized leather jacket with the sleeves pushed up. He looked like an extra in a John Hughes movie. We rode in silence, each stewing over his own misfortunes. The park was full of families on blankets and men drinking beer in folding chairs, but Andresito didn't seem to know anyone. We leaned against a fence and waited for the show to begin.

After a while he said, "I'm not afraid of the doctors in Mexico."

"Okay."

"I just won't get sick."

"That's good."

He slumped against the fence and let his head loll to the side.

"When's your article going to be done?"

I told him I didn't know.

"People used to write articles about my dad all the time."

I nodded.

"I was always like, what's the big deal? I mean, it's not like he won for being *president* or something."

"It's because he was the first person to do what he did."

"So what? I'm the first person to do *this*!" He jumped out from the fence and struck a contorted pose, glancing at me through his outstretched, crooked arms.

"Probably not, actually. That has probably been done before."

"What about this one?" he said, twisting into a new position.

"Probably that one too. Everything's been done before."

He slouched back to the fence. We stared at the crowd. "Everybody always wanted to talk to him about it. And now nobody wants to talk to him. The guy from New York even wanted to talk to *me* about it."

"What did you tell him?"

"I don't know. He was nice. He showed me pictures of New York on his computer. He said you could be anything you wanted there." He jammed his hands in his pockets and kicked the dirt. "I'm going to go there as soon as I turn eighteen."

The first explosion erupted over our heads. Soon the sky was filled with light and color. For a small city like Coalinga, it was a robust display, but it couldn't come close to the mayhem I'd witnessed back in Zacatecas during Mexican Independence Day, on September 16. There, the fireworks had been launched out of the central courtyard of the *palacio del gobierno*, some of them barely clearing the sides of the building, some exploding in showers of sparks on the roofs of nearby houses, and all the while men, women, and children as young as six were firing off rifles real and toy and shouting with their heads tipped back, throats taut and humming. The contrast between that scene and this one recalled a line from Paz's book: "On great occasions in Paris or New York, when the populace gathers in the squares and stadiums, the absence of people, in the sense of *a* people, is remarkable: there are couples and small groups, but they never form a living community in which the individual is at once dissolved and redeemed."

The next two days passed in a numb pantomime of journalism. Again and again I failed to muster the resolve to inform the King that my entire visit had been founded on bad research. How to explain it? A dangerous combination of professional incompetence and a three-year-old devil's curse? It was easier to go along with the charade. The King was so intent on showing me what fools the *chingasos* at City Hall were that I ended up having to carry out all kinds of false research trips and fraudulent interviews. We ate bowls of menudo and plates of *barbacoa* with leaders of local migrant groups. If the King thought I wasn't writing down enough of what someone was saying, he would nudge me and make a little writing gesture.

The pages of my steno pad filled up quickly, as he fretted about Andresito and railed against corruption. The fact that his story had already been told had not dampened his interest in having it told again. He was a fountain of talk and opinion. He criticized the Los Angeles Dodgers' front office and told me about a funny thing that happened on a business trip he'd taken to Salem, Oregon. Stories would remind him of other stories, which would remind him of the plots of action movies, which would remind him of people he used to know in Mexico. He waxed on about the simple lives of the Aztecs and Maya. He said he was no longer happy in the U.S. He had made very good money here, but he now felt like he was in a *jaula de oro*, a golden cage, just like the song said. He sang the song for me. All he really wanted was to make things better back home so that people wouldn't have to imprison themselves in this golden gringo cage. My hand cramped and my pens ran dry as he ranged over a dizzying array of topics—music, license plates, pool cleaners, the difference between homemade and store-bought pork rinds, the smell of sawdust. It was more talk than I had heard in months, and the more of it I transcribed, the more unthinkable it became to confess to him that none of it would ever be turned into a magazine article. One morning I tried forgetting my reporting materials at the hotel, but the King noticed immediately and sent me back to the room to get them. That afternoon he took my pad, fastened a homemade strap to it, and hung it from my neck with a satisfied chuckle. "Now you won't be leaving that thing behind all the time," he said. A small pencil, the kind doled out at libraries and golf courses, dangled from a string.

By the time we left for Mexico, on Monday, July 7, I had filled two steno pads. The King picked me up early, with Andresito scrubbed clean in the backseat, his eyes puffy and red. We headed south through the bountiful fields and fruit-laden orchards of California's Central Valley into the sprawling conurbation of Los Angeles, where we picked up Interstate 10 and headed east. Soon the city was a hazy bulk on the horizon behind us, and tall white windmills spun on the bald hills ahead. The land flattened and emptied. In the side mirror I saw Andresito nodding gently to his Walkman and watching with trepidation as the terrain drained of green.

The plan was to spend the night at a Days Inn on the Pecos River and in the morning make our way down to Piedras Negras for the crossing. The King had followed this route many times before, usually alone, and he relished landmarks such as this Days Inn as if they were old friends. He was full of recollections about his original journey across the river, stories that would have pricked up my ears had I not already read detailed accounts of every one of them in "The King Who Would Be Mayor." In fact, reading Tolen's article had given me a pretty good sense of what to expect from the whole trip. I knew that in El Paso, the interstate would draw up alongside the Rio Grande, affording us our first passing view of Mexico and prompting the King to make a speech about how "the dirt ain't different over there"; that a few hours later we would pass a Border Patrol checkpoint at Sierra Blanca, where he would declare that it still gave him "the woollies" to get the once-over from the men in green; and that, the next day, when we made it safely into Mexico, he would buy a bouquet of plastic flowers from an old woman in a rebozo, lay them at the base of a small roadside altar to Saint Christopher, the patron saint of travelers, and announce with solemnity that this was the very same altar at which he had stopped to pray for safe passage when he was a poor boy heading north with nothing but a pair of work boots and a framing hammer.

The King was now a politician, so his predictability shouldn't have surprised me, but it was annoying nonetheless and before long it drove me to quit taking serious notes. If he glanced over at me and made the writing gesture, I'd just scribble meaningless strings of letters and numbers, make elaborate borders, or draw stick figures or 3-D boxes. My mind wandered as we began to make our way into the interior. The highway crossed a lunar swath of desert, but the road itself was lively, full of cars and trucks and federal police and buses and vendors and shepherds grazing burros on the shoulder. It was like some sort of giant *plaza mayor*, narrowed and elongated, to which the public had been drawn as much for companionship as for travel. The American roadway is much safer—you never see stones used for lane markers or chickens on the loose—but it does not have the same atmosphere of fellowship as its Mexican counterpart. Octavio Paz would probably chalk it up to the difference between Protestantism and Catholicism.

A number of Paz's observations had stayed with me. "Americans have not looked for Mexico in Mexico," went one of them. "They have looked for their obsessions, enthusiasms, phobias, hopes, interests—and these are what they have found. In short, the history of our relationship is the history of a mutual and stubborn deceit, usually involuntary though not always so." When Paz wrote this in 1979, six years after the King had entered the United States, he was thinking of "writers or politicians, businessmen or only travelers," gringos dipping down below the border for strong tequila, pretty churches, and a favorable exchange rate. Now it was more mixed up—now you had the King, a Mexican looking for an image of Mexico conjured by the obsessions, enthusiasms, phobias, hopes, and interests that had plagued him since he left it; and Andresito, an American kid who just wanted to go home; and me with my steno pads. Had I deceived even myself, willed away unuseful facts at the gate to some other realm where the King was still mayor and I had a story?

Mutual and stubborn deceit. What else could it be? A border is the beginning of deceit.

"WHAT AM I GOING to *do* here?" Andresito's concern was genuine. We were north of Saltillo, passing through a rolling wooded stretch with some sort of military *campamento* chopped out of the trees, where sinewy soldiers kicked a ball around a grassless soccer field, and an old man in a bugler's cap crouched by a water spigot, filling jugs.

"Go to *bailes*, dance with girls, go ride places in the truck," the King said firmly. "You can drive when you're younger here, you know? They don't got all the same rules they got up there. You want to learn how to drive?"

"Yes."

I was afraid the lesson would commence immediately, but the King made no move to pull over. After a while he said, "You'll like it. The *chavas* they got down here . . ." The King gave me a wink.

"What's that?"

"Girls. The girls down here are pretty, *m'ijo*, you'll see."

"I don't like girls."

"Just wait till you meet some Mexican girls."

"I don't like any kind of girls."

"You like to dance, though."

"Not with girls. I do solo."

"We'll change that."

"I don't *wanna* change it."

The King was getting agitated. He shifted angrily around in his seat, glowering at Andresito's face in the rearview mirror and clenching the steering wheel. "We need gas," he said, swinging abruptly across the road onto an off-ramp. We'd been passing Pemex stations all day. Often they were the only signs of life for miles in every direction—deliverymen smoking, and buses disgorging sleepy, stone-faced men to pee and buy Sabritas, and families in trucks with tarp-pinned loads tending their overheated engines and children as in some Dust Bowl tableau.

The green-jacketed pump men came out to wash the King's windows and fill the tank. Andresito refused to get out, so we left him and headed into the store, which was full of travelers—migrants and truckers and a cop or two. Out back near the diesel pumps I spotted a group of Huichols, dressed in their traditional white shirts with bright embroidery. The King noticed them too, and we went to have a look. I knew a few things about the Huichols, having briefly considered trying to write an article about their annual pilgrimage across Zacatecas to their ancestral peyote lands in San Luis Potosí. They were standing around the tailgate of a pickup, drinking sodas and shading their eyes. The King and I stared quietly, both of us lost in contemplation. At the center of the group was an older man with long gray hair and a deeply lined face. It was the right time of year for them to be returning home from the peyote hunt, and I took the old man for the *mara'akame*, or shaman. I had a rough idea of his duties. He would have blindfolded the rookies, led everyone to the "cosmic threshold," and chanted loudly while the search for the holy cactus went on. When it was found, he would have shot it through with an arrow and given the others some to eat and then guided them on their spirit journeys into the "Otherworld," crossing a "Wisdom Bridge" to reach the ancient source of "Heart-Knowledge" from which all life springs.

"Dad!" Andresito's high-pitched voice pierced the trance. He was coming out the back of the store, holding aloft one of my steno pads; it was open to the pages filled with random nonsense. "Look," he said, showing the King.

I tried to grab it, but the King body-blocked me. He flipped through the pages, backward, forward, forward, backward.

"What the hell?" he said. "Where's the notes?"

An hour seemed to pass. Finally I said, "There will be no article." I did my best to explain why, but the misadventure was too ridiculous for them to believe. The clanking station wagon, the nuts and bolts hopping down the highway, the Green Angel, the conversation in the bar, the drunken Googling—they thought I was lying about everything. I took them back to the truck, retrieved my first two pads, and showed them page after page of real notes—long monologues from the King about Vicente Fox, Chuck Norris, immigration policy, and the invasion of Iraq; drawings of pallets; demographic information for the entire Pleasant Valley. After that they didn't know what to make of me. "Lemme get this straight," the King said. "You didn't even know they threw out the *election*?"

"No, señor."

"That was like a year ago."

"As I said, my research was flawed."

"*Flawed?* Your research was fucked. That's what it was. It was fucked."

"You lied to us," Andresito said.

"That's right," the King said. "You've been lying to us for days now."

I didn't argue. The King stared at the ground, snorting and shaking his head. At first he was more amazed than angry, but then the balance started to tip. We pulled back onto the highway and rolled along in silence. The King seemed to be reviewing my visit in his mind's eye, going interview by interview through all the deceitful days. Finally he banged the wheel with his fist and said, "I gave you my time, Jacobo, I gave you my story, I even gave you my food. And the whole time you're sitting there, knowing it's for nothing. You treated me like a fool."

"I'm sorry, señor. I didn't mean to. I thought you enjoyed talking about all that stuff."

"Bullshit. You think I'm some dumb wetback just happy to tell my story? You think I don't got better things to do? I'm a fucking international businessman. I'd be a fucking mayor if those *chingasos* at City Hall didn't steal it from me."

"You're right."

"You think you're the first reporter to write about me?"

"I'm well aware that I'm not."

"You ever heard of Joe Tolen? He's won a goddamn Pulitzer prize. He came on this trip and wrote an article about me for *The New Yorker*. That was a good article too. Did you read it?"

"In your book of clippings, yes."

"Only thing he got wrong was about the salad dressing. Maybe I do like Thousand Island dressing, but I ain't addicted to it."

"I think he meant it sort of hyperbolically."

"Of course he did. How could anyone be addicted to salad dressing?"

"Well, he probably assumed people would get that."

"But not everyone will. There are people going around right now saying, '*Conoces El Rey de las Tarimas?* That *juevon* is addicted to Thousand Island dressing.' What do you think that does for my future in politics?"

"I don't know, señor."

"You know what the problem is with journalists? You don't have enough responsibility. You don't realize that anything you say, any rumor you put in there, people will think that's the truth. You can't ever make them change their minds after they saw it in the paper."

He stomped on the gas and swerved into the left lane to get around a slow-moving bus.

"I've read a lotta stories that were about me, and none of them was exactly right. Even if the facts are straight, they leave things out. They pick and choose to make it into whatever they want. They don't tell my story, they tell their story. But it's my story."

Andresito piped up from the back. "It's my story too."

The King glanced in the rearview mirror. After a few minutes he said to me, "Give him your notes."

"What?"

"Give my son your notebooks, all the notes you took."

"But I—"

"What do you need it for? That's our story, all that stuff in there. That's our lives."

THE KING DROPPED ME at the apartment near the bus station and roared away without saying goodbye. I slept on the floor until Sigg came around the next day and pounded on the door.

"Where have you been?" he said. "I need to show the place."

He drove me to Edison's to check on the Toyota. Apparently, the constant velocity joint had arrived but the car was still not ready to drive. There was some other problem, and Edison feared the worst. He had been waiting to proceed. "I didn't know how much you wanted to spend on this," he explained. "It could go up." Nine thousand dollars was all that remained of my pirate money, and it was easy to see how salvaging the Toyota might dent these funds. Sigg recommended abandoning the car entirely. It had never impressed him very much. He thought I should sell it, ship my belongings to Texas, buy a bus ticket to Tuxtla Gutiérrez, and catch a ride back home with his road race, which was only a couple months away.

He took me to a *yonke*, or junkyard, on the edge of town and helped me hammer out a deal for the Toyota. Sigg was a ruthless negotiator. With his omnipresent dark sunglasses it was impossible to get a read on his thoughts; when the yardman's offer was not to his liking he would just stare at him silently, like a cop. Somehow he managed to work the price up to five hundred American dollars, which was half of what I'd paid for the car fifteen thousand miles ago. The money would cover a good portion of the trip down to Tuxtla Gutiérrez and back up to Laredo.

The night before the Toyota was to be towed I went to Edison's garage to clean out the glove compartment. The car was sitting in the corner of the lot, bumper familiarly askew. I knew every inch of her—the dried ketchup splotch on the steering wheel from a road meal en route to New Orleans, the missing radio tuner knob where I'd fashioned a handle with a square-bend U-bolt, the pattern of wear on the gas pedal's rubber cover, the look of the yellow seat stuffing where the vinyl upholstery was torn. She had treated me well, and I felt ashamed to be abandoning her on the high plains, thousands of miles from home, to be dismantled by some crude scrapper. In the previous four years, I'd spoken more words in the direction of her cracked brown dashboard than at any one human ear, and although there was no record of it, I knew that in some sense she had transcribed my monologues.

Now it was all gone. "The feeling of solitude," Paz says, "is a longing for a place . . . We have been expelled from the center of the world and are condemned to search for it through jungles and deserts or in the underground mazes of the labyrinth." Outside Edison's shop some kids were blasting firecrackers, laughing as they scampered away from the tiny explosions. I waited at the bus stop far down the block, listening to the periodic booms and the sharp happy screams. Then the bus came, and I left.

Chapter VII

"HE WAS PERFECT!"

A video showed a car skidding wildly across a section of highway somewhere in Mexico. The car, painted brightly and covered in decals, was heading for a small child who had wandered into the middle of the road. The tires screamed. The child froze. Suddenly the car flipped up into the air. Miraculously, the zenith of the flip was met directly over the head of the terrified child. The car cleared him by several inches and rolled harmlessly on the shoulder. The whole thing looked to have been choreographed.

"The car, it went over him, you see? He was perfectly fine. Perfect!"

I was in the banquet room of the Centro de Convenciones in Tuxtla Gutiérrez, eating tiny ham sandwiches as fast as they brought them. A crowd of racers gawked at the screen. The man doing the reassuring was Eduardo Leon, automobile enthusiast and president of La Carrera Panamericana, Sigg's road race. The race was actually a revival, in the form of an amateur road rally, of a professional race that had run for five years in the 1950s, during which time it had attracted the top car companies and best drivers in the world. There were still some very good drivers involved, but few, if any, were professionals, and some were rank beginners. I'd shared nacho plates and *micheladas* with a number of them at the Hotel Camino Real, where the massive entourage had begun to gather two days earlier, and found them to be a friendly bunch, as eager to enjoy their Mexican sojourn as to break the sound barrier on the parched flats of the Chihuahuan Desert. Some of the crews had high-dollar entourages and some were budget operations, like the two Canadians driving an old Corvette with no fuel gauge, no odometer, no speedometer, and "shitty tires," or the hot-air balloonist from Minnesota who had convinced a local diner to sponsor his Morris Minor. There were swaggering veterans and wide-eyed rookies, like a first-time navigator who was copiloting her brother's Chrysler Windsor and going by the nickname "Grandma Speedy."

"No problems with the kid," Leon persisted, as our jaws got back to work on the ham sandwiches. "But this is why we say to be safe. To finish first, you first have to finish."

I'd fallen in with some members of the Mercedes-Benz Club of Houston who had an extra seat in their service vehicle. They had run a 1965 230SL convertible in the race every year since 2000. The driver, Mike Haney, was an architect; the navigator, Gary Bartley, was a retired chemical engineer. What store of speedway cultivation the team possessed lay with its mechanic, seventy-four-year-old Helmut Holder, a German émigré who'd gotten his start, Haney told me, building Messerschmitts for the Third Reich. After the race Holder had enjoyed an illustrious career as the race mechanic for European motorcycle champ Hermann Gunzenhauser. Bartley's wife, Sylvia, former secretary of the Mercedes-Benz Club, and Holder's wife, Mimi, a nurse, filled out the squad. Loitering in the lobby, I'd met a few other teams who'd seemed like they would make interesting companions, but Go-Green-Go was the only one with an ex-Nazi mechanic running the show.

The team name was a reference to the dark green paint job on the car, which belonged to Haney and answered to the name Heidi. She was one of the 1,107 230SLs built in the German factory in 1965, Haney told me. Like a pleased parent, he could recite from memory every detail of her life history. Her first owner, a German, had defaulted on his payments before the year was out. The second owner took possession of the car only to plow into an old lady on a rainy Stuttgart night. Under German law, the man's driver's license was revoked. Next in line were Kathi and Warner Hoffman, American teachers living abroad. They bought the car from the Metz und Pabst Autohaus for $3,500 and took her to Rhodes, Greece, where they ran a school for employees of Voice of America. Over the next few years, the Hoffmans moved all over Europe with the car, whom they called Cede. Finally, they returned to the United States, settling in Houston, where they were forced to put Cede up for sale. She fell into the hands of a wild-boar hunter of French-Jewish ancestry named Jason Hebert. Hebert's brother promptly blew her engine hot-rodding the Houston frontage roads. After trying unsuccessfully to force the block from a 230SE into her slender base, Hebert gave up and sold the car to Haney.

"Did the old lady in Stuttgart die?" I asked him.

"Yep," he said, proudly stroking the sleek green hood. "Heidi has killed."

■ ■ ■

IN THIS, I soon discovered, she was not alone. Sigg had told me very little about the history of the race, but it turned out that during the brief but savage years of its initial operation, in the 1950s, La Carrera Panamericana had achieved a well-deserved reputation as the most dangerous road race in the world. Every year someone died; most years it was a handful. Livestock were splattered, houses wiped out, walls knocked down, trees uprooted, vehicles knocked to atoms. Footage of the event shows cars crashing through small Mexican towns like pinballs. Accounts I read called to mind Octavio Paz's description of the Mexican Revolution as a "bloody fiesta." Since Leon had launched the revival in 1988, the death toll had been much more reasonable, but it was still not unheard of for participants to perish; one of the requirements of the rules committee was that all cars must display on their doors the blood types of their driver and navigator.

The race's hazardous renown was at odds with its original intent, which had been to celebrate the completion of Mexico's section of the Pan-American Highway. The president at the time was Miguel Alemán, a lawyer, businessman, and real estate developer who once declared it his ambition that all Mexicans have "a Cadillac, a cigar, and a ticket to the bullfights." Having spent his youth in a country torn to flinderation by the lofty ideals of the Revolution, he was now eager to set her marching steadily toward modernization down the freshly paved highway. The boostering of tourism! The flourishing of trade! No simple ribbon-cutting would suffice to advertise an accomplishment so profound. It required a road race. Entries were restricted to hardtop stock cars piloted by a driver and a navigator, the winner's purse was set at 150,000 pesos, and on Cinco de Mayo, 1950, beneath a blazing sun, 126 vehicles representing at least ten countries roared off the starting line at one-minute intervals onto a brand-new ribbon of road closed to all other traffic and guarded by soldiers authorized to shoot on sight any stray farm animal caught wandering the shoulder.

Within the fanfare, a few discordant notes could be heard. An editorial published two months before the race in the newspaper *El Monitor* argued that a modern road connecting Mexico to the "Colossus of the North" would lay her open to a "methodical and total occupation" from U.S. forces. Once the desert barrier in which Sebastián Lerdo de Tejada took his comfort had been tamed, *El Monitor* assumed that nothing would stop the rapacious gringo. The completion of the highway had "introduced into the country a Trojan Horse of enormous proportions which harbors within the power of the United States of America . . . in building the highway, Mexico has taken one more step toward her own destruction."

There turned out to be some truth to this dark forecast. The road brought with it the race, and during the five years of its initial run, the Carrera Panamericana was one of the most destructive road races ever. Yet despite, or perhaps due to, the deathly shroud it wore, the race's popularity grew quickly. "Not since 'Allá En El Rancho Grande' was a coast-to-coast hit in the U.S. have Mexican public relations been given such a boost," noted a contemporary report from *Motor Life*. "While across the Atlantic the Panam matches Cortez' first conquistadorial report to Charles the Fifth for making Mexico a key point on the globe to millions of Europeans." It was everything Alemán had hoped for, but the attentions of the international race crowd posed a far greater challenge to the young Mexican thoroughfare than its intended traffic of long-haul trucks, Sunday drivers, crowded buses, and family wagons. By 1954, "the world's toughest road race" had claimed so many lives and damaged so much property that Alemán's successor, Adolfo Ruy Cortines, could see no good reason why it should continue. Everyone knew by then that Mexico had a new highway. Much to the dismay of the world's speed hogs, Cortines shut down the Carrera.

The roads stayed clear for thirty-four years.

OUTSIDE TUXTLA GUTIÉRREZ'S Centro de Convenciones the sun shone off a roaring sea of polished steel: Jaguars, Impalas, Hudsons, Mercuries, Mustangs, Buicks, Oldsmobiles, Falcons, Porsches, Volvos, Volkswagens, Shelbys, Studebakers, Corvettes, Chryslers, and a Facel Vega. As a tribute to the original race (and as a means of keeping race car velocities from exceeding reasonable limits), entries in the new Carrera were restricted to cars built between 1940 and 1965. Souped-up and loudly painted, these vintage autos looked like historical cartoons. Local men wandered among them, nodding their approval and pointing out details to the women on their arms. Children posed for photos and asked drivers for autographs. Decals on the race car doors announced the home countries: Mexico, the U.S., France, Belgium, Sweden, Argentina, Portugal, Britain, Germany, Canada, Italy, and Finland. In many cases the voyages had been harrowing, and a frantic storm of activity now engulfed the courtyard, as mechanics rushed to repair cracked distributor caps, dead alternators, wrongly tuned carburetors, unfastened skid plates, outdated safety equipment that would not pass scrutineering, and a host of other problems. High above it all an inflatable bottle of Corona, the race's main sponsor, bobbed gently in the air.

The race had not yet begun, but I could already sense a great groundswell of chaos readying to erupt with the first toss of the green flag. This sense of doom was boosted by accompanying Bartley to the Navigators' Meeting, at which Clerk of the Course Carlos Cordero attempted to explain the route book, a hefty spiral-bound tome that details every speed bump, railroad, rock-slide hazard, low-water crossing, village, ravine, hill, stoplight, river, and sheer two-thousand-foot cliff between Tuxtla Gutiérrez and the finish line in Nuevo Laredo. The book was an impressive compilation, but Clerk Cordero's English was not up to the task of elucidating its confusing charts and tables, and the meeting rapidly came apart in his hands. With so much riding on a thorough grasp of the symbology, as Clerk Cordero called it, no terrified novice was willing to forgo the advice of a well-informed, English-speaking neighbor for the mangled declarations of the fellow in charge. The din rose. Shouting was widespread, much of it random and meaningless. "Five!" the woman beside me, a glass-blower from California, screamed. "Roman numeral five!" As a return to order began to seem more and more hopeless, navigators leaned across the U-shaped table and grabbed frantically at Clerk Cordero's arms, shouting their questions in stiff, unconjugated Spanish.

The widespread anxiety did not extend to Bartley, who sat coolly flipping pages, betraying nothing more than idle curiosity. He had that preternatural calm of certain Texan men for whom hysterics are as unbecoming as a pair of tasseled loafers. No matter what sort of mayhem was taking place around him, Bartley displayed no more excitement than if he were floating along in Galveston Bay, his feet up on the rail of a houseboat.

Bartley's tranquillity was also the product of experience, however, and as I considered this, a disturbing realization began to take shape in my mind: there was almost no chance I'd be permitted to ride in the actual race car. Somehow, I'd failed to contemplate this unlikelihood. I'd imagined a magazine article full of white-knuckled cockpit testimony and firsthand descriptions of long straight ribbons of highway whipping underneath me at unholy speeds. Sure, Bartley was the navigator, but I'd figured they'd let me have a crack at it for at least one day. Yet, observing the visible fear in the eyes of the rookies around me, it became abundantly clear that I would be stuck in the service vehicle all the way home. What did I know of the symbology? How could I keep Haney from plunging Heidi off some deadly escarpment? Luis Reguer, the director of the race, who'd come to Clerk Cordero's aid, directed our attention to a curve marked in red. "And even for you see that right curve is simple," he said. In the room next door, convention center staffers were testing speakers for a wedding, and the low, steady thumping of their bass lines filled our room, as if a collective navigational heart pounded. "Please be alert," Reguer continued. "Be aware there, because when you go up in the apex of the curve, you will not stop. We drove this three or four times and you always feel like you are losing the car. If you are very speedy, you can lose the car in there very much."

I STILL HADN'T SOLVED the problem when the Drivers' Meeting rolled around that night. It made for a sharp contrast with the navigators' confab. Reclining in rows of chairs with beer bottles hanging between two fingers, the drivers displayed a general attitude of vague disinterest. They hadn't come down to Mexico to go to meetings. They had come down to look death squarely in the eye at a hundred and thirty miles an hour. Patiently they endured the necessary pageantry. The top race officials sat on a dais behind a blue-buntinged table flanked by two oversized inflatable Corona bottles. A row of Corona girls in spandex stood along the wall behind the officials, each of whom had before him a Diet Pepsi, a glass of water, and a Corona. Leon made a few announcements: This was the first year a Portuguese had entered the race! Reporters from the Mexican television network Televisa would be traveling with us! Victoria Motors, once again, would be doling out new engines to the winning cars! Don Piccard had something to say!

I'd been hearing about Piccard since my arrival. The first person to cross the English Channel in a hot-air balloon, he was considered by many to be the Father of Sport Ballooning, and in fact, his entry in the Carrera this year was merely a means toward accomplishing an ambitious balloon flight. He'd explained the scheme to me earlier that afternoon. The highest he'd ever risen in a balloon was 35,000 feet; his current goal was to make it to 150,000. This was more than twice as high as the world record and would essentially put him in outer space.

"The pressure's only one-one thousandth of the ground pressure," he had said, "which means I have to have a thousand times more volume in the balloon. I have some new design ideas to take care of that, but the tech people say, 'Well, we're very excited about it, but do you have a younger man who's going to pilot it for you?' So I'm doing this race to establish that I'm not a normal seventy-seven-year-old."

Piccard was tall and thin, with a long white mustache and the look of a daft but insightful country doctor. He shuffled up to the stage and presented a signed copy of the fiftieth anniversary issue of *Automobile Year,* a British motoring magazine put out by his cousin, to Inspector Jefe Julio Tovar, the chief of the Policia Federal de Caminos, under whose stern command the Mexican highways would be cleared in our path. "But can I take another moment?" the balloonist inquired, drifting about with the cordless microphone. "One thing that balloon races do is have balloon mail. I have not been able to find any evidence of motor-car racing mail. So in this Carrera, I think for the first time, we will have a limited amount of Carrera express couriers, who will carry mail from Tuxtla to Laredo in only one car in each category." Behind him, one of the Coronas began to deflate, leaning flaccidly away from the table and down to the floor. A Corona girl went to have a look. Bending over in her skin-tight suit, she grasped the bottle with both arms and began rubbing it, looking for a puncture hole. The crowd laughed into its sleeve. Several cheers went up. Piccard, unaware of the scene unfolding behind him, seemed to think they were meant to belaud his plan. "Now in case the car doesn't get there"—he grinned—"we have crash stamps put on for the next car to pony-express them to Laredo." Having discovered the bottle's plug disconnected from its outlet, the Corona girl stuck it back in. A pump whirred on. In seconds the yellow rubber swelled and stood up rigidly. The audience roared lustily, and Piccard, pleasantly surprised at the reception his scheme had provoked, raised his voice with gusto: ". . . the mail will be from schoolchildren!"

The glow was still on him an hour later at a drunken gathering on the hotel's patio. Standing a foot or so taller than most of the group, Piccard was easy to monitor as he made his rounds, lining up mail carriers from each class. Haney had already volunteered to bring the mail for our Historic B class, and now he was puffing on a cigar, swapping horror stories with two rotund lawyers from L.A., who split the driving in a Chevy. One of them said that the previous year a guy had been going 140 miles an hour on a speed run near Mexico City when the steering wheel had come off in his hands. Haney shrugged. "What about the Italian guy in the wheelchair?" he said. "Rigatoni? He crashes every year. Last year he drove an Alfa. Looked like he drove it into a giant pulverizer." Piccard edged into our circle. His presentation at the drivers' meeting had intrigued one of the lawyers, who inquired after the family's accomplishments.

"It was my first cousin once removed that ballooned around the world," Piccard told him. "And it was his father that went to the bottom of the ocean, it was *his* father that was the first in the stratosphere, it was his cousin who was the publisher of *Automobile Year*, and it was his grandfather's brother who made the Piccard-Pictet, which won the last automobile Grand Prix before real brakes."

The lawyers were eager to participate in the race mail scheme, and Piccard deputized them on the spot. He gave them a canvas mail bag, which he claimed would someday be more valuable as a collector's item than the cars themselves. The mail itself would be forthcoming; on the way down from Mexico City the truck carrying the commemorative Carrera postcards had crashed, and in the confusion everything had been stolen.

THE NIGHT BEFORE the race began, I lay in bed mulling my conundrum. Perhaps it was better to be in the service vehicle. Riding in the navigator's chair, I'd be privy to just one car's perspective. From the service truck I could see them all. I'd take in a wider scope of action. The most dramatic moments of the race, I was beginning to understand, were the accidents, and when someone skidded into a rockslide or bounced off a tree, I'd be there, ready to record the clamor of fear and excitement.

It was therefore a tremendous blow to discover the following morning that the race and service vehicles proceed along different routes entirely. Riding in a service truck, it turned out, prevents you from seeing the race at all. You leave the hotel, drive to the Pemex or parking lot where the midday *servicio* stop is planned, wait for the cars to pull in, and then drive to the next hotel. You are not on a race, you are on a road trip—counting the miles, observing the speed limit, arguing about music, eating granola bars that Sylvia purchased in bulk at the Costco in Houston so as to avoid stopping at Mexican restaurants of questionable hygiene.

We rattled out of Tuxtla Gutiérrez at dawn, the women in the backseat and Holder at the wheel. Immediately the world of the Carrera slipped away. At a military checkpoint on the edge of town, torches blazed in the half-light, and doves cooed from the box-trimmed trees. The road ascended, thinning from four lanes to two as it described long dramatic curves around deep gorges of fog. Unfinished brick houses poked rebar crowns out of the jungle. Tattered corn crops filled yards where tethered burros grazed. Children on bicycles twice their size, the handlebars weighted with hanging plastic bags full of eggs, tortillas, cheese, and Coke, rode past whitewashed bus stops with the names of towns block-lettered in black. El Tempisque. Cintalapa. A funeral procession lumbered down a side street, carrying a brown wood coffin behind a shining blue hearse. Trumpets, an accordion, and a *guitarrón* brought up the rear.

Desperate for a taste of the reckless thrills I had been denied, I turned to a book of Carrera history that Holder had brought along. It was a collection of newspaper and magazine accounts from each of the infamous first five years. I started with the 1950 race, which was as grisly as I'd heard. Just nineteen miles in, the first fatality had been recorded when a Guatemalan pilot hit a grade crossing and lost control of his Lincoln. That year, the course comprised eight stages of unfettered city-to-city runs, and cars were lost on every one, as drivers plunged into ravines, flipped over gullies, skidded off bridges, slammed into posts, battered houses, rammed aqueducts, and plastered what livestock had slipped past the troops. Paved with a mixture of volcanic ash, the road turned out to be more abrasive than anyone expected, and only 57 of the 126 cars actually reached the finish line in the tiny border town of El Ocotal, Chiapas (at that time the course ran north-south). "The road was so rough it tore up tires like carrots in a food processor," said the winning driver, Hershel McGriff. On the fourth leg, a Schenectady man lost control of his car and swung into the crowd of spectators lining the shoulder, killing a spectator named Tomasa Lopez. Despite all this, the racers enjoyed a hero's welcome from the crowd of five hundred thousand gathered around the Paseo de la Reforma in Mexico City. Whether the fans were cheering the modernization of the highway system, the thrilling velocities of the cars, the bravery of the drivers, or the pure spectacle, none of the accounts in Holder's book ventured to say.

Reading about the 1950 race turned out to be an adequate substitute for observing the action on the ground in 2003. That night in Oaxaca the news at the nightly meeting was that a Red Cross medic had joined poor Tomasa Lopez on the list of innocent bystanders killed during Carreras. On the day's third speed section, a Studebaker piloted by Axel and Nicolas de Ferran, who some said were brothers and some said were father and son, had blown its engine and dropped its oil; coming along behind them, Frank and Evelyn Currie, an elderly married couple from Southern California in a white Mustang, had hit the slick, spun wildly off the road, and slammed into an ambulance parked beside the shoulder. Race car drivers do not make good witnesses, and reports varied. Some said the ambulance had been launched into a photographer, who had also been killed. Some said the medics had survived. According to all, the Curries had not been injured, but it was possible that they had been put under house arrest in Chiapas somewhere, or that they had undergone a battery of tests in a Tuxtla Gutiérrez hospital, or that they had been remanded into the inspector *jefe*'s custody and were headed toward Oaxaca. The de Ferrans had fled the country or were at the hotel checking their email. Eduardo Leon, who seemed as confused as everybody else, promised us that better information would be forthcoming. With the race now under way, the effort required to stay atop such a wide range of disasters had turned his eyeballs red. A highly placed Mercury Monterey had erupted in flames at the race's outset, and there was talk that the car had been sabotaged by a rival team or maybe by a gang of Tuxtla Gutiérrez *taxistas*. Since the whole point of a race is to leave things behind as quickly as possible, Leon was in a difficult position when it came to dispelling wild rumors. As I talked to racers around the hall, the Red Cross medic came back to life, briefly flourished, and then lost both her legs.

The majority of the racers were just as harried as Leon and the other officials. Our caravan numbered somewhere in the two hundreds, and throughout it coursed an admixture of uncertainty and adrenaline that was to give the remainder of our journey the air of a hasty, ill-equipped, and irrelevant military campaign. Solid reports on the state of the field were a near-impossibility, but it seemed that mechanical breakdowns were already widespread—a Hudson had slung a rod; a Ginetta had run out of gas; and dark hearsay swirled around the poor showing of temperamental Frenchman Pierre de Thoisy, five-time winner of the race.

Heidi had not fared so well herself. On the day's second speed stage she'd puttered out and lost four minutes sitting on the side of the road. Although she started back up and ran fine the rest of the day, the time was gone, and Go-Green-Go could now only hope to recover through the malfunctions of its foes. Having spent the day reading about the terrific crack-ups of the past, I felt we were lucky to be running at all, but morale could not be lifted with this historical view. Holder was particularly disconsolate; he spent the whole evening frowning down into Heidi's open hood beneath a giant African tulip tree on the hotel grounds. The problem sounded electrical, but then she would not run on high rpm's. He suspected she had been running too rich, but the spark plugs showed that if anything, she had run too lean. A leak in the fuel lines could be the culprit, but there was no dip in pressure. Every explanation he came up with she refuted. Long after the sky had darkened he remained there, staring hopelessly into her innards while the tulip tree rained its woody pods upon his balding pate.

DURING THE NIGHT Holder's angst at the car's mysterious overheating developed into an unpleasant stomach condition. He kept nothing down. "I got a bad case of de *tofowl,*" he explained. Mimi had him on the tequila-and-toast restorative but what he wanted was schnapps, cherry schnapps, a sip of which he said would cure him instantly. We had no luck tracking any down at the hotel bar, nor at the Pemex on the Oaxaca-Tehuacán toll road where the second day's *servicio* stop pulled in. Even with *tofowl,* he had refused to relinquish the driver's seat, grasping his gut. He parked near the bathrooms and sat in the truck with his door open, gazing weakly through the rising dust and waiting for Heidi to appear.

The mood was tense, as dozens of other mechanics waited for their charges. Nearby I found Piccard's technician, his young face knotted with worry. Having recovered from some faulty wiring, a broken starter, and host of other problems, the Snail, as Piccard was calling his Morris Minor, had barely made it through the first day, bottoming out on several *topes,* or speed bumps, and blowing her sway bar, which had severely dented her oil pan. Her mechanic nervously toed the dust and cracked his knuckles until the familiar wooden panels hove into view. "Yes!" he screamed. "She's made it!"

Piccard debarked and wandered off, muttering about how his top speed was still too low. His navigator Ed Ryan, who was also his ophthalmologist, climbed out and leaned trembling against a service truck. "I got talked into this thing and I had some uncertainties," he shouted over the rumble of engines. "I'm just amazed at what a piece-of-shit car we're driving."

Heidi had finished the morning's runs without incident, and soon we were back on the road, gunning for the hotel. The tropical greenery of Chiapas gave way to a rockier terrain that swept into vast canyons flecked with pale green chollas that looked from afar like military gravestones. My journalistic ambitions once again thwarted by the itinerary, I cracked open Holder's book for a glimpse of the bygone action.

President Alemán had always intended the Carrera to be a onetime event, but success undid his plan. The motoring world was so enthralled by the display of wild abandon the first Carrera had presented that a second running soon became inevitable. For the 1951 Panamericana, factory teams from Ferrari and Lancia entered the fray. Organizers reversed the course to head north. Ninety-three cars started, three racers died in the first two days, and just thirty-five finished. By the time the rattling caravan reached the one hundred thousand fans gathered at the river, the army had shot 750 stray cattle. The top two finishers were both Ferraris, an outcome with profound implications. As *Motor* magazine noted, "It can be said that for the first time there were opposed on a normal highway cars of American manufacture and those of European manufacture, and for the first time there was dispelled the belief that the American car is the one more suitable for modern roads."

The clamor rang throughout the winter, leading Carrera organizers to split the field for the next year's race into two divisions, Sports and Stock. The move had a sobering effect; a Mexican in a Jaguar who cracked up and died on the second stage was the sole fatality in the 1953 edition. Mercedes-Benz entered the race for the first time and took the top two slots with its brand-new 300 SL.

We passed a massive landslide that cut the highway down to one lane, and Holder fell to ruminating on the past. He'd been working for Mercedes in 1953, he said, and the victory in the Panamericana had been a great source of national pride. Only seven years earlier, the factory had been completely destroyed by Allied bombers. "I compare it right now with Iraq," he said. "Many persons don't know how bad it was." It turned out that Holder had never built any Messerschmitts. He'd worked for a spell in a glider factory that was converted over to war production, and then he'd fought in the SS. "He was in the Hitler Youth Group," Mimi told me that night, as we waited for the race to pull into Puebla's Parque de Nalco, a small green off Avenida Cinco de Mayo where the plastic flower vendors set up. I tried to press her for more details, but our chat was busted up by a person costumed in a large rubber Corona bottle. The cars were coming.

DOUG MOCKETT, the reigning champ, who'd started the day eight seconds up, had opened the lead over Juan Carlos Saramiento's Studebaker to ninety-two seconds and was in excellent shape. De Thoisy, whom Bartley liked to refer to as "de Twah-lette," had advanced from sixth place to fourth, but he was now more than three minutes behind the overall leader. It was still entirely unclear to me whether any of this would make a good magazine article, but I did my best to behave as it seemed like a journalist would, scurrying among the racers, trying to get a sense of what I had missed in the service truck. "Ze rear end was broken," de Thoisy said when I asked him what the trouble had been, "and it broke ze pipe of brake liquid. So we didont have *any* more brake. In a speed *sec*tion. *Imagine*! No brake at all. So ah drive with ze engine brake, shifting ze gear down. It makes zis sound—*awwwwwww*. Ah was driving with ze shif*tair*! It was very uncomfortabool." He stood beside his car in a padded white fire suit, surveying the tumultuous scene through small, intense eyes. "It twill be diffi*cult* to catch him," de Thoisy said, gesturing at Mockett with his nose.

Mockett's machine was a 1954 Oldsmobile with a 1981 Camaro front clip, a five-speed gearbox, and a very big motor. Mockett himself was sixty-three years old and extraordinarily calm. Even biting his fingernails he seemed calm, as if the nails were too long and he was only making adjustments. I went over and asked him how he handled the fear. "I think it's a matter of taming the beast and keeping it under control, and having it do what you want it to do," he said.

That sounded pretty good coming from the champ, but not everyone had so obedient a vehicle. Earlier that day, Richard Morrison and Joe Hardin's Mercedes 220SE had bounced forty feet down a ravine when its rear wheels had quit holding the road. A wrecker dropped the crumpled heap in the hotel parking lot. Grass and dirt still clung to creases in the metal. "The tail just came out," Hardin said, his hands quivering. "These are notorious for trailing throttle, but I was on the throttle and it came out anyway." He shook his bald head. A small crowd stood around inspecting the damage. Piccard leaned in the window, smoothing his mustache. "I'd like to make an offer for the handles on the dashboard," he said.

He'd had problems of his own that day. The Snail's oil pan, battered unceasingly for a day and a half by an onslaught of *topes*, had finally dropped its lube. No one would say it, but all feared the engine had been cooked. His mechanic spent the evening fuming around the battered machine, which was parked alongside Heidi, whom Helmut had vowed to repair before sunup. Mike had driven well the first two days and clawed his way up to third place in our Historic B class, thirty-sixth place overall. If we had any chance of holding on to the bronze, Heidi's overheating would need to be addressed. Ignoring the fires in his stomach, for which we had still been unable to locate a soothing glass of cherry schnapps, Helmut hunched over the engine, poking and prodding it and pouring water into it and listening to it and peering into its innards. Finally, he declared the problem to be the thermostat coil. It had stopped compressing properly, even once the engine was hot. He removed the thermostat and the tiny coil inside it. We cursed it silently. Then he chucked it in the trash. Although it took Heidi much longer to warm up the next morning with all her water circulating, the fix seemed to work. When we met her at the *servicio* in Mexico City, having crossed through a region of piney woods that Holder likened to the Black Forest, she was running smooth.

A TAUT AIR HUNG OVER the mall on the city's outskirts where the crews had converged. The racers had yet to run a speed stage that day. All morning they'd taxied through a long transit stage, allowing plenty of time to consider the vertiginous frights awaiting them that afternoon on Mil Cumbres, an infamous section of serpentine Michoacán highway that traverses the Sierra Madre Occidental. Nerves wound up with brittle strands of anticipation. Reports of rain and fog threatened the afternoon's course.

The Ginetta raced in. The driver, a bouyant Englishman named Peter Davis, leapt out in his filthy yellow jumpsuit, tore off the hood, and immediately threw himself hammer and tongs at the steering rack. All morning long the slightest ripple in the road had swung the car wildly from left to right. "If we get in a stage like Mil Cumbres," his equally perky navigator observed, "we'll be off the edge." When I pointed out that, indeed, this was the very section he faced that afternoon, it seemed to only bear him up the more. "We ought to get done with the alternator, steering, and the carburetor jets in here," he said, casting a jovial eye about the lot. "And may have time to give it a polish."

This tally-ho routine was impressive, but the Ginetta broke down at the first sight of Mil Cumbres and had to be trailered to Morelia with a Mini Cooper's service crew. On the way, the service truck was sideswiped by the press car traveling with de Thoisy's bold and stylish French delegation. Packed in among the backup tires, the Ginetta survived the accident, which ruined the trailer and set at odds the Mini Cooper's driver, Tom Davies, and de Thoisy, a quarrel pitting a Texan in a Mini against a Frenchman in a Stude. The road was beginning to take its toll. Keeping track of what had happened every day required a herculean effort on my part. The service truck-and-press car crack-up was only one of four major accidents that afternoon. Along the boulevard leading to the Holiday Inn, a local *taxista,* in a moment of derangement, had skipped multiple lanes of traffic and cannonballed a perfectly restored Porsche. Most dramatic of all was the news that on the day's first speed stage, the popular Swede Mats Hammarlund, "El Vikingo Loco," had spotted the head of Mockett's navigator, Alan Baille, peering up from the side of the road in a daze. Hammarlund had steered his yellow Volvo into a culvert, jumped out, and run back to Baille, who'd gasped out his tale: The Oldsmobile had swung off the road, rolled down a hill, flattened some trees, smashed into a creek, and become wedged on a boulder with the nose pointing straight downward. The champ hung unconscious in his five-point harness.

This had cleared a path for de Thoisy, who finished with the day's best times. "Ah ween today," the Frenchman hotly declared. "Mock*ette* crashed. It is a peety but zat is ze race. He was mah hardest competi*tore*. Now ah am against Mexi*can*, Mexi*can*, Mexi*can*." He pointed out his rivals with violent jabs at the air. "Ah will beat zem."

Wandering among the frenzied mechanics disserting on the day's events, I came upon Piccard, who was reattaching a pair of long hood horns to the trailered Snail. They hadn't made it very far that morning before Dr. Ryan had heard an entirely new sound. Fearing they were about to make a hash of the engine, most of which, it turned out, belonged to the Square Peg Diner in Minneapolis, they'd pulled out of the race. "Well, you know," Piccard said, not looking up from his horn project, "you let things get out of hand and that's what happens. You know, I knew that I needed to have some kind of *tope*-protection. The minute I dropped this car off the jacks and saw how low these tires made it, I said, 'We've got to have a boilerplate underneath, and it's got to go over to Gene Olson's.'" He shook his head. Gene Olson couldn't do anything now.

Piccard held up a tiny horn screw and squinted at it. Laying out had put him in a philosophical mood. "Everything is good," he opined. "You cannot say that anything that happened in the past is bad." I asked him how the race had compared to his experiences on the ballooning circuit. He torqued a screw and inhaled deeply through his nose. Driving a car and flying a balloon, he observed, were very different things. It was a matter of control. "When you're walking you have very much control. When you're driving an automobile you have less control, and when you're driving a bicycle you have even less. Some people on a horse have full control, some people on a horse have no control. When you ride in a locomotive steam train, you have no control. The engineer has a very little bit of control." He looked up at the sky. "In a balloon, you're in complete control."

WITH THE RUNNING of Mil Cumbres the country's toughest sections of road were now behind us, and all that remained was to blast through the fertile plateau of the Baijo and floor it across the northern flats of creosote bushes and prickly pear to the mud-brown Rio Grande. We spent a night in Aguascalientes, where Mimi's grandfather had been kidnapped and held for ransom. She was vague on the details but I gathered it had happened during the Revolution. At the Drivers' Meeting, Leon introduced a group of young women dressed in old-time hoop skirts with tight herringbone bodices and feathery hats, just the sort of outfits that had riled up the peonage in Mimi's grandparents' day. The trotting out of local maidens in regional attire was customary wherever we made our camp, but in Aguascalientes, worn out from four days of driving, the drivers had even less patience than usual for the fashion show. Leon hurried the ladies offstage and ran through the day's results, which showed de Thoisy, true to his word, making an aggressive run at the heirs to Mockett's lead. He was now just thirteen seconds back of Juan Carlos Sarmiento. The Mexican was driving it for all he had, desperately trying to hold him off, but it did not look good for the home team. The word at the hotel was that de Thoisy had it in the bag. His car had mysterious powers. The Mexican Carlos Anaya had driven it to three Panamericana victories, then sold it to de Thoisy, with whom it promptly won five in a row. "*Es un supercoche*," one man told me.

I asked Mike about it that night as we lay in our beds. Did he believe that some cars were more than the sum of their mechanical parts? He seemed to feel it was so. The list of his own automobiles was studded with eccentric, particular machines—a 1955 Chevy, a Maserati Bora. In high school he drove a 1938 Buick limousine to school each day. "It looked like an Al Capone gangster car," he said, locking his fingers behind his head and grinning at the ceiling. "The back doors were suicide and the front doors were regular, and you had running boards on it, so basically people could walk between the front and back seat while you're driving down the road. Then there was the Starfire. What a piece of shit that was. You couldn't go anywhere without the heater on full blast or it'd overheat. Let's see, I also had a '74 Datsun pickup, that half of the engine was of my own design out of J-B Weld, which is like this epoxy stuff you mold into shapes. I was so poor that, when the exhaust manifold broke, I would just make a new one out of J-B Weld."

Mike was getting excited. He sat up and counted on his fingers. "I had the Dodge red Ram, a 1950 Ford truck." He frowned, trying to remember other cars. "There was a little Honda Civic . . . what else . . ." Suddenly he threw his hands in the air. "Lupe! Ah, God, how could I have forgotten her?"

He lay back down, savoring the rush of memory. "Lupe was another of my creations. She started off as a 1980 Dodge 024 fastback. I drove her for four years, and then the engine died. I let her sit for about a year. Then one day this guy who wanted my '55 Chevy calls me up and says, 'I've got an eighteen-thousand-mile Dodge Shelby Turbo Daytona, a very high-performance car, that flipped end over end three times. Factory defect, the rear axle snapped on it. The woman sued Chrysler, got millions. She doesn't want the car, the whole back of it is destroyed. But the drive line isn't damaged at all.' Well, Lupe was like a little sister to that car. So I agreed to the trade and the guy delivers the front half of the car. We pull the drive line out of Lupe, strip the drive line out of the Turbo Daytona, roll it under Lupe's body, and start cutting. It took us a year and a half to get it in there.

"Now, a Shelby Turbo is a hundred-and-forty-mile-an-hour car. Lupe weighed eleven hundred pounds less and had the same drive line. So she was *very fast*. I outran Corvettes, I outran Trans Ams, I outran Camaros. And it looked like I was driving some little piece-of-shit econo hatchback. My proudest moment was this one time, middle of the fucking night, I'm heading back to College Station on 290, and a Dodge Shelby Turbo Daytona pulls up beside me. He's, like, *vrooomm*, *vroommm*. And I'm thinking, We have the same engine, but you're packing around an extra eleven hundred pounds of steel. So we took off, side by side, and he doesn't know I'm not at full throttle. We got up to about ninety, and he's looking over at me, and I can see from his eyes he's thinking, How the fuck are you keeping up with me? And then I nailed it and just left him."

He laughed for a good while. Finally he said, "How many cars have you owned?"

I told him about the Toyota.

"That's it?"

"Yeah."

"*Jesus!* I don't even want to ask how many girls you've slept with."

■ ■ ■

THE NEXT AFTERNOON we reached Zacatecas. It was a strange sort of return. I'd barely left, but already nothing of mine remained—no boxes to pick up, no electric company deposit to claim, no overdue Telmex bill to settle, no car to retrieve. We were staying at a nice hotel on the *plaza mayor* a few blocks from my old apartment, which was still vacant, or so it seemed. While the cars roared up and down La Bufa on the day's speed stage, I went looking for Sigg, but his office mates told me that he was running all over town making accommodations for the race. I was secretly relieved. Sigg had been bullish on the Carrera story, but what did I really have to show him or anyone else? I knew all about sport ballooning, Messerschmitt airplanes, and Panamericanism, but I had not seen a shred of the action.

I took a taxi up to La Bufa to rectify this situation but the cops had shut down all the access points. The best I could do was to sit on a cinderblock and listen as the giant engines thundered off the red rock walls above me. The day's results put a sixth title clearly within de Thoisy's grasp. He was now in second place, mere seconds behind Sarmiento. The standings relaxed him, and at the evening's event—a *callejoñada*, or small Zacatecan parade led by a brass band—he lightened up, donning a cable-knit sweater knotted loosely over his shoulders and tossing back shots of mescal with a jaunty flick of his elbow. The thin air of the desert upland hastened the inebriation of the sunburned, road-weary crowd. Women shook their hips. Men made crude attempts to imitate the shouting they'd heard on records of Latin jazz. In the midst of the ruckus, I finally spotted Sigg. He stood motionless while three tangoing blondes stumbled past. Despite the fact that night had fallen, he was still wearing his sunglasses. I went to say hello. He pumped my hand and grinned. "Didn't I say it was beautiful?" he shouted. I nodded. He was eager for a full report, but before I could deliver, Leon pulled him away, and a surge in the crowd pushed me in the other direction. "Sigg!" I shouted, but I was drowned out by the boisterous first verse of the "Marcha de Zacatecas." The last I saw him, Sigg was nodding intently, arms crossed over his chest, face impassive, sunglasses reflecting in miniature the swarming festivities.

The mobile party had reached the point at which fun begins to diminish and increasingly more ridiculous antics are employed to keep it from disappearing entirely. A conga line was formed, the dance of last resort. De Thoisy grasped the hips of a man who'd yanked his T-shirt up over his head to expose his pale stomach. He was chomping on a cigar and wearing a gigantic sombrero. Gigantic sombreros floated everywhere atop the multitude. With their first free moments in Mexico, the racers had rushed to satiate an apparently universal desire for novelty hats. From windows and doors along our route, Zacatecans gazed out as we made our raucous way over the cobblestones. Watching them watch the hooting and reeling crowd of drunken gringos in sombreros, some shouting "*Arriba!*" while others yelled "*Olé!*," it was hard not to think of the ominous words published in *El Monitor* as the great road neared completion: ". . . introduced into the country a Trojan Horse of enormous proportions which harbors within the power of the United States of America . . . in building the highway, Mexico has taken one more step toward her own destruction."

■ ■ ■

THE SUN had not yet penetrated to the cold stone streets in the old city's core when we left Zacatecas at dawn and headed upcountry through Saltillo toward Monterrey on a straight road through a flat plain flecked with cacti and bunchgrass. There were no more trees. The landscape had made its final change, and it now seemed as if in our northerly progress across the country we had mile by mile been stripping Mexico of its frills and were now looking at the bald inheritance of earth on which the rest of the republic had made improvements. It was hard to judge the distance from ridge to ridge. Every now and again, on the roadside, an enormous gravel parking lot funneled down to a small cinderblock *llanteria*. These tire-repair shops abound in Mexico, from the biggest city to the most remote spur, and from their ubiquity you can only conclude that people in Mexico are either constantly having blowouts or constantly opening jinxed *llanterias*. Some had adjoining restaurants.

Holder roared ahead, swerving around the overburdened half-ton pickups that clogged our lane. We passed a truck full of men hunched in the back, their heads bent against the dust and wind, hoods up, shirts tied across their faces, hands stuffed deep into their pockets. It was a familiar sight that conjured a familiar line. "There was a magnificence to this," old drunken Malcolm Lowry had noted back in 1947. "Some symbolism for the future, for which such truly great preparation had been made by a heroic people, since all over Mexico one could see those thundering lorries with those young builders in them, standing erect, their trousers flapping hard, legs planted wide, firm." I'd never seen one of these trucks without thinking of this line, but it came to me now, near the highway's end, that the young builders Lowry had admired might have been on their way to pave the Pan-

American Highway. The great preparation was a road, and rolling over it ahead of us was the future—delivery vans painted with cartoonish bread loaves, milk bottles, and chip bags, pulling off the blacktop in dusty towns to distribute the brightly packaged tokens of a distant industry.

"Well," Sylvia said, "I need a new dentist." It turned out that she had been a patient of Clara Harris, the Houston dentist who had recently been sentenced to twenty years for running over and killing her unfaithful husband with her silver Mercedes S430.

"This note came in the mail saying all her patients would be referred to another dentist," Sylvia said. "I had always tried to get her to join the club, but she never had time."

"People who do something like that must be completely out of their minds," Holder said, shaking his head.

"That's why she shouldn't be in jail," Mimi said.

"Some people say it's gonna hurt Mercedes," Sylvia said, "but I said no way. Women are gonna be linin' up to buy them after this."

This point was hotly debated for a few minutes, but before long, the sense of loneliness rising up off the empty desert returned us to our silent thoughts. The trailer rattled along behind us. The sense that Mexico was ending quieted us all down and made us think of home. I consulted Holder's book to see how the story of the race's first iteration would end.

Clara Harris's autocide made an apt introduction for the clippings from the 1953 Carrera. The winner of that year's race was Juan Manuel Fangio, who drove a Lancia on a factory squad, but he toasted his victory in the shadow of the worst death toll to date. Felice Bonetto, a well-known Italian champ, was killed when he drove into a lamppost during a ferocious duel with Piero Taruffi.

Antonio Stagnoli and Giuseppe Scotuzzi both perished when their Ferrari left the road near Juchitán, flew 180 feet through the air, and exploded in a fiery ball. The worst accident came just moments before that, at a curving bridge spanning the Tehuantepec River. Bob Christie's Ford cleared the bank and tumbled down into the mud below, drawing a crowd of officials and fans, some of whom dashed across the road for a better view. The next driver was Californian Mickey Thompson, ace of the Utah Salt Flats, who came roaring around the turn to find a child crossing the highway. To avoid hitting the child, Thompson steered blindly off the bridge, plummeted eighty feet, and landed in the crowd that had collected around the first accident, killing six.

Throughout the winter and spring, the status of the 1954 race remained in question. Vehicles now ran at speeds unheard of when the highway had opened. It was no longer clear that the road would be able to hold them. To complicate matters further, shortly before the tentative race date, torrential rainstorms washed out portions of the desert highway and caused tremendous rockslides in the mountains, where in some places the road was entirely buried.

The president decided to push ahead. He sent three thousand laborers to clear the roads, had the National Railway suspend grade crossings, and assigned seventeen thousand soldiers to patrol the highway, twice as many as the previous year. Despite his best efforts, the 1954 Carrera was an even grislier saturnalia of blood than the 1953 edition. Four competitors died just getting down to Tuxtla Gutiérrez. The first racer off the line, Jack McAfee, in a 4.5-liter Ferrari, blew a tire trying to outgun the Marqués of Portago and slammed into a rock wall, killing his navigator instantly. On the third day, a driver lost his legs and a second navigator died. The fourth day polished off a third navigator. Fans undeterred by the carnage enjoyed a closely fought duel between the heavily favored Italian, Umberto Maglioli, and Phil Hill, a California racer. Maglioli's was the newer and more powerful of their twin Ferraris, but Hill stayed with him until the country flattened out, earning the nickname "El Batallador" from the raucous Mexican crowds. The sobriquet suited the scene. Violent retirements were heavy throughout the race. *Motor Life*'s account of an accident involving a Pegaso entered by the Dominican dictator Rafael Trujillo illustrated a typical scene:

> Just 26 miles out of the capital, Karl Guenther's Borgward left the road on a downhill curve and crashed in a maguey field. Military medical personnel rushed to his aid and were getting the situation in hand when the Pegaso was heard roaring toward the curve much too fast. It hit the ground just before the Borgward, throwing driver Palacios against *Motor Life* photographer Bob Flora. Then the Pegaso bounced over the Borgward, struck and badly hurt a soldier, rolled several times and burst into flame—a total loss. No sooner had the two drivers and the soldier been carried off the field of action than a Dodge and a Chevy crashed in the same spot.

Of the 149 starters, 87 crossed the finish line. Cortines had seen enough. For five years the highways, cornfields, riverbeds, and ravines of his country had hosted these racers, and the president no longer found a profit in it. The Carrera Panamericana, he declared, would never run again.

I looked up from the book. We were approaching Nuevo Laredo, the last town before the border, and the *yonkes* had begun. Yonke Alesso, Yonke Sammy, Yonke Don Kikon. Any Mexican town worth its salt has a *yonke* or two, but to my knowledge, the Yonke Row of Nuevo Laredo is without peer. Whole fleets of improbable cars could be put together from the piles in these junkyards. For miles they occupy both sides of the highway. Yonke las Carcachitas, Yonke los Chachos, Yonke los Chepes. The chance seemed good that flotsam from Carreras past might even have swirled into these eddies at the roadway's gulf—sheet metal from "Wild Bill" Vukovich's Lincoln, or the grille off Carroll Shelby's Austin-Healy. Holder slowed and cast admiring glances over the great collections. Yonke Beto, Yonke La Gringa, Yonke el Nacional. Some of the *yonke* men were sitting in tin-wrapped booths, watching tiny televisions or cracking open sunflower seeds, while the rusting mountains rose behind them like store heaps of the past. Some of the men picked through piles with customers. Others stood patiently at their gates and surveyed the highway, perhaps imagining what the passing cars might look like in twenty or thirty years. They must only wait. Eventually, everything ends up in a *yonke*.

THE FINAL CORONAS had been blown up between Restaurant Bar Tokio and Telas Parisina at one end of Nuevo Laredo's Avenida Guerrero—a dingy boulevard of curio shops, discount pharmacies, mattress outlets, and dentists. Nearby stood a giant bronze of Vicente Guerrero, hero of Mexican Independence and short-lived president of the young republic, who was declared, in 1828, "mentally incapable of governing" by the Congress and executed by firing squad shortly thereafter. The statue showed the insurgent leader at a happier time, a sword in his hand, a breeze in his hair, and a glint in his eye as he gazed over the scene of total mayhem collecting around the finish line. The Corona girls were out in force, wandering among the buzzing race fans, the plastic doll vendors, the pizza and hot dog and taco men, the boys with miniature checkered flags, the mothers and fathers trailing their children, and the officials radioing gravely back and forth on walkie-talkies. Gold-plated lowrider bicycles snaked through the crowd. From a bandstand a sweat-drenched man shouted, "*Viva México! Viva México*!" Miss Nuevo Laredo toured the avenue, waving while a high school bugle corps blared discordantly in the shade of a furniture emporium. It was only a few days until Día de los Muertos, and behind their drums and horns the musicians were costumed as witches, monsters, *banditos*, vampires, and blood-streaked pirates. One bugler wore a Ku Klux Klan robe. Many had painted their faces white, their lips black, and their eyes red. Honking discordantly under the watchful eye of their drillmaster, a late-period Elvis, the teens gave the afternoon a ghoulish air, as if someone had felt that a macabre reception best suited the Carrera, which had claimed so many lives and limbs.

De Thoisy arrived first. Gunning his Stude over the final stages of flat desert, the Frenchman had easily secured his sixth title. He stopped a few feet from the low wooden victory arches and climbed up on the roof of the car to blow kisses. Someone handed him a Corona, and he shook it up and sprayed it in the air as if it were champagne. The rest of the cars made their way through the arches, where they were greeted with strident, off-key bugling. Flattened green butterflies covered their grilles. They had dents in their hoods, cracks in their windshields, and missing pieces.

They limped down Guerrero like heroes of a distant campaign, the struggles of which would never be understood by the citizens now cheering in the safety of their return. These autos had rampaged two thousand miles across the nation, through jungles, up mountains, down rivers, and over deserts. They had borne *topes* innumerable, wandering livestock, rockslides, fog, and sabotage. You couldn't help but read in their animalian grilles expressions of relief.

The last cars crossed the line, but Heidi was nowhere to be found. We took a nervous taxi ride back to the hotel, where the sight of her tied sadly to a trailer confirmed our darkest fears. "Pulled that plastic filter out," Bartley said. "Gave her a hysterectomy with a screwdriver. I'm bettin' there's a hole in the side of the block. Threw a rod." Haney was mute, Holder aghast. "I feel like a dog without his tail," he said, leaning on his cane. Bartley smoked and coughed and tried to give as accurate an account of the breakdown as possible, but it was academic. Having held fast the whole span of Mexico, Heidi's engine had exploded just a few kilometers from the finish line.

Showered and downcast, we made our way to the trophy presentation, held a few hours later in the lush grass courtyard of a gymnasium beside the hotel. A warm wind blew down from the north, lifting the long white tablecloths on the round dinner tables. Palm trees tossed and the blown-up bottles nodded. Sylvia took a table at the back of the lawn, near the beer tent, with no view of the stage. We didn't intend to stay long. Holder wanted to eat some *cabrito* before leaving Mexico and there would be no more opportunities after tonight.

Eduardo Leon thanked some dignitaries and passed out the awards. I watched the stage expectantly. Throughout the eight-day campaign, I'd held out the hope that sooner or later, in his evening pronouncements, when the times were posted and the dancers were through, Leon would get around to telling us what the meaning of all this was, but as he handed over the stage to a boisterous mariachi band and staggered into the wings, it was clear there would be no explanation. What meaning there was lay in the past, and even a revival like the Panam doesn't really bother with the past. Reaching the future is what matters in a race. It is what matters in a road. I excused myself from the table and walked down to the edge of the lawn, where a short chain-link fence defended the gymnasium's lush grass from a dirt field strewn with litter. Several hundred feet across the dark ground was a two-lane highway that ran alongside the field for a ways before curving between two small hills. Red and white lights trailed back and forth in pairs. I stood and watched them come and go and come and go and come and go.

Chapter VIII

BAKER TENHOLTZ IS A SIX-AND-A-HALF-FOOT phonographer who used to cut bee trees. It was through cutting bee trees that he first developed an interest in phonography. When hunting hives, he explained to me, it is necessary to have a way of remembering which trees contain honey. There might be fifteen or twenty honey trees scattered around a small wood. Chasing the bees around to determine which trees they're using—"lining" the bees, or "coursing" them—a hunter has no time to lose. When he finds some bees swarming into a knothole, he marks the bark with his knife or ties a ribbon on the trunk before running on to the next tree. Afterward, he strolls through the wood, locating by his marks the bee trees, harvesting the wild comb honey with a smoking rag.

Tenholtz was born in 1932 in Eudora, Arkansas, and as a boy he made a good summertime living off bee trees. He marked his trees with a ten-inch bowie knife. After a few seasons he found that he was more interested in coming up with new markings than with pulling out comb. He had a basic hash mark that indicated whether or not the trees had bees, and by crossing the hash mark perpendicularly at different heights he could indicate the location of the knothole. Dots arrayed around the mark recorded the bees' particular ferocity.

"I became very interested in this," he told me. "I was wondering, how much information can be conveyed by a few simple marks on a tree? My range was limited by tools and materials, but in no time I discovered that with a small alphabet of symbols, I could express a wealth of information. Not only were the bees aggressive, but where had I first picked them up? Was it by a stream? Had I seen a wild turkey on the far bank? And how was the weather? Did it look like rain? I got pretty good on those kinds of questions, and then I started trying to record other matters. Soon enough, on a tree with good smooth bark, I could put down most any current event. I'd never heard of Isaac Pitman at that time. I was just pursuing a childish diversion. Of course, I had to practice. I filled up half the notebooks in town, working out my characters with a pen and paper, but what I really liked was to carve something on a tree, where it would stay put and stupefy anybody who happened to come upon it. Nowadays, the trees have grown so much I would imagine my inscriptions are unrecognizable."

Several years later, in a typing class, Tenholtz came across an old edition of Pitman shorthand, the first comprehensive system of abbreviated writing to be taught in the United States. On the page, it looks somewhat like Arabic, with short, hooking characters and flickering embellishments. It has a phonetic basis, which is why some people call it phonography. Tenholtz's first glimpse of a text in Pitman shorthand was very nearly a mystical experience. The system made his bee tree glyphs look crude and unwieldy, but it also seemed familiar, strange, and beautiful. He said it was like "looking at a note you might have written to yourself in your sleep and cannot remember writing." He learned it in four days. From Pitman shorthand he moved on to Gregg shorthand, a loopier script that looks more like cursive. Soon he was an adept at virtually every form of shorthand known to man. He picked up Boyd's syllabic, Eclectic-Cross, Gabelsberger, Thomas, Pullis, Forkner, Dutton Speedwords, Salser-Yerian Briefhand, Universal, and even, as more of a party trick than anything else, some small bits of Tironian notes, named for Marcus Tullius Tiro, a Roman scribe who devised the four-thousand-character system to record the speeches of Cicero.

Most stenographers end up as court reporters, but Tenholtz never did, mostly because he disliked machine shorthand, which was standard by the 1950s. Machines took all the fun out of it, he felt, and, more importantly, they were bulky and inconvenient. Nevertheless, he mastered the Stenograph and in 1954 won the National Court Reporters Association speed contest with no errors on the 280-words-per-minute jury charge. Afterward he made headlines for publicly denouncing the association's endorsement of shorthand machines, claiming that "no device has done more to ruin the fine and noble pursuit of shorthand pen writing."

Tenholtz and I first crossed paths on March 28, 2004, in a supermarket in Houston. He was standing in front of a refrigerated case of ready-to-eat dishes—buffalo wings, wilted Caesar salads, thick squares of King Ranch casserole—shaking his head and muttering, "What is the point of this?" As I walked past, he turned slightly and caught my eye, and although I was in the sort of mood that makes casual conversation with strangers seem nearly impossible, I hesitated and smiled ruefully, as if to agree, though I had no idea what he was talking about.

"Why do they do this?" he asked me, his voice raspy with age. His hair consisted of forty or fifty wisps above a liver-spotted dome and his gaunt frame was bent slightly over a wooden, rubber-footed cane, which he gradually lifted and used as a pointer to indicate a sign above the display case that read MEALZ TO GO. "There isn't any point, as far as I can tell, to that letter Z," he said. "It doesn't make the word any shorter, or easier to read." I agreed that the spelling was both useless and idiotic and continued on my way, but he was not done. He brought his cane down, drew a notepad from his breast pocket, and scribbled furiously for a few moments. Writing up his complaint, I thought. He seemed like one of those tiresome, half-mad geezers who search public buildings for something to dislike, a self-appointed inspector of the world's many defects. I could imagine him pestering the store's manager, refusing to accept that the S had been changed to a Z simply to enliven an otherwise pedestrian sign. "But it does nothing of the sort," he would protest, "it only gives it the impression of having been written by a ten-year-old."

And the manager, frustrated but slightly bemused: "Listen, buddy, I don't know what to tell you. I don't make the signs. I just put them up."

"Of course you don't. No one is responsible for anything anymore."

Not that I disagreed with him. My outlook at the time shared much with that of a dyspeptic old codger. From Nuevo Laredo, I'd trailed back to Houston with Go-Green-Go, lacking any idea for how the city might occupy me. I had eight thousand dollars and no clue how to turn my race notes into a piece of journalism. I'd found a cheap apartment in a low-rise complex off Bissonet inhabited mostly by Mexican immigrants, men—they were all men—who knew Zacatecas well and were baffled and amused to find a gringo who'd lived there. They had all heard of the Pallet King, and some knew of the Carrera Panamericana too. My Mexican sojourn had done nothing to advance my career in journalism, but it had made me a source of endless curiosity for my neighbors.

Some of these men had interesting stories, but I didn't bother to draw them out or take notes. I was through with journalism. I spent most of my time under the air at the public library, aimlessly searching Craigslist for some barter item or job opportunity that would give my life a new purpose. Piano lessons? An Olympic weight set? A four-month-old painted Welsh pony? Teaching English in rural Java? One day, scouring the rideshares, I came across someone looking for a companion to share the driving out to Terlingua, a small desert town south of Marfa. The anonymous author of this query would depart on April 22 and return three days later.

The next morning I replied to the ad, offering my services. The poster wrote back with several paragraphs. There was no signature, but I gathered from the address—anne1944@aol.com—that she was a woman. There was a lot to digest in her email. She explained that she was going to Terlingua to take part in an adobe workshop hosted by a woman named Ruby Prentice, a disciple of the world-famous Mexican adobe architect Joaquin Tenorio. "My interest in mud brick architecture stems from my interest in this remarkable woman," anne1944 offered. She said she no longer drove long distances without a companion because she had bad night vision and wouldn't like to end up sleeping on the side of the road if the trip took longer than expected. "Surgery might help," she wrote, "but I refuse to let a doctor fiddle with my eyeballs. Doctors nowadays think they can fix everything but half of them can't even take your temperature. Besides, I'm not sure they should be allowed to fix everything. It's only a way for them to run up their bills. People should learn to live with their defects."

Needless to say, I was taken with my correspondent's digressive style and began to look forward to our ten-hour drive, convinced that I would be hearing a great deal more not only about Ruby Prentice, Joaquin Tenorio, and the shortcomings of modern medicine, but also about anne1944 herself. Who was she? A lonely River Oaks dilettante? An aging hippie swept up in the green building craze?

Neither, as it turned out. She wasn't even a woman. She was Baker Tenholtz, a six-and-a-half-foot-tall phonographer who used to cut bee trees.

"**NOTICE THE LOW** clearance here," Tenholtz said, gesturing with his cane to the small gap between the undercarriage of his car and the cracked pavement of his driveway. He wore gray slacks and a yellow shirt under a frayed blue sweatshirt. Although it had not even been a month, he didn't remember our brief exchange at the supermarket until he consulted the pages of a notepad he carried. His house, a small bungalow in Bellaire, was run-down and badly in need of a coat of paint. Weeds bordered the front walk and piles of rotten fruit lay on the ground beneath an overgrown lemon tree. Up on the porch were three huge bookshelves curtained with plastic sheeting to protect the spines from sideways-driving rain.

Despite the disarray of his property, Tenholtz was exacting

about his automobile, a well-maintained 1982 maroon Mercury Zephyr. The car was like a museum piece, with the original eight-track player and all the cheap fake wood trim pieces in place and unbroken. He had me take it around the block a few times so he could examine my driving, which he found to be a little reckless, despite the fact that I never topped fifteen miles per hour. After the Toyota, the Zephyr's long frame took some getting used to. There was plenty of car hanging out fore and aft, and it seemed to take twice as many revolutions of the steering wheel as I expected before the wallowing bulk would drift in the desired direction. Tenholtz sat across from me on the bench seat, peering at my pedal work and bracing himself against the dashboard. It nearly derailed the entire trip when I let it slip that I had gone on a road race the previous fall.

"A road race?"

"In Mexico."

He studied me for a minute. "I cannot abide any hot-rodding with my vehicle," he said. "Our highways are for the transport of goods and people, not for your illegal entertainments."

"That's okay. I didn't even go in the race car. I spent the whole trip in the service truck reading a history book. My last car couldn't even go faster than fifty-five."

This settled him down. He told me to take the first leg and directed me onto the freeway. I drove as cautiously as possible, letting the Zephyr find its speed. After a few minutes he apologized for his outburst. "I am impossibly burdened by the past," he said. He shifted around in his seat, trying to get comfortable. I assumed that after a cryptic comment like that he would offer some kind of explanation, but he just let it hang. He kept his notepad on his lap and jotted things here and there, glancing up and down from the pad like a sketch artist. After a few minutes he popped open the glove compartment and pulled out a hard-boiled egg, which he banged on the door panel and peeled out the window. He ate it in one bite and made a note in his pad.

"What are you writing on there?" I asked him.

"Everything."

"Are you a journalist?"

Tenholtz shook his head. He said he was a phonographer, a master of shorthand writing. He taught classes in the Business, Management, and Administration Department at Lone Star Community College. Carrying the pad around was a way for him to practice. It was a second language, after all, and like any second language, you had to keep using it or risk losing proficiency.

"So that's why you were taking notes at the supermarket?" He nodded. "I thought you might have a short-term memory problem."

"I've had students with such difficulties," he said. "This is a great application for pen shorthand. Patients recovering from brain tumors, or cranial injuries, or severe psychological trauma. There are, you will be unhappy to learn, many ways to lose your memory. Certain drugs for Lyme disease can have damaging side effects to the short-term recall."

"So your students all carry pads like this?"

"Imagine that you cannot remember names, what you ate for lunch, what you said to someone on the phone. Imagine that movies with complicated plots are hard to follow. It seems to me that they all have complicated plots these days. Well, you won't be able to carry around a Stenograph machine; you won't be able to use one of those silly PalmPilots. Pen shorthand is your best hope."

He bent over his notepad and filled a page with squiggles, glancing out the window and around the car as he wrote. His hand seemed to move of its own accord, drifting back and forth across the page in firm, straight lines while his head cocked this way and that in birdlike observation. He was like some kind of instrument, a Richter scale of human experience scratching involuntarily at the scrolling passage of time.

"So the adobe workshop is just . . . ?"

"An enthusiasm," he said, while continuing to scribble. "It may not surprise you to learn that while it may pay the bills just fine, teaching note-taking to business admin students does not entirely fulfill the mind's natural curiosity. So I cultivate enthusiasms, one of which is the building arts. Did you know that the Egyptian god of writing was also the god of building?"

"No."

"Can you understand why?"

"I'd have to think about it."

"Permanence. That's why. Her name was Seshat. They also called her the goddess of history."

"Really?"

He nodded. "And what about you?" he asked. "You don't seem to be in high finance or directional drilling."

"Journalism. Well, I used to be a journalist. Or I was trying to be one, at any rate. I even thought about learning shorthand once. Deborah Gallatin uses shorthand. You know who she is?"

"No."

"She writes for *The New Yorker*."

"I don't take it anymore."

"Well, she uses shorthand. Someone told me that once."

"It's easy to learn."

"That's all right. I'm not a journalist anymore. It didn't work out."

"Why's that?" In his peculiar way, Tenholtz was an able interrogator, and over the next hundred miles, transcribing the whole time, he pried it out of me—the job at the *Sentinel*, the Sanchez letter, Deborah Gallatin and the drought, the escape to New Orleans, the Famous Poets Society, the broken compass treasure, Zacatecas, the McDonald's, the Pallet King and Joe Tolen, Sigg, the fruitless trip across Mexico in the Go-Green-Go service truck. The story seemed to interest him.

"You do realize that the treasure was almost certainly of much greater value than they let on, don't you?"

"Yes."

He shook his head and wrote a few lines in his pad. "And how could you have waited all afternoon to see what those fellows had uncovered in your yard, back in Marfa I'm talking about now. I'm certain I would have been out there immediately demanding that they quit filling the hole back in until I'd had a look."

"I suppose I knew it would be blank."

"Even so." He thought about it for a minute. "Is this your motive in returning to West Texas? Have you discovered a new lead?"

"No. Just taking a trip."

Tenholtz didn't say much for the next half hour. He wrote for a bit and then slouched in the corner and closed his eyes. We circled San Antonio and headed up through Comfort and Kerrville along that last stretch of Hill Country highway before the road tops out at Junction and the horizon expands. He leaned forward and stared out the window, watching as the cedar trees thinned out and the cacti and yuccas took over. The Zephyr was doing fine, but it burned up gasoline like a furnace. The gauge was already scraping bottom. I stopped at a station in Junction, and Tenholtz handed me a twenty. He sat with his door open and his feet on the pavement, fanning himself with his notepad.

There was no one else at the gas station and few cars on the highway at one p.m. on a Thursday. I bought some cold waters and a packet of beef jerky and a bag of peanuts in the shell. Tenholtz scarfed the nuts, dropping pieces all over his lap, but passed on the jerky, which was too tough for his seventy-year-old teeth. We got back on the road. He poured some water on a yellow handkerchief and buried his face in the cloth. Then he wound it up and tied it around his neck, pulled out his pad, checked his watch, and made a few notes.

"What are you writing now?" I asked him. He held up the pad to show me the squiggles, then read: "One-ten—stopped for gas, peanuts, water. Paid twenty dollars. Used kerchief to cool down. Continuing westbound on Interstate 10. Desert flora beginning to predominate. "

"You really don't do anything with these notes?" He shook his head. "You don't go back and read them ever?"

"Oh, sure. I read them. I consult them. I use them to remember things." He smiled. "Our memories are not without their defects. I doubt you can recall every single thing that's happened in the last forty-eight hours. For a man of my age, my memory works fine, but it is not flawless. And it may cease to function at any moment. "

"Cease to function?"

"It has happened before." He was quiet for a few minutes and I thought the conversation was over, another mysterious comment dropped and abandoned. Then he said, brusquely, "I have not been able to trust my memory since the day in 1944 when I woke up in a car on the side of Highway 65 outside Pine Bluff, and found my parents and sister were gone. They were never found, and I have never been able to remember what happened." He took a breath. "Do you mind if we get some lunch?"

We pulled into Sonora, an interstate town with a row of fast-food joints right on the highway and a decrepit town square a few blocks off it. A Mexican restaurant with serapes hanging in the dusty windows looked okay, and over green enchilada plates and iced teas, Tenholtz told me the full story of his family's disappearance. He had been twelve years old at the time. Much of what he had been unable to remember himself he had managed to fill in by speaking with relatives and memorizing the police report. The family had been on a trip from Eudora, which is in the southeast corner of Arkansas, up to Little Rock. It was a Friday morning. They stopped in the little town of Dumas at a place called Bert's Café, and according to a waitress who worked there, Tenholtz had eaten a hamburger and drunk two glasses of milk. His mother always made him drink a lot of milk, he said, and milk made him sleepy.

"After leaving Bert's, I fell asleep in the car. When I woke up I was lying across the entire backseat, so my sister may have crawled into the front and sat on my mother's lap, as she often did when I stretched out. 'Baker is crowding me!' she always said. 'Quit him crowding me!' She was little, only four years old. We drove through Gould and Grady and Pine Bluff. Seventeen miles north of Pine Bluff, just past a small wooden bridge, we got a flat tire and my father pulled off the road. The police determined that the flat tire may have been caused by the uneven surface of the road and the bridge. I slept through the whole thing. Everyone got out of the car except me. My father's tools were still on the ground beside the tire. He hadn't even put the spare on. That suggests that someone or something interrupted him, and not that he and my mother and sister simply walked down the road, back the hills, and left me behind forever.

"When I woke up I was immediately scared. I knew something had happened before I even lifted my head up and looked, as if my dreams had been trying to tell me all along. I crawled out of the car and walked around, calling their names. It was spring and on the side of the road the grass was bright green, the color it is after hard and heavy rains. I wondered if I was still dreaming. All that day and all the next I wondered if I was dreaming. Back then the roads were not so crowded as they are today. It was ten minutes before a car drove past. They stopped to see what the matter was, a man and a woman dressed nice, and happy. The woman stayed with me while the man drove back into Pine Bluff to alert the police.

"They searched a ten-mile radius and found nothing. They knocked on every door in the area. They dredged the Arkansas River. Weeks passed and the investigations went on. I was sent to my mother's parents' house back home in Eudora. I didn't know what to do, and that's how I started cutting bee trees—for the extra money and because I liked the solitude. You can't imagine how much attention my story attracted. I was the little Tenholtz Boy. You ask anybody over a certain age and they'll remember the case. Newspapers all over the country sent reporters to interview me. Nowadays they would put me on one of these cable television news shows around the clock. It was that sort of thing. And the police came around again and again, asking me the same questions over and over. But I could never remember anything."

The waitress came over to clear our meal. Tenholtz hadn't eaten much. He watched her pile the plates. Once she had wiped everything down he asked her name. "Mariana," she said. He jotted it down.

"But you were asleep. How could they expect you to remember something that happened while you were asleep?"

"Even before I was asleep. Had anyone followed us from Bert's Café? Had we stopped anywhere else that morning? Why were we going to Little Rock in the first place? I couldn't remember anything."

"So you started taking notes."

"When I was still convinced that my family would reappear, I thought I would have a chance to fill them in on what had happened since then, go through the pages with them and say, 'On this day, here's what happened.' There would be so much to tell. How could I remember it all? At some point I guess I knew I would never see them again, but by that point it had become a habit. This year my mother would have turned a hundred and four and my father a hundred and twelve. Obviously they're long dead. Even my sister Anne, who was nine years younger than me, might as well be dead. She had a vascular birthmark on her left cheek, a port wine stain, as they call them. Once I thought I found her in a restaurant in Memphis."

Tenholtz paid our tab with another twenty and we drove back to the interstate. He made no move to take the wheel, and I understood now that he wouldn't. My coming along had nothing to do with his poor night vision; he needed someone else to do the driving so he could take his notes. I asked him if the case had ever been solved. He shook his head.

"The police had many theories for how my family could have

gone missing. Most involved all three of them being murdered. But as no bodies were ever found; and as my mother's handbook was sitting untouched on the dashboard with twelve dollars in it; and as there was no blood anywhere, no sign of a scuffle, I have never accepted that conclusion myself."

"What do you think happened?"

"I don't know."

"But you don't believe they're still alive."

"How could I?"

"So who are you keeping your record for, if you don't mind the question?"

He rolled up his window and withdrew his pad. "I just don't like to forget anything," he said.

IT WAS DARK when we arrived in Terlingua, an old mining town west of the Chisos Mountains whose chief attraction now that its lodes have been extracted is its dramatic isolation from the modern world. In the 1880s, when the area was still controlled by various Indian tribes, Mexican and American prospectors came looking for cinnabar, a kind of quicksilver known as "red lead" that the Indians prized for its pigment. By 1900 the Indians had been persuaded to find other face paints; twenty years later, 40 percent of the quicksilver mined in the U.S. came from Terlingua. Many of the era's lighthouse lenses, barometers, thermometers, herbicides, laxatives, handheld maze games, and road-leveling devices contained a portion of the local diggings. The good times soon passed, however, and by the end of World War II, Terlingua was a ghost town. Thirty years later, it was rediscovered by renegades, solitary souls, bearded rockhounds, and the sort of people who like to be able to see a visitor coming from several miles off.

Ruby Prentice's compound was at the end of a dirt road flanked by ocotillos and prickly pears. I inched along, mindful of the Zephyr's low clearance. My attentiveness had paid off—Tenholtz had agreed to let me drop him off and take the car up to Marfa. A sign beside a wooden gate said THE CENTER FOR BUILDING IN BALANCE. A man with a long braid down his back came out and let us through the gate. He said his name was Dwight. It was dark and I couldn't get a feel for the place, but from Dwight's flowing, earth-toned garments and his vaguely monkish bearing, I gathered that the Center for Building in Balance was the sort of place where the baking and stacking of mud bricks was not only a building art but also a form of new age worship. Tenholtz was too sleepy to notice any of this. He stood up slowly, stretching his long arms and legs, and said, "Thanks for the ride and the companionship. We'll have more to discuss on Monday." Dwight grabbed his suitcase and pounded the top of the Zephyr twice. I drove up to Marfa, passing the devil's cave and the profile of Lincoln, checked into a crappy motel, and slept for ten hours.

The next few days passed awkwardly. I went to Carmen's, the post office, the courthouse, the old Blackwell School, and the library. I had not told anyone I was coming, but a few people waved me over, stuck their heads in the passenger-side window, and asked where I'd been. Mostly the streets were empty. I kicked around the fields where Michael had taken me to search for the missing graveyard, and drank Lone Stars at the bar where Frank had told me about the devil. I drove out to the Marfa Mystery Lights viewing area at night and sat for hours on the hood staring into the dark.

On Sunday I checked on the ranch house where I'd lived. The irrigation system had transformed it into a paradise. The blue grama grass that had been patchy and sunburned under my care was now a rolling carpet of bright green that ran all the way from the road down to the house, where a lush bounty of flowering bushes and native grasses tossed in the breeze. Out in the middle of the grama, a man in a red bandanna rode a lawn mower in circles. Dogs swarmed as I crunched down the driveway under the soft pink blossoms of desert willows thriving in a neat row. A large woman emerged from the little house that had once been mine and yelled at the dogs to scatter. Squinting in the sun, she told me that she and her husband were the caretakers. That was him out there on the riding mower. The owners were in Houston. I told her I'd once been the caretaker too. She frowned. "Are you the one that just ran off?" she asked.

I nodded.

"They weren't too happy with you."

"It was unprofessional."

"That's one word for it. Lalo and me had a ton of work to do when we got hired. The weeds were out of control."

"Sorry about that."

"Why'd you do it?"

"Family illness."

She stared at me, shaking her head. "Least you could have called. There's a box of your stuff in the garage."

There was nothing in the box I really wanted. I threw it in the back of the Zephyr and returned to town. What was I looking for? Some fork in the road where I'd chosen the wrong path? Some secret I'd missed the first time around? There was nothing in the wide, dusty boulevards, only that same blankness and vacancy that had frustrated me the first time. I went by the *Sentinel* but the office was closed. The paper in the outside box blared familiar headlines—city council, drought, a concert at the Am Vets hall. I dropped fifty cents and took a copy.

A story on page five caught my eye: "Center for Building in Balance Hosts Annual Adobe Workshop." It was a standard sort of press release, reprinted in full, that outlined the center's mission statement and described in glowing terms its history of service in the Big Bend region. What stopped me was the photograph. It showed a woman, identified as Ruby Prentice, standing beside a pile of mud bricks with a trowel in her hand. A large port wine stain covered the left side of her face.

I MAY HAVE PUSHED the Zephyr a little too hard as I hurried down to Terlingua the next afternoon. How long had Tenholtz known about the birthmark? I struggled to recall everything he had said about Ruby Prentice on the drive and in his emails. Could she really be his sister? If she was, would he be returning to Houston at all? How could it be proven? Where had she disappeared to?

The gate was open. I parked next to a heavily bumper-stickered Subaru. In the daylight I could see that my notion of the place had been correct. An asymmetrical collection of mud huts were arrayed around a domed building. Prayer flags hung from the eaves of some of the huts' deep porch roofs, below which giant plastic rain-catching tubs sat half empty. A bearded man crouched on a porch washing his feet in a tin basin. Three women stood on the shady side of the domed building, talking in low voices. At the top of a ladder, a skinny kid was repairing some roof tiles. The place had the feel of a commune, or a monastery. The clean, dirt courtyard seemed to be the center of a Venn diagram in which vision-questers and off-the-gridders overlapped. I asked the foot-scrubber, a member, it seemed to me, of the latter category, if he knew where I could find the old man who carried a notepad.

He stared at me from behind his bristly mound, which up close resembled the nest of an untidy bird. "Number seven," he said, pointing down a row of huts. "You a friend of his?"

"Sort of."

"Can you reiterate a message to him for me?"

"I guess."

"It's cool if he wants to write everything in that pad all the time. That's his movie. I respect that. But in my movie nobody knows my coordinates, okay? And it's got to stay that way."

He wrung out a washcloth and scrubbed his big toe, glancing up at me with narrow eyes.

"Your movie?"

"Yeah, my movie. The one I'm living in, man."

"You're saying you don't want him to publish anything about you?"

He dropped the washcloth in the basin. "Publish? Fuck, no. He didn't say anything about that. Is he from *Architectural Digest* or some shit? I need to be off the record. You make sure he knows that. Off the record one hundred percent. That's my movie. You got that? I'm off the record. No names. No physical descriptions. Make sure he gets it."

I explained that Tenholtz was not from *Architectural Digest* and was not even a journalist and would do nothing whatsoever with the notes he'd been taking, but the foot-scrubber didn't look convinced, and kept insisting with quiet indignation that he had a right to "live my movie." He told me again to reiterate his message and turned back to his toes. The huts were connected by a gravel path. I crunched along it. In a large field behind the buildings, a giant gridwork was laid on the ground, in which hundreds of adobe bricks lay baking in the sun. Substantial stacks of finished bricks were piled neatly. A group of eight or nine people listened to a short Mexican man in jeans, a tight cowboy shirt, and a wide palm-leaf hat as he gestured at the bricks and made rectangles with his hands. Some of the doors to the huts were open and I caught sight of the simple furnishings inside—a bed, a couple chairs, and a table, all of it in a rustic Mexican style, with colorful saddle blankets draped over everything and wide-brimmed hats hanging on the walls. On every porch there was an old-fashioned straw-bristle broom and a bamboo mat for shoes, which ran the gamut from bright orange clogs to mud-caked ropers.

The door to Tenholtz's hut was closed. I knocked a few times and he appeared in a white T-shirt that emphasized his age and spindliness. "Oh, good," he said. "Come in." It took my eyes a moment to adjust to the darkness. There was no lamp. A thin shaft of sunlight from the half-open window shutters hit the floor a few feet from a small square table. Sitting at the table was Ruby Prentice. She wore jeans and a white blouse. Her gray hair was knotted at the back of her head, which she held perfectly erect, like a queen balancing a large, encrusted crown, though her own hat, another palm-leaf gardener's job, hung from the back of her chair. The vascular birthmark, as Tenholtz had called it, was dark purple and splotched across her left cheek in the shape of some remote and windswept island nation.

Tenholtz made the necessary introductions, to which I replied that I had heard much about Mrs. Prentice and even seen her photograph in the *Big Bend Sentinel* the day before. Tenholtz nodded. He gave me a stool and took his seat at the table. His notepad lay open before him, covered with the familiar squiggles and dots. It was impossible to tell, from looking at their faces, at what point I had entered their conversation, or what, if anything, had already been said.

"We were just discussing the historical mud brick," Tenholtz said. "Its use by the Egyptians. Apparently, Moses and his fellow Hebrews in bondage in ancient Egypt were *adobaderos*." He stumbled over the Spanish word and Prentice corrected his pronunciation. She had a calm but firm voice, as if in her years of building squat, solid huts she had taken on some of the characteristics of her materials. There was a complete lack of frivolity about her, a sense of the core essentials and nothing else.

"In Exodus they mention a mud-and-straw brick," she said. "This is because the surface soil in the Nile floodplain had a very high clay content, and a brick that is more than thirty percent clay will crack without some form of binding, straw or dung usually."

"Permanence," Tenholtz said, as he finished transcribing her words. He looked up from his pad. "We are always looking for permanence, and we never find it. Even with the straw, all those buildings are long gone, aren't they?

Prentice nodded. "There are a number of undecayed examples of ancient adobe architecture, though. The Arg-é Bam Citadel in Iran dates from five hundred B.C. This was the largest mud structure in the world until it was destroyed in an earthquake last year. The village of Chan Chan in Peru. Without care, yes, mud-brick architecture deteriorates over time and ultimately melts back into the earth. Properly maintained, it may last for millennia."

Tenholtz scribbled away. "You are kind to indulge the enthusiasms of an old man," he said, standing up and walking over to one of the walls. He smacked it a few times for dramatic effect. "This stuff has really been around forever, hasn't it? And yet *this* is what our experiences always come to." He turned and looked out the window, where a long flat dust plain stretched off to a row of brown mountains. Staring at the bleak vista, he continued with his monologue, which began to drift into disorganization. "Dust to dust. Oblivion. The word comes from *ob*, 'over,' and *levis*, 'smooth.' Smooth as this desert dust. The missing and the lost. Do you realize how easily everything might be forgotten? I mean thoroughly erased. We would know nothing about ancient Egypt were it not for the scribes. Speeches of the pharaohs and the lives of commoners survived only because the scribes put them in writing and gave us accounts of the straw in the bricks of the Hebrew bricklayers. The writing has lasted longer than these reinforced bricks. The written word is as old and necessary as the building arts. They come from the same basic need—to have shelter. Words can be a shelter, can't they? I have always found it interesting that the Egyptian god of writing was also the god of architecture and building, but I suppose you knew that."

"She was called the goddess of history," Prentice said.

Tenholtz turned from the window and stared at her. When he spoke next his voice was a rasp and his eyes burned. "May I ask you a personal question?" he said.

"What is it?"

"It says on the website that you were born in 1941. I would like to know the date."

"July twenty-fifth."

He continued to stare at her. "Are you certain?"

"Unfortunately so," she said with a laugh.

"There is no chance that you're mistaken?"

Prentice turned and gave me a bemused look, then returned her level gaze to Tenholtz. "I was born on the day Lefty Grove won his three hundredth game, July twenty-fifth, 1941. He was pitching for Boston by then, and we rooted for the Orioles, of course, but my father had played sandlot ball with him in Baltimore and always said he was the best left-hander the game ever saw. Robert Moses 'Lefty' Grove. Pride of Maryland." She chuckled.

Tenholtz sat down hard in his chair and began to write in his pad. He did not look up. The sun had crawled up the table legs and flooded the tabletop, causing the silver accents on his ballpoint pen to shine. His hand moved more slowly across the page than it had before. "Thank you," he whispered.

THE RIVER ROAD was empty and the sky cloudless as we headed through Lajitas and Redford. We would pass the night in Marfa, which Tenholtz had wanted to see, and leave for Houston at dawn. In Presidio I asked if he would mind stopping at the devil's cave. I had not planned on a visit to the hillside grotto, and in fact had driven past Presidio twice already without making the detour, but it suddenly seemed like the place to go. Not only for my own obscure purposes, but for Tenholtz's.

We passed Abarrotes "Nellie" and forked down the road toward the cemetery. The route to the base of the mountain was still rough, but I drove it with more confidence this time around, easing gently through the crusty arroyo and riding up on the rocky fringes to avoid potholes big enough for sleeping dogs. It was rougher driving than the Zephyr was used to, but Tenholtz made no effort to stop me. He didn't even seem to notice. We parked and walked the short ways up. The sun bore down, and when we got to the cave, which was cool and shady, Tenholtz sat on a rock and stared out the opening at the valley below.

After a few minutes he spoke. "The one in Memphis had the stain on the wrong side of her face, so I knew even before I asked her, but I asked her anyway. I sat and talked to her. She had grown up in Denver, the daughter of a railroad man. We ordered dessert, pecan pie for her and I had a bowl of strawberry ice cream. The waitress's name was Francine.

"Another time I saw a woman get on an elevator in Tulsa but the doors closed before I could get to her. I waited all day for her to come back down, sitting in the lobby with a shoeshine man named Junior. Turned out she was English, born in London in 1949."

"How many have there been?"

"This was the ninth. Maybe the last. I'm getting too old to keep chasing birthmarks."

He was quiet for a moment. Down in town a distant motor revved. "Why did you want to come here?"

I said it was hard to explain, something about returning to old haunts and hoping to find the feeling that no time had passed. A do-over. I told him about the last time I had come to the cave, with Bryant Holman, in the midst of my hunt for Bierce's bones, and the run of bad luck that plagued my efforts to become a journalist after that.

"Yes." Tenholtz sighed. "Journalism. You mentioned that before." He stood up and walked to the mouth of the cave. "What is the problem, exactly?" he said, leaning his head out and looking down.

My answer wandered. Lord Macaulay. John Reed. Bernal Díaz

del Castillo. There was a believing and an examining frame of mind, I told him, and whereas poetry required an ability to believe, journalism required an ability to examine, since it was a tool by which secrets were revealed and truth uncovered. Without a sufficiently skeptical mind, the right questions would not be asked and a man might find himself spending a year looking for bones that will never be found, or traveling thousands of miles to interview a mayor who is not actually a mayor, or going on a road race and missing entirely the racing. Tenholtz was unimpressed, peering at me as if I were one of his shorthand students who had just confused Pitman and Gregg.

"What do you think is the common feature of those few ancient Egyptian monuments that have survived the passage of time?" he asked.

"An arid desert climate?"

"That's everything in Egypt. What else?"

"The building material?"

"That's right. Forget mud bricks. The monuments that survive are made from stone." He turned back to the valley. "Stone was reserved for the dead and the gods, understand? Journalism is not a matter of examining or believing. It is a matter of memorial." He waved his bony hands ceilingward, then thrust them at me with a vehemence that caused me to recoil slightly. "You must preserve our memories. At the end we will have nothing else."

He began to write and he wrote as we descended the hillside and got back in the car and wrote as we bounced back to the cemetery and wound our way past Abarrotes "Nellie." A line of cars waiting to get into the U.S. had backed up to the center of the International Bridge—Mexicans crossing for the weekend or for dinner in Presidio, Americans coming home, trucks with mysterious loads—and we sat there, in no country, baking in the sun over the lifeless brown river. Tenholtz kept writing. His hand curled and darted over the pages. When the pages were full he carefully turned them, and each time, for a moment, the white paper turned translucent in the slanting afternoon sun, showing through the symbols, impenetrable to me, with which he had encoded his dashed hopes, and in which, as they accumulated on line after line, he took his consolation.

about the author

JAKE SILVERSTEIN is the editor of *Texas Monthly* and a contributing editor at *Harper's* magazine. He lives in Austin, Texas. This is his first book.